REBECCA BRANDEWYNE

is a bestselling author of historical and contemporary novels. Her stories consistently place on the bestseller lists, including those of the *New York Times* and *Publishers Weekly*. She was inducted into the *Romantic Times* Hall of Fame in 1988, and is the recipient of the *Romantic Times* Career Achievement Award (1991), the *Affaire de Coeur* Golden Quill Pen Award for Best Historical Romance and the Silver Pen Award.

PEGGY MORELAND

published her first romance with Silhouette in 1989 and continues to delight readers with stories set in her home state of Texas. Winner of the National Readers' Choice Award, a nominee for the *Romantic Times* Reviewer's Choice Award, and a two-time finalist for the prestigious RITA® Award from Romance Writers of America, Peggy frequently sees her books appear on the *USA Today* and Waldenbooks bestseller lists. When she's not writing, you can usually find Peggy outside, tending the cattle, goats and other critters on the ranch she shares with her husband. You may write to Peggy at P.O. Box 1099, Florence, TX, 76527-1099, or e-mail her at peggy@peggymoreland.com.

The Bounty

REBECCA BRANDEWYNE

A Little Texas Two-Step
PEGGY MORELAND

Silhouette Books

Published by Silhouette Books
America's Publisher of Contemporary Romance

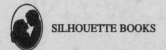 SILHOUETTE BOOKS

Copyright in the collection:
© 2002 by Harlequin Books S.A.

ISBN 0-373-48476-3

The publisher acknowledges the copyright holders
of the individual works as follows:

THE BOUNTY
Copyright © 1995 by Rebecca Brandewyne

A LITTLE TEXAS TWO-STEP
Copyright © 1997 by Peggy Bozeman Morse

Visit Silhouette at www.eHarlequin.com

Printed in U.S.A.

THE BOUNTY

Rebecca Brandewyne

* * *

For my karate instructor,
Sensei Nanci Smith.
In friendship and with appreciation.

Dear Reader,

When my editor, Tara Gavin, called me about writing this novella, I was thrilled because this would be my first contemporary work, and so a real challenge for me. How would I take all those characteristics that had always made my historical heroes so dangerous and exciting and put them into today's man? Obviously I wasn't going to do a story about the boy next door! So I started thinking about some of my own less-than-tame hobbies, such as karate and target shooting, and that led me to consider all the action-adventure movies I've enjoyed over the years. Then I knew I had to have a wild, seductive hero that somebody like Mel Gibson, Steven Seagal or Jean-Claude Van Damme might play on film. So thanks to those guys for Martin Riggs, Casey Ryback, Chance Boudreaux—and for my own Rafer Starr. Thanks, too, to my friend investigator Mauro Corvasce for his tale about the female bounty hunter with whom he once worked—and who, despite her skirt, "got her man" with a flying tackle. I hope you enjoyed how my own heroine, Hayley Harper, got Dolan Pike and her hero, Rafer Starr, each in her own special fashion!

Rebecca Brandewyne

Chapter One

Twenty-five thousand dollars. That's what Dolan Pike represented to Hayley Harper. Money in the bank, money she desperately needed and could make last a year, if she were careful. So, no matter what it took, she wasn't about to let it—or Pike—get away. Thus resolved, she deliberately leaned forward to provide him a better look at the swell of her full, generous breasts displayed by her liberally unbuttoned, red-bandanna blouse as, after collecting the empties, she plunked another ice-dripping, long-necked bottle of beer down on the cork coaster lying on the chipped, wood-grained Formica table before him. The wide, inviting smile she flashed him had in the past beguiled criminals even more hardened and cunning than he, and like that of Pavlov's dog, Pike's tongue was already hanging out in response.

"Will there be anything else, lover boy?" Hayley drawled, just softly enough that he had to bend near to hear her above the blaring jukebox and the raucous talk and laughter of the Saturday-night crowd gathered at the Watering Hole, the local favorite—possibly because it was just about the only—honky-tonk for miles around. Despite that outside the spring night air was cool, the barroom itself was hot. Perspiration glistened on Hayley's upper lip and trickled down her exposed cleavage, mingling sensually with the potent, musky fragrance of her perfume. Pike's nostrils twitched as he inhaled the scent of her. "I like to keep my customers happy…if you know what I mean?" Her heavily green-shadowed, kohl-rimmed eyes spoke volumes as her tongue darted forth to suggestively moisten her mouth, bright red with lipstick.

The man would have had to be a complete fool to misunderstand her—and Pike hadn't managed to commit more than a dozen armed robberies, to jump bail after his last arrest, and subsequently to evade recapture for the last two and a half years, by being a fool. He might be a high school dropout, but what he lacked in education and intelligence, he compensated for with a dangerous, animal cunning and a vicious dearth of morals. Inside his skull lurked a brain as sly as that of a weasel stealing eggs from a hen house before bolting back to its hidey-hole. He'd got away clean from all but the last of his several bank jobs by being clever enough not to step foot inside any bank itself. Instead, his MO—as in modus operandi—had consisted of his pulling his pickup up to one of a branch bank's drive-up windows and loading into the receptacle not a withdrawal slip, but a bomb triggered by a remote-control detonator, whose explosive device he'd then sent through the tube to the teller, along with a note threatening to blow up the bank if the teller didn't empty the contents of all the cash drawers into money pouches, which were then to be hand delivered to him outside. With a pair of high-powered binoculars, Pike, his face concealed by a black ski mask, had watched from his truck through the bank's windows to be certain his instructions were carried out to the letter. With everybody in the bank terrified at the thought of his depressing the red button on the bomb's detonator should he hear the sound of sirens wailing or see patrol cars approaching, no employee had ever proved brave enough to set off the bank's alarm system. Still, like most criminals, Pike fancied himself smarter than he really was, smarter than the law, unlikely to be caught—despite his rap sheet of previous arrests, all but the last for more minor offenses—and, if ever once more apprehended, able to make good his escape a second time.

Now, a knowing, anticipatory grin split his thin lips, revealing crooked, tobacco-stained teeth as he leered up at Hayley smugly, drunkenly. The beer she'd just brought him was his sixth; she'd kept track, just as she'd kept the black plastic bowl of salty pretzels on his table filled to brimming all night to ensure his thirst. Drink befuddled a man, slowed his wits and reflexes, gave her an advantage that, being a woman, she sometimes needed to hook him.

"Jest lookin' at you's enough to make a man think he'd died and gone to heaven, angel." Pike's beady, bleary eyes roamed over her cascade of gleaming, honey blond hair, her svelte, curvaceous figure licentiously as he lounged in his chair, hips thrust forward to emphasize the obvious bulge in his ragged jeans. Ostentatiously unfolding a wad of bills he took from the pocket of his T-shirt, he peeled off enough to pay for the beer and a generous tip, besides, making sure Hayley noticed the amount of the extra cash he laid on her metal, cork-lined serving tray. Then he slowly slid his hand up her left leg to cup her buttocks, enticingly encased in a pair of very short, very tight denim cutoffs. "How 'bout it, angel? You wanna spread your pretty wings for me, so's I can teach you how to really fly…higher 'n you've ever been before?"

Imperceptibly, Hayley's cat green eyes hardened and her cherry red mouth tightened at his crude, boastful question, and at the unwelcome, offensive feel of his hand upon her backside. Pike was scum, everything she heartily despised in a man: an ignorant, racist redneck; a conceited, sexist pig; a felonious lawbreaker. She wouldn't be at all surprised if, in addition to robbing banks, he belonged to one of the White Supremacist groups scattered throughout the Northwest. No doubt, it was from them that he'd learned how to build the bombs he'd used during his bank jobs, having favored a sawed-off shotgun at convenience- and liquor-store holdups in the past, graduating to the big time only after a stint in prison. It was all Hayley could do to keep from snatching up his beer bottle and bashing him over the head with it, knocking him senseless right then and there. But she'd learned the hard way not to let her temper get the best of her on a job. So, instead, swallowing her revulsion, she forced herself to pick up Pike's money and to make an entertaining show of slowly tucking it down inside her lace, demi-cup bra, so the bills nestled temptingly in the valley between her breasts. All the while she thought with grim satisfaction how she was really, if he gave her any trouble whatsoever later, going to enjoy giving him the business end of her stout *kapo* before handcuffing him, throwing him into her small recreational vehicle and then hauling him off to the nearest sheriff's office, in order to collect the $25,000 bounty on his head.

"You keep those tips coming like that, lover boy, and after my shift ends, we'll be soaring all night." Hayley's voice was low, smoky, sexy, like molasses heating over a fire.

The idea of actually going to bed with Pike gagged her. And not for the first time, she pitied the other barmaids, who, unlike her, were the genuine article and, provided a man had been forthcoming with his tips—and sometimes even if he hadn't—were seldom averse to going home with a customer after closing time. Hayley couldn't have lived like that. She didn't understand how other women did, despite knowing that unfortunate circumstances often drove them to it. Sometimes it was the only way they could make ends meet, especially if they had small children to support—the result, in far too many cases, of their having got mixed up with the wrong man: a worthless bum, an alcoholic, a doper, an abusive brute, or a hard-core criminal like Pike.

Every time Hayley dragged a bail jumper back to face justice, she felt she was striking a blow not only for law and order, but also for every poor woman who had ever suffered at a man's callus hands. Sometimes she even fancied herself on a crusade with her one-woman bounty-hunting agency, cleaning up filth so the streets would be safe for women and children alike—after which women everywhere could direct their attention to educating otherwise basically decent men, who just hadn't seen the light yet when it came to equality of the sexes. During her investigation of Pike's case history, background, acquaintances and habits, she'd discovered that his ex-wife and three little kids were living in a shack, subsisting on welfare and food stamps, struggling just to keep their heads above water. Given his disadvantaged upbringing, typical of so many law offenders, Hayley would have had more sympathy for Pike if he'd resorted to armed robbery for his family's benefit. But it appeared that he'd selfishly blown his loot on himself instead. The purchase of a shiny new "Dually" pickup, complete with a well-stocked toolbox bolted across the bed, and endless bouts of carousing had punctuated his last-known crime spree.

A sucker for beer and beauty both, Pike had clearly taken the bait Hayley had dangled before him; now, all she had to do was reel him in. Surreptitiously she glanced at the round, luminous-dial-faced clock that hung above the mirrors behind the brass-railed bar that ran the length of the barroom's east wall. Another thirty minutes, and it would be "last call." She'd waited two and a half years to nab Pike; if she had to, she could endure another thirty minutes of his crass leering and grabbing, managing to fob him off until closing time, when she'd give him something—although not at all what he was expecting—to remember her by outside in the Watering Hole's gravel parking lot. With feigned reluctance, Hayley turned from her prey, intending to sashay away with a toss of her head that would set her dangling hoop earrings to dancing provocatively, and with a sway of her hips that would keep Pike firmly hooked until the vigorous ringing of the cow bell suspended over the bar, which sounded "last call." But Pike had other ideas. Before she could make good her escape, he grabbed her wrist and, in a slobbering caress, pressed his lips to her upturned palm, his tongue snaking out to lick off the last traces of the melted ice from the beer bottle.

"What's your hurry, angel?" he asked, practically drooling.

Hayley's hand clenched convulsively on her serving tray. Thoughts of whacking Pike in his weasely face with it, bloodying and breaking his sharp, pointed nose, crossed her mind. But again, with difficulty, she tamped down her temper—although she was unable to repress a shudder that, fortunately, Pike mistook for being sexual in nature.

Just grin and bear it, Hayley, honey, she told herself sternly. *Pike might not be prime stock, but he's still cash on the hoof. And having to put up with a few uncouth passes is a small price to pay for the chance to keep the agency going a little while longer.*

"Oooh, you *are* a lover boy, aren't you? I can hardly wait till closing. But right now, I've got to get back to work. Buckshot gets awful mad if the barmaids slack off on hustling drinks." Hayley nodded toward the big, beefy proprietor of the Watering Hole. He was perched on a high stool behind the old-fashioned cash register that sat at one end of the bar, the buckshot-loaded shotgun that had earned him his sobriquet propped up close at hand as a deterrent against brawls. He was glaring at her censuringly for wasting so much time with Pike when the barroom was packed full with free-spending, beer-swilling customers. "You don't want me to lose my job now, do you?"

Pike snorted at the prospect. "Buckshot'd be a fool to fire a woman like you. Bet you sell more beer 'n a brewery!"

"Miss. Hey, miss! *Miss!* Yeah, you, blondie!" The man hollering at Hayley from the nearby pool table gazed at her coolly as, finally realizing he was addressing her and not one of the other barmaids above the cacophony of music and babble, she glanced over in his direction. As he leaned against the pool table, casually chalking the tip of his cue, his eyes flicked from her to Pike and then back to her again. Then one brow lifted demonically and his lips twisted sardonically, making his disgust for her—and her apparent taste in men—plain. Mortified, Hayley blushed with shame and embarrassment before she reminded herself that she was *not,* in reality, a cheap barroom tramp on the make, for which the pool shooter had obviously and, given the circumstances, understandably taken her. "You think you could pay a little less attention to your boyfriend there and a little more to your customers? I've been waiting so long to be served that my tongue's swollen from thirst. Can I get a beer over here or what?"

Hayley had noticed the man earlier but hadn't paid him much attention. Now, from long habit—her sixth sense beginning to prickle, warning her that he might be trouble—she mentally sized him up.

Perhaps spruced up and dressed in an Armani suit instead of the old, short-sleeved blue chambray work shirt and faded jeans that he was currently wearing he might have been not just handsome, but actually drop-dead gorgeous. Even as it was, there was something curiously, compellingly, attractive about his rough, unkempt appearance. The mane of dark, woodsy-brown hair that brushed his broad shoulders and the small, thin gold hoop in his left earlobe both marked him as a rebel by nature. The stubble of beard that shadowed his lean, hard visage revealed a careless attitude toward what he deemed unimportant. The casually open collar of his shirt, which partially exposed the fine mat of hair on his chest, hinted at sensuality. The copper-tinged skin indicated a strain, somewhere in his genes, of American Indian blood, a heritage not particularly uncommon in the Northwest, but seldom resulting in facial bones so strongly but finely sculpted, the product of noble ancestry and in sharp contrast to those of most of the Watering Hole's patrons. The pool shooter had got the best of both worlds—and his arrogant stance, one thumb now hooked in the leather belt slung low on his narrow, provocatively-thrust-forward hips, said he knew it, too. King only of the barroom beasts, he might be, but he was a king all the same—a lion among jackals, prowling and dangerous.

Framed by thick, unruly brows and spiked with thick black lashes that appeared as though they often concealed long, brooding thoughts, his dark, deep-set hazel eyes held a predatory glitter in the dim, smoky light of the barroom as they raked her. The nostrils of his chiseled nose flared as though he'd caught her musky scent; his carnal mouth curved, baring even, white teeth in a wicked smile that mesmerized and beguiled, as a carnivore might hypnotize its prey in that heartbeat just before fatally striking. His hard, determined jaw, which bespoke a man accustomed to getting what he wanted, was softened only by the cleft in his chin, alone of which suggested that his savage temperament could be gentled, if not tamed, by those who knew the way. He was tall, a couple of inches over six feet, Hayley's expert eye judged, and would weigh more than he looked, because his sleek, rangy body was corded with the kind of muscles that came only from manual labor or regular workouts—probably the former, she speculated, taking in the unusual tattoo on his bare right forearm.

From past experience, she knew that tattoos usually indicated a military, blue-collar, or criminal background. But if this last were the case, she didn't recall the pool shooter's face staring back at her from any of the more recent Wanted posters she'd carefully examined, before stashing them in a drawer in her RV. Regardless, she would have remembered the tattoo—an "identifying mark"—had she seen mention of it on the sheets. Still, that didn't mean he wasn't bad news. Instinctively she knew he was a man who wouldn't back down from a fight, and beside her, Pike was already bristling like an eager, untried timber wolf about to defend his territory.

"'Last call' isn't for another thirty minutes. So just keep

your shirt on, mister. I'll be right with you,'' Hayley called to the pool shooter, relieved that he'd at least given her a good excuse for pulling away from Pike.

Unfortunately, as she'd feared, Pike didn't see it that way at all.

"Why don't you git somebody else to wait on you—or else git lost, man!'' he snarled, slurring his words and glowering threateningly at the pool shooter. "Angel here's taken, ain'tcha, angel?''

Without ruining all her deceitful, demeaning but necessary efforts to gain Pike's interest, Hayley could hardly disagree. Inwardly she sighed, now certain there was indeed going to be trouble. Unwillingly she forced a smile to her lips and nodded her head, silently reminding herself of the role she'd so carefully established and played over the past few weeks, once she had cajoled Buckshot into hiring her. Her success had been based on a not-quite-so-false hard-luck story, a stream of crocodile tears born of an onion in her handbag, and a low-cut, pullover knit shirt coupled with the clinging denim cutoffs she was currently wearing.

"That's right...I'm taken,'' she agreed, disliking the hard glint that had come into the pool shooter's narrowed eyes at Pike's insulting words and knowing how a verbal barroom confrontation more often than not rapidly escalated to a physical one—which, in this case, might wind up totally destroying not only her well-laid plan for tonight, but two-weeks' worth of hard work that she could ill afford to lose. "But I'm sure Jolene there wouldn't mind taking your order,'' she added hastily, indicating one of the other barmaids, in the hope of staving off an altercation.

"Well, I don't want Jolene. I want *you*...angel,'' the pool shooter insisted perversely, his voice low, insolent. His eyes smoldered like twin embers as they deliberately ravished her, lingering covetously, unmistakably, on her breasts and the juncture of her inner thighs, igniting within her a sudden, jolting heat that coursed through her entire body, as though an electric shock had leapt from him to

her. Confused and unnerved, Hayley shivered; she could
have sworn that just moments ago, there had been nothing
in his glance but contempt for her. Now it was as though
he desired her and intentionally aimed to rile Pike by taking
her from him, notions the pool shooter's next words appeared to confirm. "So, why don't you go fetch me a beer
and tell old ferret-face there to take a hike—preferably a
long one."

"Hey, I don't like the way you're talkin', man—and I
like even less the way you're lookin' at my woman!" Savagely scraping his chair back from the table, Pike leapt to
his feet, enraged. He had a volatile temper, Hayley knew,
its fuse frequently shortened, as now, by liquor. As a child,
he'd often been beaten by his loutish, backwoods father,
besides. As was the result in so many battered children,
instead of turning him against violence, his father's brutal-
ity had left Pike equally as quick to resort to his fists. "You
shut your friggin' mouth, and leave her alone, you bastard—or I'll kick your sorry half-breed Injun ass!"

At Pike's threat, a tight, mocking grin that did not quite
reach his flinty eyes curved the pool shooter's lips.

"Well, come on!" he taunted. "If you think you're big
enough!"

Even Hayley, her every sense alert, was taken by surprise
at the speed with which events progressed. Pike charged
forward, fists swinging, connecting, to his astonishment,
with nothing but air as the pool shooter stepped lightly,
agilely, aside, using his cue like a *bo*, a Japanese long staff
that was Hayley's own specialty when it came to martial
arts weapons. Turning swiftly to land—legs spread, knees
bent—in the traditional horse stance, the pool shooter
jammed the butt end of the cue into Pike's stomach, dou-
bling him over. Then, deftly pivoting into a right front
stance while bringing the cue level and around, the pool
shooter slammed the length of its tip end into Pike's jaw,
sending him reeling. After that, flinging the cue onto the
pool table, the pool shooter grabbed Pike by both the scruff

of the neck and the left arm, the latter of which he twisted up behind Pike's back as—apparently wise to Buckshot's means of settling barroom disputes—he roughly, rapidly, half marched, half shoved Pike through the crowded barroom and out through the Watering Hole's front door. It all happened so fast that Hayley could see from the corners of her eyes that even the sharp-eyed, avaricious Buckshot remained unaware of the brief commotion. He had not budged from his perch to reach for the shotgun with which—as the pitted plasterboard ceiling and walls testified—he maintained what passed for acceptable behavior in his establishment, thereby keeping the cost of glass and furniture breakage to a minimum.

Fury and anxiety roiling inside her at the pool shooter's unwitting interference with her scheme to capture Pike, Hayley tossed her serving tray onto the nearest table and raced after the two men, slapping away grabbing hands and, with fists and elbows, proficiently driving aside the cowboys, lumberjacks, wildcatters and bikers who formed the bulk of the Watering Hole's clientele. She pushed past one of the two burly bouncers to rip open the front door; the cool, fresh, spring night air and the quiet hit her in a welcome blast after the heat, smoke and clamor of the barroom.

For a moment she just stood there on the flat concrete pad of the shake-shingled vestibule, catching her breath while her eyes and ears adjusted to the relative darkness and hush beyond. The string of outdoor floodlights that lined the top of the Watering Hole's painted signboard mounted on top of the roof—Buckshot was too cheap to spring for neon—did double duty by illuminating not only it, but also a portion of the gravel parking lot beyond the vestibule. Still, half the bulbs had been shot out by rowdy drunks or had burned out on their own. The night seeped like a black, amorphous stain around the edges of the light, and the tall trees of the fecund woods, which threatened to engulf the patch of open ground upon which the Watering Hole sat, cast long shadows in the silvery shower of moonbeams that dripped through the soughing branches. In the parking lot itself, cars, pickups, motorcycles, four-wheel-drive and off-road vehicles all beaded with droplets from the sweet, clean-smelling rain that had drizzled earlier, were parked helter-skelter around the crater-size potholes that now had become muddy puddles. The vehicles glowed dimly in the diffuse light, like the irradiated refuse of some post-apocalyptic world.

Damn Pike!—and damn that interfering pool shooter! The minute Hayley had taken his measure, she'd known he was going to prove a pain in the butt. Where in the hell were they? Stepping from the vestibule, she spied the two men at last. Pike had somehow managed to wrest free of the pool shooter's tight grip; now, they were engaged in combat beneath the feathery boughs of a towering pine rising up at the dark border of the parking lot. Pike was getting by far the worst of the fray. The pool shooter, it would appear, was indeed—as his stances and the way he'd used the cue earlier had seemed to indicate—a martial-arts expert, a black belt in karate, if Hayley were any judge of competency and style. Despite her own matching rank in that art, she wasn't sure she wanted to take him on. Watching him, she knew he was good. And while she'd found that a man's height often worked against him when battling her, a smaller opponent, the fact that the pool shooter outweighed her by at least seventy-five pounds was *not* to her advantage—his weight alone would take her down if he jumped on her.

On the other hand, the local sheriff might not be too happy if she dragged in Pike, with him having been beaten to a pulp. Just as they did private investigators, law-enforcement officers sometimes had a tendency to treat bounty hunters like second-class citizens. She was trained in Ryu Kyu Kempo, an Okinawan form of karate similar to the Shotokan style popularized on film by Jean-Claude Van Damme. And with her *kapo,* she *had* planned to clobber Pike over the head if he'd proved recalcitrant—not that the sheriff would know that, of course. Still, unless Pike spoke up in her defense, which seemed unlikely if she turned him in to the law, *she* might be suspected of having done the number on him. Hayley had enough problems as it was, keeping her small agency afloat; she didn't need any additional hassles, especially one that could conceivably lead to the suspension or even the revocation of her bounty-hunting license.

Digging her key ring from the pocket of her cutoffs, she ran to her RV parked to one side of the Watering Hole, unlocked the back door and climbed inside to grab her *kapo* and handcuffs off the counter within, where she'd laid them earlier next to her handbag with its gun inside, in preparation for Pike. The cuffs she shoved down inside her back pocket, but the *kapo* she kept in her hands. The solid, burnished ebony wood of the Japanese nightstick shone lethally in the moonlight as, after slamming the RV's door shut behind her, she started determinedly toward the two men, a martial glint in her eye.

By this time Pike was down on his hands and knees on the ground, scrambling to escape from the well-placed jump kick that caught him in the ribs before he could elude it, tumbling him over onto his back and knocking the wind from him. Groaning, gasping for breath, he curled into a tight ball, rocking to one side, arms clutching his ribs, knees drawn up to protect himself from further blows. Intent on their conflict, neither man noticed Hayley sneak near, flitting stealthily through the shadows, using the trunks of the trees along the boundary of the parking lot for cover, her feet making no sound on the moss, wild grass and weeds that carpeted the earthen floor of the woods.

"Had enough, dirt bag?" the pool shooter demanded harshly, scornfully, his whipcord body bent forward, hands on knees as, breathing labored, he scowled down at Pike.

"Go to hell...Injun trash!" Pike ground out between rasps for air. Blood dripping from his nose, he lay there sickly, looking as though he might puke at any moment.

Gingerly, with the back of his hand, the pool shooter wiped away a trickle of blood at the corner of his own lips, then he spat in the gravel to rid his mouth of the bad taste.

"Come on! Get up! You ain't hurt that bad! A broken nose and a couple of busted ribs, maybe, is all. You're lucky it ain't worse. I don't take kindly to insults from pond scum like you. Now, get up, you redneck!"

Still, Pike made no effort to move. At that, with a snarl of anger and disgust, the pool shooter hunkered down, powerful hands grabbing hold of Pike's faded old Jerry Jeff Walker concert T-shirt—which had prompted the last gibe—to haul him roughly to his feet.

She would get no better opportunity, Hayley knew. Stepping up behind the pool shooter, she swung her arm back, raising the *kapo,* then, with an expert flick of her wrist, she brought it down hard. But some sixth sense equal to her own evidently warning him, the pool shooter glanced up over his shoulder at the last minute, snapping his left arm up and over in an upward block, just in time to deflect the intended strike. He grunted with pain as the nightstick buffeted his inner forearm, knocking him off balance so he stumbled over Pike and nearly fell. Quickly, before the pool shooter could regain his footing, Hayley lunged forward to attack again, this time delivering a crack upside his skull, which drove him like a poleaxed steer to his knees. A practiced roundhouse kick to the opposite side of his head finished him off. He stared at her dazedly, disbelievingly, for a moment, before his eyes slowly fluttered closed and he slumped into a crumpled heap upon the ground.

Lord, what if she'd accidentally killed him? Hayley wondered uneasily as she warily crept forward to take a closer look at his fallen figure. That second clout she'd dealt him with her *kapo had* been pretty hard; she'd been so worried about not doing him in with the first, about his getting the jump on her as a result, pinning her with his muscle and weight. As she stared down at him, an image of the pool shooter's hard, corded thighs straddling her, imprisoning her, pressing her down, came unbidden into her mind. She remembered how his eyes had strayed so hotly, so desirously, over her body, the answering heat that had surged inside her; and she shivered—although not entirely with apprehension.

It had been years since her divorce, months since she'd slept with a man. She was a strong, intelligent, independent woman who hunted hardened criminals for a living. Most men couldn't handle that, backing off, like her ex-husband, once they discovered that beneath her beautiful exterior lay not the joke-provoking dumbness of the stereotypical blond bimbo, but a smart mind and a steely will that demanded respect and equal status. Hayley wished that just once in her life she could meet a man unafraid of that challenge, a man willing to face it head-on, to meet it halfway. But, then, even if she did, her gypsy life-style of living in an RV, wandering from place to place, with only a post office box to call home, would in the end no doubt make the relationship unworkable. No matter how he'd looked at her or how she'd responded, the pool shooter was no different from all the rest of the men she had ever known. Only her father, "Gentleman Jim" Harper—so called for his pugilistic abilities, which had been in keeping with those of the famous Gentleman Jim Belcher and which had in his younger days won him a Golden Gloves boxing championship—had valued her strength, her intellect and her abilities, teaching her to value them, too. After all this time since his death, she still missed him.

Kneeling beside the pool shooter's sprawled form and cautiously laying two fingers at the side of his neck, Hayley sighed with relief as she felt his pulse beating steadily. Thank God, he was still alive. Still, his being out like the proverbial light didn't mean he wouldn't come around soon. When that happened, she wanted Pike handcuffed, stashed in her RV and both of them well away from the Watering Hole, in case the pool shooter proved stubborn enough to attempt to finish what he'd started. Rising, stuffing her *kapo* through a belt loop on her cutoffs and jerking her cuffs from her back pocket, she turned to the spot where Pike had been lying, doubled up, a few feet away.

Damn! He was gone!

He must somehow have managed to get to his feet and to stagger off while her attention had been focused on her examination of the pool shooter's unconscious body. Her face tightening with vexation and despair, Hayley glanced about feverishly. She just couldn't lose Pike! She just couldn't! It would mean the waste not only of the months she had spent tracking him, but also of the past two-weeks' worth of hard work, of standing on her feet all night, slinging beers and humiliating herself by dressing up and acting like a cheap tramp, letting Pike paw her—for nothing! Not to mention the loss of the $25,000 bounty she so desperately needed.

The sudden, deep-throated growl of a monstrous 460-HP engine springing to life, the piercing of the darkness by a pair of brilliant headlights, followed by the loud crunching of gravel, alerted Hayley to Pike's whereabouts. He was in his Dually— getting away! Crying out in protest, she bolted toward the black pickup now bumping and fishtailing along a crooked path through the parking lot toward the narrow backwoods road beyond. Each pair of dual rear wheels, which had given the truck its nickname, were spinning, and in their wake both gravel and water came flying out of the puddled potholes.

"Wait! Wait!" Hayley shouted, running toward the Dually, waving her arms wildly in a futile attempt to flag down Pike. He did stop—but only just long enough to plaster a feeble grin on his swelling lips and to yell out the open, driver's-side window, "Some other time, angel." He gunned the pickup's engine deafeningly before he lurched onto the blacktop, tires screeching and burning rubber as he sped west down the road into the darkness.

He was gone. And in the RV she would never catch him—at least, not tonight. She'd lost him. Hot tears of bitter frustration stung Hayley's eyes at the realization. Angrily, ashamed at her unaccustomed display of weakness, she dashed them away with the back of her hand. Then she slowly tucked her cuffs into her back pocket. By God, it was all that damned pool shooter's fault! she fumed. If not for *him,* she'd be on her way to the nearest sheriff's office by now, with Pike securely cuffed and stuffed in the RV. Pike had got away...but maybe all was not yet lost; maybe that pool shooter *was* wanted, she thought suddenly, her eyes narrowing speculatively at the idea. Maybe he was worth something, after all, and she just didn't know it. She'd find out who he was, Hayley decided resolutely, as she strode toward the place where she'd left him. Then, with the internal modem of her laptop computer, which was inside the RV, she would run a make on him.

Good thing for the pool shooter that he was still lying passed out on the ground, because she was so mad right now that if he hadn't been, she'd have knocked him witless again. Her mouth set in a grim, determined line, Hayley bent and, having taken the precaution of cuffing his hands behind his back first, began methodically to rifle the pockets of his jeans. Locating his leather wallet, she slipped it out and flipped it open.

"You've caused me a whole lot of trouble, Pool Shooter. So, now, we'll just see who you are. If there's a warrant out for you for so much as a lousy parking ticket, you're going to be sorry!" she declared aloud, glaring down at his unresponsive figure. Then, manipulating his driver's license so she could get a better look at it in the faint light, she inhaled sharply as she read his name: *Rafer Starr.* "Damn, Hayley!" she whispered to herself, stricken. "You've really done it this time—dumped the fat out of the frying pan and right into the fire! And not a fire extinguisher in sight! Great...that's just great. Way to go, Hayley." A man like him, with a name like his...she couldn't possibly be mistaken. It had to be *him!*

Her hands trembling, she hastily unlocked her cuffs

about his wrists, then crammed his wallet back into his jeans, her heart pounding as he began to moan and to stir. She had to get away! She had to get away before he came to, otherwise, there was no telling what he might to do her! Leaving him where he lay, she raced to the RV, yanked open the door on the driver's side and clambered into the cab, punching the key into the ignition.

"Come on, come on," she muttered to the engine as it balked and sputtered lamely, *rrr rrr rrr,* refusing to start. Bad battery, bad alternator, bad starter? No, not now, not now! The engine was just a little cold, that was all; please, let that be all. Nerves strung as taut as thong, she pumped the accelerator a couple of times, then turned the ignition again. This time, to her vast relief, the engine roared to life. "Go, Hayley, go!" she urged herself frantically, wondering dimly in some far corner of her mind if, living and working alone for so long, she weren't growing prematurely senile, talking to herself all the time. Maybe she should get a dog or a cat.

Or a man, she could almost hear her father prod... and then chuckle at her indignation.

Grimacing wryly at the image, she expertly whipped the RV around, tires slinging gravel as she barreled through the parking lot toward the road, hitting a pothole that jolted her head into the ceiling, causing her to wince and to swear. That was another thing for which she owed Rafer Starr! On the radio, Waylon Jennings was belting out "Ladies Love Outlaws."

"Like hell, they do, Waylon," she muttered with annoyance, abruptly twisting the knob to the Off position.

Rafer Starr was an outlaw—of a sort.

Hayley tried hard not to dwell on that disturbing thought as she swung onto the blacktop and, following Pike's trail, headed west into the night.

Chapter Two

On the Road
Wyoming

She shouldn't have panicked. There had been absolutely no reason for her to panic. In her line of work it was not only unprofessional behavior but also dangerous, as her father had taught her. Panicked people didn't think straight—and she hadn't. Still, as she plowed along the narrow, wending, backwoods road, pushing the small RV faster than she ought, Hayley's hands gripped the steering wheel so tightly that her knuckles shone white in the spray of moonlight through the windshield. And she could not seem to prevent herself from checking the rearview mirror every few minutes, searching for a pair of headlights coming hard and fast behind her.

Rafer Starr. That name was legendary among bounty hunters. He was the best in the business, maybe the best there ever had been or ever would be. Even her father, Gentleman Jim Harper—himself a bounty hunter extraordinaire—had spoken well of Starr, had respected and regarded him highly.

"The man's something else, Hayley," her father had said once, shaking his head and smiling wryly, although not without admiration, even so. "Before he resigned his commission, he was a captain in the Marines—Special Forces.

Even then, as now, he was a law unto himself, they claim, notorious for disregarding orders, daring—downright reckless, some would tell you, especially after that wild stunt he was reported to have pulled down in South America. Plus, it was rumored that he beat the tar out of a fellow officer afterward, calling him a fool who'd jeopardized men's lives on a mission. Still, the fact that, despite his antics and insubordination, Starr was never dishonorably discharged speaks for his abilities. It's said that his men would have followed him to the gates of hell—they had that much faith in him. This I do know, however—whatever else Starr might be, he's one hell of a man—strong, smart and capable, a professional…the kind of man *you* need, Hayley, instead of another namby-pamby like Logan. Money wasn't all *he* reeked of! Why, every time I think about the night that knife-wielding mugger attacked you, and how Logan went running back inside the restaurant—"

"He went to get help, Dad," Hayley had interjected, but her voice had lacked conviction, for she'd felt, as her father had, that instead of fleeing the scene, her ex-husband, Logan Anthony Deverell III, should have come to her aid. As they had so often during their marriage, they'd quarreled that evening; it had long been a bone of contention between them that after their wedding, she'd continued to work for her father. Angry as a result, Logan had been several steps behind Hayley when the mugger had leapt out from between two cars in the shadowy parking lot to grab her around the neck, pressing a bowie knife to her throat and demanding her purse and jewelry. Instead of trying to defend her, Logan—fearing for his own safety, and assuming that, being a bounty hunter, she could take care of herself—had raced back inside the restaurant where they'd just finished eating a late supper, leaving her to deal with the threatening mugger on her own. Shattered by Logan's lack of caring, his callous desertion of her in the face of her endangered life, Hayley had divorced him a month later. "And at least he did call the police."

"Mighty damned generous of him!" Her father had snorted with disgust. "Man was a coward! Always had things too soft, too easy, stepping right into his daddy's shoes, taking over the family's oil business instead of having to work his way up in the world! If he'd have had to get a little bit of that oil, a little bit of that grease and dirt from his daddy's oil fields on his hands, it might have made a man of him instead of his turning out to be such a wimp! But Rafer Starr, now…there's a man! *He* wouldn't have cut and run, abandoned you to the mercy of a mugger's knife! No, ma'am! Too bad he's such a loner; we could use him in the agency now that my old ticker's not what it used to be and you've still got some learning to do, puddin'."

"Don't you worry about me, Dad. I'll be fine," Hayley had insisted, distressed at the idea of her father's bringing an outsider into their small agency. She knew she would do everything in her power to look after Harper & Daughter and her father both, just as he'd always taken care of her since she was a child and her mother had died in a car accident. Further, although Jim Harper had never liked or approved of her ex-husband, he'd loathed even more the thought of her being left all alone someday, he being her only family. To Hayley's dismay, after his heart attack, her father had taken up matchmaking on her behalf. She hadn't liked the notion he'd had about Rafer Starr's being the man for her. Logan had taught her that no man, no matter his profession, wanted a "macho-woman" bounty hunter, as her ex-husband had called her, for a wife, and she wasn't about to make another mistake when it came to men. "And besides, the doctor says you'll be back up to speed in no time, Dad."

But much to Hayley's deep shock and grief, instead of regaining his former good health, Jim Harper had unex-

pectedly suffered a second—and fatal—heart attack. It had
taken Hayley a long time to recover from his death. Holi-
days, especially, had been hard, with her having no other
family to turn to. On top of her sorrow, she'd soon discovered how difficult it was going to be for her to keep the
agency solvent without her father—how few people, despite all her training and credentials, took her, a woman,
seriously as a bounty hunter. Still, determined not to fail
her father, to keep the agency that was his legacy alive,
she'd thrown herself into her work, managing somehow to
survive. It had been three years now since Jim Harper's
death, three years since she'd thought of their conversation—and of Rafer Starr.

"What's Starr think he's doing…poking his nose into
my business, anyhow?" Hayley asked herself crossly as she
glanced nervously at the rearview mirror again. "Dolan
Pike is *my* bounty, damn it!—not his."

Still, deep down inside, she had a sinking feeling that
not only was Starr *not* going to see it that way, but also
that he was going to see *her* just as she'd seen him: as an
unwelcome interference, one to be got rid of as quickly as
possible. That's why she'd panicked. His reputation was
such that she wouldn't have put it past him not just to have
subdued her physically, but actually to have gagged and
handcuffed her and left her locked in the toilet stall of her
RV or something. He was wild, brazen, unpredictable and
ruthless—an "outlaw" in the country-western vernacular—
not known for being a particularly nice guy if he felt that
someone was poaching on his preserve. Without exception
he always worked alone, never in tandem with another
bounty hunter. His one-man agency—Shooting Starr, Incorporated—was one of the most successful in the business,
renowned for bringing down the big game. Pike's $25,000
bounty was hardly even worth Starr's time—and it meant
everything in the world to her!

Now, some of her anxiety fading at the lack of headlights

behind her, and her anger rising at the thought of Starr snatching her hard-earned bounty right out from under her nose, Hayley wished perversely that she'd hit him even harder, had taken a chapter from his own book and had cuffed him and stuffed him into the Watering Hole's Dumpster out in back of the rundown building, where he might have been stuck for at least a day or two before being discovered, giving her a jump on him. He'd treated rivals similarly in the past, she'd heard through the grapevine, so it would have served him right to have been given a dose of his own medicine. Now, not only did she have to worry about catching up to Pike, but she'd have to be constantly looking over her shoulder, too, for Starr. He'd seen her face when she'd whacked him and he would remember it. If he ever saw her again, he'd probably leap at the chance to even the score between them, especially if he learned that she was after Pike, also.

Hayley was so tired and upset that she drove off onto the sandy verge when a deer suddenly crashed from the woods to bound across the road in front of her. When the glare of her headlights illuminated it, she had just time enough to slam on her brakes and to swerve to avoid hitting the startled animal. It came within inches of being clipped by her front bumper but, to her relief, somehow managed to escape. Still, since she was an animal lover, the incident rattled her so badly that after she'd recovered her composure and spent several minutes searching for a turn-off, she found a place to park the RV in the woods on the side of the road for the night.

After making sure all the doors were locked and the blinds drawn, she stripped to her French-cut lace panties and pulled on her favorite old nightshirt, which had the words *Hard-hearted Woman* emblazoned across the front. She'd bought it after her divorce, to remind herself never to be a fool in love again. At the sink she gratefully scrubbed off all the makeup that, in keeping with her barmaid role, she'd applied with an atypical heavy hand to her face; then she brushed her teeth. After that she retrieved her automatic pistol from her purse and climbed into the wide bunk over the cab. Making sure the gun had a round in the chamber, she tucked it securely into one of the berth's cubbyholes in which she kept it at night, within easy reach. It was a Glock 19, given to her by her father. The polymer used in the construction of the compact pistol made it lighter and so gave it less of a recoil than most nine-millimeters, so it was easier for a woman to handle. In addition, it fired fifteen rounds and had a trigger safety, meaning it was always ready when she needed it. Hayley had been compelled to use it only a few times in her career, but she was always prepared to do so. A woman in her line of work couldn't be too careful.

Flipping the light switch, so only the RV's night-lights glowed, she flopped over onto her stomach, pulling the blankets up about her and her down pillow sideways under her head, so she could wrap her arms around it—not so comforting as the presence of another human being or even a teddy bear, perhaps, but it was all she had. Somewhere in the night, a solitary animal cried, echoing the loneliness she resolutely kept at bay, locked away in her heart.

To her perturbation, when she slept, her dreams were of Rafer Starr.

With her laptop computer's internal modem, knowing there was no time to go through proper channels, and re-minding herself that she was leaving the files exactly as she'd found them, Hayley spent the better part of the morning guiltily hacking into various credit card data bases to see if Dolan Pike had used any major credit card late last night or early this morning—to pay for a motel room or breakfast—so she could pick up his trail. But much to her frustration, her investigation proved fruitless; she turned up nothing under his real name or any of his known aliases.

He could be anywhere by now. That being the case, she saw no choice but to keep traveling west until she reached the next town. It wouldn't be much of a town, Wyoming having the smallest number of residents in the nation. Even its largest city, Casper, had a population of only 51,000 people. But at least she could purchase some groceries at the local market, ask around, find out if anybody had seen Pike or the Dually. Her biggest fear was that Pike would head deep into the wooded mountains, where she'd lose him for sure, because to track him there, she'd have to possess special knowledge and training—like Rafer Starr—which she lacked.

Finding nothing worth listening to on the radio to entertain her while she drove, Hayley popped Styx's *Paradise Theater* CD into the compact disc player, programming the song sequence so only her favorite tune by the '70s rock band would play, over and over—a habit that had driven her ex-husband up the wall. He'd never understood how certain music put her in certain moods, how she wanted to listen to a song until she couldn't stand to hear it again for a while. Right now, she wanted the sounds of what she'd always thought of as hard-driving, bluesy rock wailing in her ears. Generation X didn't know what it was missing, she thought as the opening strains of "Snowblind" filled the RV; today's music was synthesized and digitized to the point that in exchange for clarity of sound, it had lost much of the rough-and-tumble heart and soul that had characterized the music of the sixties and seventies belonging to the Baby Boomers.

Nowadays, musicians didn't have to be able to play their instruments, only to produce a few chords; singers didn't have to be able to sing, only to "rap." There were no Lennons and McCartneys, no Hendrixes and Claptons, no Joplins and Arethas anymore. At the thought, Hayley reflected wryly that she was getting old; in a few more years, forty would be just down the road for her, through the

woods and over the mountain—or over the hill, as the case
might be, although not if she had anything to say about it.
Still, her "biological clock" was ticking. Although she
didn't regret divorcing her ex-husband, she did wish that
they'd had children, that something to be treasured and cel-
ebrated had come of their marriage. She would have liked
to have had a family. But Logan hadn't wanted any kids—
something else, like assuming she'd give up being a bounty
hunter, he'd neglected to tell her until after their wedding.

As she listened intently to the lead guitar's intricate,
soaring, sliding notes, emphasized by the Marshall's
preamp being kicked on overdrive; to James Young's and
Tommy Shaw's powerful, emotion-filled vocals; to the
dark, soul-stirring lyrics about emptiness and being "snowblind" with a desperate, aching hunger and need, which
emotions were adroitly only implied by and so must be
derived from the words, Hayley unwittingly recalled the
way Rafer Starr's eyes had appraised her in the Watering
Hole, making his desire for her plain; and again, that
strange, thrilling heat shot through her. Unlike Logan, she
couldn't imagine that Rafer Starr would have any inhibi-
tions about stating flat-out what *he* wanted and expected
from a woman. Somehow she knew instinctively that he
would mate like an animal, would be blind with passion,
savage in his hunger and need for a woman he wanted
above all others. Her heart pounded peculiarly at the notion.
For the umpteenth time since hitting the road after lunch,
she glanced in her rearview mirror but spied no one behind
her. Starr must have passed her by in the night or else had
taken a turnoff somewhere between the Watering Hole and
town. Either way, she'd succeeded in eluding him, Hayley
thought, confused and disconcerted to find that she felt not
elation, but a curious pang at the realization.

The men once under his command would have recognized that not only was Rafer Starr's present mood an ill

one, but also that while it was upon him, he should be avoided at all costs. He was not, under the best of circumstances, a man to cross; when in the grip of one of his infamous black rages, he was lethal. Last night, Dolan Pike had escaped from him, and even now, his head still ached and bore a lump on it the size of a goose egg where he'd been struck by Pike's beer-slinging, *kapo*-wielding girlfriend—a real knockout in more ways than one. Damn her! Rafer still couldn't believe how she'd managed somehow to sneak up behind him and to cosh him, conking him out cold. It had been a long time since a man—much less a mere woman—had got the best of him like that! She'd made him feel like a complete fool, a raw greenhorn in the bounty-hunting business. Because she was a woman, a cheap barroom tramp, Rafer had broken the number one rule of survival: know your enemy. He'd not only underestimated, but wholly discounted Pike's girlfriend as a player in the events that had unfolded at the Watering Hole. He would *not,* however, make that mistake again, Rafer assured himself grimly as he stared at her through the leafy branches of the bushes behind which he was currently crouched for cover.

His off-road Jeep could go where her RV couldn't and was a hell of a lot faster, besides. Last night, having lost Pike, he'd decided that the woman represented his best chance of sniffing out his quarry's trail, that sooner or later she'd lead him to her ferret-faced boyfriend. In fact, given how she and Pike had hung all over each other in the Watering Hole, Rafer had thought that it was a pretty good bet that Pike was living with her in the RV, which doubtless, like the Dually, was an ill-gotten gain bought with the loot from the bank jobs. Thus reasoning, Rafer had turned off the two-lane blacktop onto an unpaved road that, while a good deal rougher, was a shorter route to the nearest town west, and that had put him there ahead of Pike's girlfriend.

At first, when she hadn't shown by lunch, Rafer had been

afraid that his hunch had been misplaced, that instead of
heading toward town, she'd turned off somewhere along
the way and that he'd lost her and Pike both. But just when
he'd been fixing to start up the Jeep to backtrack toward
the Watering Hole, Rafer had spied the woman finally rolling into town. She'd stopped at the local market on the
corner, buying a bag of groceries, chatting at some length
with the clerk at the checkout counter while she'd paid for
them. Then she'd stepped outside to survey her surroundings carefully, either looking for Pike or making certain she
hadn't been followed, Rafer had surmised as he'd watched
her covertly from his Jeep.

When she'd finally driven out of town, he'd fallen in
behind her, taking care to hang well back so she wouldn't
spot him, since, obviously, she'd suspected she might be
tailed. No doubt Pike had warned her not to lead anyone
to him. At sundown she'd pulled off the road into a little
clearing in the woods, placed a call on her cellular telephone—presumably to Pike—then pitched camp, building
a fire over which she was currently cooking a pot of chili
and a pan of spoon bread. Rafer's mouth watered at the
savory aromas. For lunch he'd wolfed down a couple of
packaged ham-and-cheese sandwiches he'd bought at a
convenience store. But they hadn't done much to sustain
him, and now he was hungry again. Still, that the woman's
supper was nearly done indicated that her boyfriend, Pike,
ought to be showing up anytime at their rendezvous. Had
she been his woman, Rafer knew that he himself would
already have been here, eating his fill of her food and drink-
ing in his fill of her beauty.

Her silky, honey blond hair, parted on the side in the
style immortalized on film by Veronica Lake decades ago,
cascaded down past her shoulders, a luxurious mass that
framed a pale, oval face with high cheekbones skillfully
emphasized by a light dusting of dusky rose blush. Beneath
gracefully arched brows, her cat green eyes were wide and

luminous, lined with a heavy fringe of sooty lashes that, in the firelight, cast crescent smudges upon her cheeks. Her classic nose was set above a mouth that was as lush as a full-blown rose and a gamine chin with a decidedly stubborn tilt. Ripe, round breasts strained against her short-sleeved, oversize, pullover burgundy shirt. Its wide neckline bared her swanlike throat, delicate collarbones and one white shoulder, and, despite its bagginess, did little to conceal her slender, hourglass figure. Her long, shapely legs were accentuated by clinging burgundy stirrup pants and a pair of high black boots.

There was something different from last night about her now, Rafer mused as he studied her. In the subdued light cast by the snapping and sparking flames of the campfire, she looked softer somehow, fragile, vulnerable and pensive—traits he would not previously have associated with her. Maybe she was not so hard as he had at first supposed; maybe she'd just had the bad luck to get mixed up with the wrong man—although why she'd picked a weasel like Pike to begin with, Rafer couldn't fathom. With that face and body she could have had any man.

Get a grip, Rafe, he told himself sternly as he abruptly realized the unwise direction of his thoughts. *Don't be a fool again. Behind that angel face lurks a devil of a woman. She damned near killed you, for God's sake!*

This stringent reminder was reinforced by the fact that the woman had a Winchester 1300, the Defender model, propped up against a rock beside her. The 12-gauge, pistol-grip shotgun had an eighteen-inch barrel and fired eight rounds, and there was not a doubt in Rafer's mind that, like the *kapo,* she would use it, if need be. That was why he intended to secure her before Pike arrived. There was no reason to have the odds stacked two against one unless necessary. Checking the wind, then moving low and soundlessly through the brush, Rafer began to circle around behind her, an expression of grim determination upon his hard visage.

Hunkered over the campfire, a potholder in each hand, Hayley carefully lifted the ceramic lid on the big, white-speckled, blue stockpot perched on the open grill and, with the ladle resting inside, stirred the homemade chili, sniffing its steaming aroma appreciatively. It was hot, ready to eat, and she was hungry. She replaced the lid. Then, so the chili would stay warm but not burn, she slid the pot off the grill, setting it alongside the pan of spoon bread on one of the rocks that ringed the campfire. Her plate, bowl and utensils sat nearby, waiting, along with a large, gay, red-checkered cloth napkin. Just because she was eating alone didn't mean she shouldn't pamper herself with a few niceties, she'd always thought, having resolved after her divorce not to fall into a miserable rut. Now, was there anything she'd forgotten? she asked herself. Oh, yes. The butter for the spoon bread was still in the small refrigerator in the RV.

Under normal circumstances, the snapping of a twig would have warned Hayley that she was no longer alone. But as she stood, turning to fetch the butter from the RV, she mistook the sound for the crackling of the cheerily blazing campfire and so let out a startled scream when she spied Rafer standing less than six feet away, looking like some wild animal looming out of the surrounding woods' long shadows, which had come with nightfall—a dangerous predator stalking his prey. She hadn't heard him. He moved like a panther, she thought, and resembled one, too, half crouched, fixing to pounce—on her! There was not a doubt in her mind that he'd crept up on her, seeking revenge. As it had last night, unaccustomed panic rose within her. Resolutely, Hayley fought it down.

"*You!* What are you doing here? What do you want?" she asked, annoyed by the nervous note in her voice, which she knew he must have heard.

"A bowl of that chili and a slice of that spoon bread would do me for a start," Rafer rejoined lightly, slowly straightening up but not making any other move, sudden or otherwise, hoping to allay her apparent fear and suspicion, thereby still to take her off guard. "It smells real good, and I'm famished. Look, you don't have to be afraid. I'm not going to hurt you. I just want to talk, okay?"

"Yeah, right. My dinner guests always show up looking like they're on the warpath or a covert military operation!" Hayley's voice dripped with scorn as her eyes took in his appearance: the two eagle feathers braided with a narrow, beaded rawhide thong into his otherwise loose mane of hair; the wide black band, its long ends trailing, tied around his forehead; his handsome face daubed with camouflage grease, and his soldier-of-fortune attire—a pair of black combat boots, jungle fatigues and a black T-shirt that, across the front, boasted a wickedly grinning white skull wearing a Special Forces beret. Framing the skull was the wry catch phrase *Mercenaries never die. They just go to hell to regroup.* Being something of a mercenary herself, Hayley didn't need to ask the obvious question, why the word *old,* which customarily prefaced the majority of all such similar slogans, was absent. There were no old mercenaries—and no old bounty hunters, either. Neither was the automatic pistol in the shoulder holster he wore nor the knife in the leather sheath at his belted waist apropos merely for a meal and a friendly chat. "Where are your tomahawk and Uzi, Rambo?" she prodded sarcastically, wishing that her heart were not drumming so hard, so crazily, at his proximity. What was the matter with her that she continually lost her professional cool in this man's presence?

"I must have forgotten and left 'em at home. And it's Rafer, not Rambo."

"Gee, you could have fooled me!"

"Consider yourself fooled then. Now, how about that chili?"

"The only 'chili' you're going to get is a chilly goodbye, Rambo. Now, get lost—before I lose my temper and do something you'll regret even more than that crack I gave you upside the head," Hayley threatened with false bravado.

"You're making a mistake," Rafer declared, maddeningly unruffled, casually beginning to walk toward her.

"I don't think so!" she shot back defiantly, although she was shaking inside as she warily backed away from his approach.

Given his appearance and knowing his notorious reputation, she didn't trust him an inch. No matter what he'd said earlier to the contrary, he had—garbed like some half-breed Indian commando—sneaked up behind her, hoping to catch her unaware. There was no telling what he intended, only that whatever it was, it wasn't anything good—at least, not for her. Despite her caveat, he hadn't left—and didn't look as though he were planning to, either. In fact, at any moment, he would be close enough to grab her. Her gaze narrowing, Hayley swiftly gauged the distance between her and her shotgun, then her and the RV. The shotgun was closer, loaded and ready for action. Abruptly moving, she dove toward it. But Rafer was a professional, too, and in that fleeting moment in which she'd assessed her situation and selected her best option, he'd read her decision in her eyes. Springing forward at the same time as she did, he seized the wrist of her outstretched hand and began to drag her struggling figure toward him.

"Let go of me—or you'll be sorry, I swear!" Hayley warned through gritted teeth as she settled into a back stance, digging her heels into the ground and exerting a determined pull in opposition to Rafer's own, while trying to wrench her wrist loose.

"You're the one who's going to be sorry," he insisted

coolly as, before she realized what he intended, he withdrew his handcuffs from his back pocket and swiftly locked
one steel ring into place around the wrist he held imprisoned with a grip like an iron band, deliberately cutting off
her circulation. "Woman, this is one battle you can't win,
so why don't you just give up now and save us both a lot
of grief."

"Like hell I will!"

Unable to haul him off balance, terrified that he would
capture her other wrist and finish cuffing her, Hayley took
him by surprise with a side kick, slamming her right foot
straight into his chest, causing Rafer to grunt with pain and
to release his tight hold on her as he stumbled back, sprawling onto the ground. Again, she lunged toward her shotgun.
But he came up fast, trying—as he realized he was indeed,
as he had previously suspected, dealing with a woman
trained in the martial arts—to grab her around the knees so
he could yank her legs from beneath her, then flatten her
with his greater weight. To counter the offensive move,
Hayley delivered a powerful roundhouse kick to the left
side of his ribs, pivoting around. But before her spinning
hook kick could connect, Rafer grasped her ankle, twisting
her leg so she fell, although she did manage to take him
down with her by hooking her arm around his elbow.

Grappling for supremacy, they rolled on the earth together, she catching his booted foot behind her knee as they
edged perilously near to the campfire. Despite the heat cast
by the flames, which she could feel uncomfortably close
against her skin, Hayley determinedly maintained her grip
on Rafer's arm, finally maneuvering him into a joint lock,
so he was forced facedown against the ground. Normally
she could have held him immobile while she handcuffed
him, but her own cuffs were in the RV, and she was on
her knees instead of standing as she ought properly to have
been for the hold, besides.

As she reached to pull his automatic from his holster,

Rafer, with his strong right leg, captured her ankle again, roughly hauling her sideways, while, simultaneously, his fist shot out. His pistol skidded away as, adroitly, she parried the blow, following through with a back fist to his jaw, which they both knew would leave a bruise in its stunning wake. Blood spurted anew from the split corner of his mouth, wounded last night in the battle with Pike. But tumbling to the side as she was, Hayley was in no position to defend against Rafer's sweep, as she normally would have done by jumping over his foot, which hit hard behind her knees, jerking her legs up and out from under her so she landed, with a cry of pain, flat on her back, the wind knocked from her. Instantly, as she'd feared, Rafer was on top of her before she could recover, mercilessly pinning her down with his heavier weight, his corded legs imprisoning her own, his strong hands snatching her arms up over her head and locking upon her unsecured wrist the open ring on his handcuffs, so both her wrists were now caged and, regardless of how she tussled, he could hold her firm with just his left hand, leaving his right one free for whatever he might choose to use it.

The sudden, explosive battle had lasted less than ten minutes, but both Hayley and Rafer were breathing hard and fast from their exertions, each all too aware of the other—hot, flushed and sweating, adrenaline still pumping, their lithe bodies pressed together intimately, his covering her own as though he were making love to her. Hayley's nerves thrummed at the thought. Her head was spinning; she couldn't seem to catch her breath as Rafer stared down at her, taking in her blond hair tangled about her in sexy dishabille, her eyes that flashed sparks of fury at him, her shirt—torn somehow in their struggle—now half revealing her lace, demi-cup bra and heaving white breasts. As she saw where his gaze strayed, realized how she was exposed to him, she inhaled sharply, shivering with both fear and some other equally strong, wild, primitive emotion she did not want to name. Deeply misliking the rapacious glint in his narrowed eyes, she began anew to struggle fiercely to liberate herself—to no avail.

"Let me go! Let me go, damn you!" she cried.

"Not a chance in hell, baby," Rafer replied grimly, a muscle flexing in the taut jaw he rubbed gingerly with his free hand, wiping away the blood that trickled from the broken corner of his lips. "I've got a knot a broody hen would mistake for an egg on my head, and now, my jaw may never work right again, thanks to you. The FDA ought to require you to come with a label—one that reads Warning: Seriously Hazardous to a Man's Health! Talk about your blond bombshells…woman, you are definitely nitro."

Rafer thought he'd never before seen a woman at once so wildly beautiful and so dangerously beguiling, like a tigress—one that badly needed taming. Undoubtedly ranked a black belt in karate, she was so damned good that if not for his superior strength and weight, she might well have won their confrontation. In a million years he had not thought to find her like—a woman who was his match, his equal, a fit mate for a man who feared no one and nothing but what lay coiled deep within his own dark, brooding, solitary soul, the emptiness, hunger and need that, being such a loner, he had too long suppressed and denied—and that now, as he lay atop her, stirred forcefully within him, no longer willing to be restrained and rejected.

For, as fighting often did a man, their conflict had not only enraged, but also excited Rafer. The soft, sensuous feel of Hayley herself—her half-bare, ripe breasts pressed enticingly, however inadvertently, against his broad, muscled chest, her long legs spread and pinioned by his own—did the rest. As though somewhere inside him a floodgate had burst, arousal abruptly surged through him, swept him up on a strong, overwhelming wave. His breath caught harshly in his throat; his loins tightened sharply. He could tell by the sudden, alarmed widening of her eyes, the flaring of her nostrils, the ragged little gasp that issued from her own throat, that Hayley, too, felt the burgeoning hardness of his heavy, heated sex against her, at the vulnerable, opened juncture of her inner thighs. In that highly charged moment of their mutual awareness of his desire, Rafer had a powerful, unbridled urge simply to rip open his fatigues, to take her then and there on the grassy ground, to fill her until she moaned and writhed beneath him, cried out her surrender, begged him for release—a primal male instinct that she sensed, he knew, and that, even though she obviously feared and would fight it, her eyes said she nevertheless understood. Her lashes sweeping down to conceal her betraying thoughts from him, Hayley turned her head away, swallowing hard as she perceived the depth of her sudden peril. Surely, he would not force himself on her! Her moist, tremulous mouth parted.

"Please," she whispered, her voice at once importuning and husky with the emotions and sensations coursing through her wildly, setting the pulse at the hollow of her throat to jerking visibly. Never had a man made her feel as Rafer did now—like a quintessential female, fragile, vulnerable, opened, waiting to be taken, to be thrust hard and deep inside of, again and again, undeniably claimed, indisputably possessed. Unbidden images of Rafer doing that to her filled her mind, filled her body with an irrepressible, wanton desire that licked like tongues of flame through her, making her go weak and molten at her core. Stricken by the sound of her soft, beseeching voice, fearful of losing control, of being swept up, too, by the hot, dark, dangerous thing that had seized Rafer in its grasp, Hayley bit her lower lip so hard that she drew blood to hold back the further entreaties that rose in her throat and that she thought would prove fruitless. Forcing herself to concentrate on the pain she'd deliberately caused herself with her teeth, she strove to regain mastery of herself and her situation, trying desperately to push him off her.

But her frantic writhing did not win her freedom; indeed, it only enkindled Rafer all the more. For what was happening so unexpectedly between them was as lethal to him as it was to her. It had been a very long time since he'd experienced such strong feelings toward a woman. He'd thought himself dead inside; now, he knew beyond a shadow of a doubt that he was still alive. The fragrance of her perfumed body was like jasmine on the wind—heady, intoxicating—as he breathed it in deeply. Her flushed skin, as luminescent as a flawless pearl, glistening with perspiration born of the closeness of the campfire and of their conflict, was as soft and delicate as a rain-showered rose petal as, with his free hand, he caught Hayley's jaw, deliberately twisting her countenance back up to his. Slowly, sensually, making her shudder, her heart leap, he drew the pad of his thumb across her generous lower lip, tugged at it gently.

"You scrubbed up real fine." Rafer's own voice was as low and smoky as hers as his dark, glittering hazel eyes drank in the beauty of her face no longer overpowered by an excess of cosmetics, but, instead, subtly enhanced by their light, skillful application.

"Too bad I can't say the same for you, Rambo!" Hayley hissed in return, staring up at his camouflage-greased visage, longing fervently to deny how the feel of his warm breath against her skin and the heat of his sex against her own were like a fever in her blood, dizzying her. Inhaling sharply, she caught the woodsy, musky scent that clung to him—vetiver, her favorite. Her heart beat fast with mingled dread and a perverse but undeniable excitement at his nearness, his dominant-male position. For the first time in her life, she'd met a man stronger than she, was at his utter mercy. To Hayley's bewilderment and dismay, despite her fright, she could not seem to suppress the inexplicable thrill

that shot through her at that knowledge, exhilarating her,
like a harrowing ride on an old wooden roller coaster, in
the last car, which always skipped the tracks. She lived on
the edge, as did Rafer. Now, they were both there together—and he was as savage as his Indian forebears in
war paint; a warrior, a dog soldier, wounded but forever
unbowed, unconquered, she thought, although she did not
speak the words aloud. "You look like a grease monkey!"
she spat out instead, fighting him, fighting herself and all
he had evoked inside her. "Now, for the last time—turn
me loose, you…you…*barbarian!*"

"I don't think so," Rafer muttered thickly, an echo of
her own words to him earlier. His eyes darkening with passion, he abruptly crushed his mouth down on hers hard,
taking her breath and stifling the whimper of protest that
rose to her captive lips.

Hayley was shattered, shaken to her very bones by the
ruthless kiss that was like none other she had ever before
known—practiced, powerful, possessive, coercing her com-
pliance, demanding her response to the mouth that de-
voured hers hungrily. No! she thought frantically, no! She
would *not* let this happen! She would not! Marshaling her
wits, she bit down hard on Rafer's lower lip, causing him
to snarl with pain and then to swear.

"So, you still want to play rough, do you, tigress?" he
grated softly as he jerked his head back, licking away the
blood from the tiny wound she'd inflicted. "All right, then.
We'll do it your way.…" He laid his hand upon her slender
throat, deliberately tightening his fingers there ever so
slightly, threateningly. "Kiss me," he demanded, his voice
low, urgent, raw with desire, his breath sultry against her
flesh as his mouth brushed hers electrifyingly. "Kiss me,
damn you.…"

Before Hayley could speak, his lips claimed hers savagely again, swallowing her breath. Despite how her mind
yet rebelled against his onslaught, the pressure of his hand

at her throat compelled her mouth to part, to yield pliantly to the inexorable intrusion of his probing tongue. It found her own, touching, twisting, tasting, exploring her moist inner recesses until, at long last, with a low moan, she ceased to struggle against him, melted beneath him, began to kiss him back with a fervor to match his own, unable to continue the futile attempt to deny the feelings he was inciting inside her. At that, Rafer's hand slid from her throat, stroking her bare shoulder before seeking and cupping her naked breast beneath the lacy material of her bra. A powerful eruption of excitement and desire radiated through her at the bold caress; her nipple puckered and hardened beneath the slow, sensuous circling of his palm, the taunting motions of his thumb and fingers. His hips thrust provocatively against hers, rubbing his hard sex between her spread legs. Unconsciously Hayley strained against him, instinctively positioning herself so the pressure kneaded her soft mound, where a desperate, burning ache was building inside her. It had been so long since she'd had a man—and never one who'd made her feel like this. Certainly, Logan had never made her feel like this. Despite herself, she wanted Rafer inside her, deep inside....

Oh, God, what was she thinking? What was she doing? Hayley asked herself abruptly, mortified as she strove dazedly once more to recapture her senses. She didn't even know Rafer; and here she was letting him kiss her, fondle her, stroke himself against her. In moments he would be ripping off her clothes and his own, pushing himself inside her. She'd been under such a strain lately that she must have lost her mind, must have gone absolutely mad! What must Rafer think of her? That she was a cheap barroom tramp? But, of course, that was exactly what he thought, Hayley realized, sick inside as she understood then what had prompted him to fall like some ravaging animal upon her. With difficulty she tore her mouth free from his, thrashing her head from side to side as he sought ardently to reclaim her lips and, when he couldn't, pressing searing kisses on her temples, throat and breasts instead.

"Wait…please!" Hayley gasped out, afraid she wouldn't be able to contain what she'd inadvertently unleashed inside him. "Listen to me! Please! You—you don't understand. I'm—I'm not what you think—"

"What I think is that you're too damned good for a loser like Pike," Rafer growled. But then the thought of his quarry brought him abruptly to his senses, and he swore softly. "Damn!"

He must be completely out of his mind—letting his lust rule his brain! Pike would be here at any moment, and he, Rafer, would be caught with his pants down—literally! He was a bounty hunter, a professional; he knew better than that, a good deal better! What was it about this woman that had inflamed him to the point where he'd permitted his desire for her to override his every ounce of common sense, his every instinct for survival? She was nothing but a cheap barroom tramp, Pike's girlfriend, and probably his accomplice, as well. No doubt, with her seductive feminine wiles, she'd hoped to keep him, Rafer, occupied until Pike arrived, and things had just progressed too fast for her to handle. Naturally she wouldn't want Pike to show up and to find her actually getting it on with another man. His eyes narrowing, his mouth tightening with anger and disgust at himself, Rafer drew back from her a little so he could see her face, although he didn't release her, even so.

His gaze took in her long blond hair, tumbled in wild dishevelment about her; her thick-lashed green eyes dark not only with apprehension, but also with the passion he'd aroused in her; her upper lip beaded with perspiration; her tempting, tremulous mouth, bruised and swollen from his hard, savage kisses; the tiny pulse beating erratically at the hollow of her pale, slender throat; the quick, shallow rise and fall of her breasts, their generous swell above her lacy bra, the trickle of sweat that moistened the valley between them.

At the sight of her, it was all Rafer could do not to finish what he'd started. But instead, his voice low and taunting, he asked, "What's the matter, baby? Did you suddenly remember your boyfriend Pike's jealous temper, grow afraid he might beat you if he should come upon us in flagrante delicto? Or did you just get more than you bargained for, taking me on?"

"Oh, God, I never dreamed that you thought Pike was…that I'd actually let him…when even just the *thought* of that weasel touching me makes me ill! But no wonder you believed that you could…that I would—" Stricken, Hayley broke off abruptly, biting her lower lip. Then, seeing Rafer's slow, puzzled frown, that he had got hold of himself, however difficultly he'd restrained his turbulent emotions, that he could at least be reasoned with now, she continued. "Look, if you'll just listen to me a minute, I can explain everything. I—I know how things must have appeared to you last night, but you've simply got to believe me. Pike is *not* my boyfriend. I don't even have one at the moment, and even if I did, it sure as hell wouldn't be *him!* And I don't sling beer in a bar for a living, either—"

"Yeah?" Rafer quirked one eyebrow devilishly, his skepticism plain, his tone sarcastic as he went on. "Well, you sure fooled me."

"I understand that, and I don't blame you for thinking what you did. But you were wrong—although, to be honest, I don't think you're going to like the truth much better—"

"Oh? And just why might that be, I wonder?"

"Because I'm a—I'm a bounty hunter, just like you." At his startled, darkening glance, Hayley rushed on, not giving him a chance to interrupt again. "I was working undercover at the Watering Hole, so I could get to Pike. I'd learned through my investigation, just as you must have, that he dropped in there on occasion. My—my name's Hayley Harper. And even if that doesn't mean anything to you, the fact that my father was Gentleman Jim Harper should. We used to be Harper & Daughter, but since his death, it's just been the Harper Agency, and I've been running it alone. I…ah…rifled your pockets last night, after I knocked you out. When I found out who you were—are…Rafer Starr, I'm afraid I just kind of…ah…panicked. You've got quite a—a notorious reputation in the business, you know, especially for dealing with rivals. So rather than stick around and try to sort things out with you when you came to, I just drove off. Frankly, I thought I could get the jump on you and locate Pike before you did."

"Pike now knows I'm a bounty hunter. He would surely have told you that—and for all I know, you might have concocted this story specifically for the purpose of deceiving me in the event that I ever got my hands on you—no pun intended," Rafer added mockingly, causing her to blush furiously as his gleaming eyes roved over her again lewdly. "So why should I believe you?" he queried dryly, although his gut instinct told him that Hayley was, in fact, telling him the truth. He *was* familiar with Jim Harper's name and work, had heard through the grapevine about Harper's death and now vaguely recalled some tale about the daughter's having taken over the agency—and having a hard time making a go of it, too.

"My ID and license are in my handbag, in the RV. If you'll let me up, I'll get them."

"Pardon me if I insist that we get them together. But I'm sure you'll understand that regardless of what you've just told me, after your whacking me with your *kapo* and back fisting me in the jaw, quite frankly, I don't trust you, woman." Rolling off her at last, Rafer stood and, reaching down, hauled her to her feet. But he didn't unlock the handcuffs about her wrists; and although after retrieving his automatic and Hayley's shotgun, he returned the pistol to his holster, he checked the shotgun to be certain it was loaded and that the safety was on, and then he trained the barrel on Hayley. "Just in case you have any bright ideas about pulling another fast one," he explained at her inquiring glance, then motioned with the shotgun toward the RV. "Now, lead the way…nice and slow."

Once inside the RV, Rafer instructed Hayley to sit down on the bench to one side. Then, carefully placing the shotgun on the counter so it was within his easy reach, he took stock of his surroundings, his gaze lighting on her nearby *bo* and *kapo*. Eyeing her askance, he removed both from her proximity and put them next to the shotgun. Then he picked up her black leather purse she pointed out to him, which was cleverly constructed to appear as though it were all one piece but that, in reality, was like a pair of saddlebags stitched almost completely together along the edges. The concealed opening on one side between the two pouches gave way to a holster inside, in which she kept her Glock 19 during the day, so she didn't even need to unzip the handbag in order to get at the gun. Plus, in the event that the purse were ever forcibly taken from her, it could be opened up and its contents checked without the automatic's presence being discovered, so the handbag—and the hidden pistol—would more than likely be returned to her. But Rafer was wise to the tricks of the trade, and the first thing he did as he examined her purse was to slip his hand between the two pouches and to withdraw her gun.

"My, my. You're just chock-full of nasty little surprises, aren't you?" With one corner of his wryly twisted mouth, he *tsk-tsked* with feigned dismay as, slowly shaking his head, he slid out the magazine and emptied the chamber before laying the automatic alongside her shotgun. Then, saying, "Turnabout's fair play, don't you agree? I mean, after all, you *did* go through my pockets and wallet," he unzipped her handbag and began to rummage through it. "What've you got inside here? A pair of brass knuckles? No, don't tell me…a stun gun. Of course. What else?"

Experimentally he depressed the button on the weapon, causing a loud crackle of electricity to erupt between the two small poles. "Bring down a lot of big game with that, do you?" He tossed the stun gun onto the growing arsenal on the counter.

"It's come in handy a time or two," Hayley said tersely, because even though she knew that the charge from the stun gun wouldn't consistently drop an assailant, particularly a heavy one or one high on drugs or alcohol or both, she believed in always carrying a couple of back-up weapons, just in case; and for that purpose, the stun gun worked well enough.

"Uh-huh. I'll bet," Rafer grunted. "If Dolan Pike only knew what a narrow escape he'd had from your clutches, he'd thank his lucky stars that I was at the Watering Hole last night. No wonder you don't have a boyfriend; most men wouldn't dare to risk closing their eyes around you, woman. You know, it belatedly occurs to me that perhaps I ought to have…ah…frisked you more thoroughly. You've probably got a knife stuck in your boot, too."

"Frisking? Is *that* what they're calling it these days?" she drawled derisively, her lashes hooding her eyes to cloak her thoughts. But she could do nothing to hide the betraying stain of color that crept upon her cheeks. And the next thing she knew, Rafer was slipping from her right boot the black-handled switchblade she'd purchased at a gun show a few years back.

"I prefer a butterfly knife myself." Grimly he pushed the catch that released the blade, testing its spring before he snapped the blade closed and tossed it onto the heap of her weapons he'd already confiscated. "You wouldn't by any chance happen to be a Boy Scout, would you?" he asked acidly as he impatiently resumed his rifling of her purse, even opening and digging through her cosmetics bag before finally withdrawing her French-style leather billfold and unsnapping it to reveal her driver's license, bounty-hunting license, gun permits and a couple of major credit cards. "Or do you just share the same motto?"

"Be prepared? Listen, Starr, I shouldn't have to tell you—of all people—what it's like out there on the job these days!—especially for a woman!"

"Well, well. We're making progress. I've been elevated from Rambo to Starr—and you are, indeed, Hayley Harper, would-be Honey West." He flashed her a tight, mocking smile as, at last satisfied as to her identity, he returned her billfold to her handbag and threw the purse aside. Then, folding his muscular arms over his broad chest, he lounged against the counter, gazing at her speculatively, thoughtfully. "Bet she was your idol when you were just a kid in pigtails. You even resemble Anne Francis a little— got that same blond hair and that beauty mark at the corner of your mouth."

"I had a ponytail. And Honey West was a private detective, not a bounty hunter, and, yeah, so what if I used to watch the show every week on TV? Anne Francis broke new ground for women everywhere with that part. She played a woman who did what was considered a man's job and who managed to retain her femininity while doing it, just as Angie Dickinson's Sgt. Pepper Anderson did in later years. What's wrong with that?"

"Not a damned thing from where I'm standing." Once more, Rafer's eyes appraised her, lingering on the swell of her breasts revealed by the tear in her shirt. "Except that I've got the strangest feeling that, also like them, you intend to get the job done—whether I like it or not."

"That's right. Pike's federal—you know that. He robbed banks and crossed state lines on his little spree. He's fair game for anybody. So, how about these?" Hayley hastily held up her cuffed hands, afraid that, knowing she wouldn't back off, Rafer might be getting any number of unpleasant ideas where she was concerned, a suspicion his next words appeared to confirm.

"What're you going to give me in exchange for the key?"

"What—what do you want?"

"You? Is that what you thought—hoped—I was going to say?" he asked, with a wide, sardonic grin as he spied the look in her expressive eyes. "Sorry to disappoint you, Ms. West, but right now, my hunger is leaning more toward a bowl of that chili and a slice of that spoon bread that I can still smell warm on the fire outside."

"Don't flatter yourself, Rambo!" Hayley rejoined, incensed and humiliated that he should so correctly guess her equally apprehensive and anticipatory thoughts about his finishing what he'd started earlier. "The only way you could disappoint me is by sticking around. So if feeding you is the only way to get you to slink back to whatever zoo you escaped from, I'll be more than happy to oblige, believe me."

"Didn't your daddy ever teach you that it's dangerous to provoke an animal?" Rafer inquired softly, intently. Deliberately he let the sudden silence stretch significantly between them, unnerving her, before, to her relief, he finally dug the key to the handcuffs from a pocket of his fatigues and tossed it to her. "Now, be a good girl and get cleaned up for supper. It is, in fact, a jungle out there, but I don't think you'll be needing any camouflage grease tonight."

Once Hayley had freed herself, a glance in her mirror confirmed that her face was indeed, as Rafer had intimated, smeared with camouflage grease from his kisses…kisses she tried hard not to think about as, together, she and he washed up at the sink. She didn't want to dwell on what had flared so unexpectedly and explosively between them. But when she forced her thoughts into other channels, Hayley unwittingly recalled her father's words about how it might have made a man out of her ex-husband, Logan, if he'd ever got a little grease and dirt on him. And then she thought that, with one of her washcloths, Rafer Starr had just scrubbed off more than his fair share of both. Why was it that the most attractive, exciting men were always such no-good rogues? she wondered a trifle bitterly. Why were they always men who didn't know what it meant to love and to cherish a woman, to be honest with and faithful to her? Logan had often lied to her and, Hayley suspected, in her absence while away on business for the bounty-hunting agency, had cheated on her more than once during their marriage. Doubtless, Rafer Starr was an accomplished prevaricator and had had his share of women, too. That the RV should seem so inordinately small and cramped because he was in it, that his maleness and nearness should prove so unsettling to her was foolish. The sooner she was rid of him, the better! Unless it were the kind she was dragging back to face justice, she didn't want or need another scoundrel in her life. Logan's rejection had stung more than she cared to admit. That she was, in some respects, still punishing him—and even her father, too, for dying and leaving her alone—and, by extension, all men, by living as she did, tracking down bail-jumping criminals who'd hurt others whose loved ones were then left behind to grieve, was a thought Hayley determinedly shoved from her mind. She didn't want or need to be psychoanalyzed, either.

In the privacy of the toilet stall, she changed her damaged shirt for a whole one. Then, he adamantly refusing to leave her alone with her cache of weapons, she and Rafer went outside, carefully extinguishing the fire and carrying the chili and spoon bread back into the RV to eat at the foldaway table, since the wind had freshened and the spring night air had grown chilly.

"By the way, just out of curiosity, if it wasn't Pike, who *did* you call earlier on your cellular telephone?" Rafer inquired casually as he ladled the still-steaming chili into bowls, while Hayley sliced the warm spoon bread and spread it with butter from the refrigerator.

"My answering service, to see if I had any messages—not that it's any of your business."

"You're on my turf, Hayley." The statement was blunt. "I'm making it my business."

"You been hired by the bondsman for Pike?"

"No," he conceded reluctantly as they sat down at the table.

"Then I'm not on your turf, am I?"

"Look, Pike's personal, all right?" Rafer's shuttered expression said he didn't want to discuss the matter further, but Hayley didn't intend to be put off.

"In what way?" she probed before spooning chili into her mouth and then breaking off a piece of the spoon bread on her plate, swallowing it down with a sip of bottled dark beer.

For a long time she thought he wasn't going to reply. But then, at last, he spoke.

"Pike's ex-wife...Wenona...she's the kid sister of one of the men who was in my unit when I was in the service. He was killed on a mission down in South America, and before he died, he told me about Pike and asked me if I'd look out for Wenona. Seems Pike periodically gets his kicks by driving out to her place and slapping her around before raping her. She doesn't have a whole lot of money or education, and she's too afraid to call the sheriff, for fear that the state will step in and she'll wind up losing her three kids."

"I suspected something like that," Hayley admitted. "She wouldn't even let me inside when I stopped by to ask her about Pike, much less talk to me. Look, Rafer, I'm real sorry for Wenona's troubles, but what difference does it make if it's you or me who puts Pike back behind bars, where he belongs?"

"The difference is that I'm going to give Wenona the bounty. I don't need it, and she does. She's attending a vocational school at night, when she can get one of her sisters to watch her kids, and twenty-five thousand dollars will go a long way toward helping her get off welfare and food stamps, and on her feet. You, on the other hand, plan on keeping the bounty for yourself.''

"The truth is...I—I need it. Otherwise, I'm going to be forced to dissolve the Harper Agency, and I just can't let that happen! It was Dad's whole life, his legacy to me!'' Even as she unwillingly confessed her financial problems, Hayley felt miserably selfish in light of Rafer's entirely unexpected generosity toward Wenona Pike. But, then, he could afford to be charitable, she thought bitterly. As the gun in his shoulder holster—a Walther P-88, $1,200 minimum, retail—attested, he didn't have any monetary worries. Neither had she—once. But despite the advice of both her father and her lawyer, she'd stubbornly refused to take so much as a dime from Logan, even though he'd been loaded. She hadn't wanted anything from him; she could make her own way in life, she'd told herself proudly at the time, and it was too late now for regrets. "Maybe we could work together, split the bounty,'' she suggested. "That's fair.''

"I work alone, and I never split bounties.'' Rafer's tone was cool, imperious. "So back off...walk away from this one, Hayley.''

"And if I don't?''

"You said yourself that you weren't unaware of my...notorious reputation. Wasn't that how you phrased it? It's true. I don't lightly tolerate rivals—not even ones who look like you.'' His eyes glittered with heat and appreciation, making her shiver as he gazed at her. Then, finishing the last of his beer, chili and spoon bread, he rose, carrying the dirty dishes to the sink and beginning the task of washing up.

"You don't have to do that. In fact, I—I think that it would be best if you left now,'' Hayley insisted a trifle nervously, as she put the remainder of the food into airtight plastic containers and away in the refrigerator.

The glance Rafer shot her from beneath his lashes was sharp.

"Man eats a woman's cooking, the least he can do is clean up the dishes afterward—and unlike a lot of men, I ain't too proud and arrogant to do my share of household chores." There was silence for a moment as Hayley digested this remark, while he, having completed the scrubbing and rinsing, directed his attention to drying the dinnerware and utensils, neatly stacking them on the counter afterward. Then, slinging the damp towel over his shoulder, Rafer turned back to her, continuing. "Besides, it's late, and I'm tired. And, so, quite frankly, I don't relish the idea of having to sleep with one eye open and one ear cocked all night, in case you get some wild notion about sneaking up on me, bashing me over the head again or jerking the plugs out of my Jeep's distributor cap, stranding me so you can get the jump on me and catch up to Pike before I do."

"What—what do you mean?" Hayley asked, her heart starting to pound far too hard and fast in her breast at the wicked, determined glint that now suddenly shone in his hazel eyes. "What—what are you saying?"

Beginning slowly to stalk her, Rafer answered softly, "What I'm saying, Hayley, is that I intend to spend the night right here, in your bed, with you."

Chapter Three

In the Woods
Wyoming

"**Y**ou—you can't be serious!" Hayley cried as she stared at Rafer, stunned and aghast, thinking that, surely, he was only teasing her, even though she knew by the expression on his face that he'd meant every single word. "You can't sleep here—and certainly not in my bed, with me!"

"Wanna bet?" Rafer smiled slowly, mockingly, his eyes raking her in a way that sent a shudder of mingled fright and excitement rippling through her. Then, his voice low, arrogant, insolent, he demanded, "Take your clothes off, Hayley."

"I—I won't!" Her turmoil and trepidation were such that she did not dare to add "And you can't make me!" because even as the thought occurred to her, she realized how childish it would sound, and she knew, besides, that he could—and that he would—compel her to undress for him, given the slightest provocation. He'd already proved that she couldn't beat him when it came to a sparring match between them—a new and not entirely welcome experience, since she was accustomed to besting and thereby getting her man. Still, her karate instructor had always warned her that, all else being equal, a woman would invariably be defeated by a man's superior strength and weight, that surprise and speed were the only elements on her side—and Hayley had now lost both. Since their battle, Rafer was on his guard against her, and his proximity in the small RV prohibited a quick escape. A verbal demand appeared her only realistic option. "I want you to leave, Starr—now!"

"I told you—I'm not going anywhere. So, we can do this easy, or we can do it rough, whichever you prefer. Just make up your mind, Hayley."

For a moment she gazed about the RV wildly, seeking a means—any means—of ridding herself of Rafer's presence, while simultaneously calculating her chances of eluding him. But all her weapons were piled on the counter before which he stood, blocking her access to them, and he was between her and the RV's back door, besides. To get away, she would have to crawl through the cab, and he would undoubtedly catch her before she could reach either the driver's or the passenger's door. She was, in effect, helpless against him, another feeling to which Hayley was thoroughly unused. Still, not being one tamely to submit to her fate, she snatched down her nightshirt, which trailed over the edge of her bunk where she'd tossed it that morning. Then, shooting Rafer a defiant glance and relieved when he made no move to halt her, she flounced into the toilet stall to change, firmly locking the door behind her.

Once inside, Hayley leaned against the wall, trembling. This just couldn't be happening to her, she thought, astounded both by her predicament and by the fact that she was only half scared by the notion of Rafer's compelling her to make love with him. She was a smart, competent woman highly trained in the art of self-defense. That she should be at his mercy galled and unnerved her, even while her body tingled with treacherous, tantalizing anticipation as she unwillingly remembered the feel of his mouth upon hers earlier, of his weight pressing her down, of his hand cupping her bare breast....

"Hayley, open up!" Rafer abruptly pounded peremptorily upon the door of the toilet stall, startling her from her reverie. "Hayley, so help me, I promise you that if you don't hurry up and come out of there, I'll kick this door in—and you know me well enough by now to know that I damned well will, that I don't make idle threats."

"Yes, I know. Just—just keep your shirt on, will you? Statistics show that it takes a woman longer than a man in here, or don't you know that?" she called crossly, motivated into hastily stripping to her French-cut lace panties and yanking her nightshirt on over her head. Nervously, afraid the thin door might come flying off its hinges at any moment from a powerful blow delivered by an impatient Rafer, Hayley used the toilet, then flushed it. Then she unlocked the door and opened it, drawing up short at the sight that met her eyes: a broad expanse of naked, heavily muscled chest matted with fine dark hair that trailed enticingly down a firm, flat belly to disappear into the waistband, its top button unfastened, of the fatigues slung low on lean, narrow hips.

"As you can see, I don't take orders well," Rafer drawled with a cocky grin as he tossed his T-shirt aside, having previously, while she was changing into her nightshirt, not only unbraided the eagle feathers from his hair, but also taken off the remainder of his apparel, save for his fatigues. "But at least your bathroom door is still in one piece."

"I suppose you think I should be grateful for small favors, huh?" Hayley gibed caustically, scowling but still unable to prevent her gaze from straying appreciatively over his coppery flesh: his corded arms, the right fore of which sported what she now knew must be a Special Forces tattoo; his broad chest, at its heart a pair of silvery metal dog tags that hung from a chain about his neck.

"*Exceedingly* grateful," Rafer declared softly, intently, his own eyes slowly taking her in: the wide neckline of her nightshirt, which bared her throat and one creamy shoulder; the way in which the thin, pale pink cotton material clung to her full breasts, outlining her nipples taut with fear and excitement; the short hem that revealed her long, graceful legs. "Hard-hearted Woman," he read aloud the nightshirt's caption, emblazoned across a big red heart on the front. "Is that a fact? Well, I'm a man who enjoys a challenge, actually." Then, before Hayley realized what he meant to do, Rafer suddenly reached out and caught her right wrist in a grip of iron, snapping around it one steel ring of his handcuffs, which he had concealed behind his back, then locking the other circle onto his own left wrist. "Even if I don't always play fair," he added coolly, with a cynical smile at her outraged gasp of protest. "So, here's the deal, Hayley—the key to these cuffs is in the right front pocket of my fatigues. You be a good girl and don't give me any trouble, and we'll both get a good night's rest. But if you wake me up—and I warn you that I am a very light sleeper—I will most assuredly forget where I stashed the key and assume that you're fumbling around in my pants for a whole 'nother reason. Do I make myself clear?"

"Crystal. You know, you really are an unconscionable cad...using sex as a weapon!" Hayley's eyes shot sparks at him, for she'd thought—half hoped—he was attracted to her. And now, she felt a pang of pique and disappointment at the realization that his desire for her had been born only of their heated struggle earlier.

"Well, correct me if I'm mistaken, but somehow I thought that's exactly what you were doing with Dolan Pike at the Watering Hole last night," Rafer jeered, his mouth turning down sourly at one corner. "Or are you denying using yourself as sexual bait to lure him outside after closing, where you no doubt planned to cosh instead of to kiss him?"

Hayley had the good grace to flush guiltily.

"It's different for a woman," she insisted defensively,

although, even to her ears, the excuse sounded lame. "We're not as physically strong as men, we have to rely on our feminine wiles. Besides, any man so arrogant and fool enough to fall for that kind of an act deserves whatever he gets!"

"Uh-huh. Well, arrogant, I may be—but fool, I'm not. You might want to keep that in mind when you bat those cat green eyes of yours at me in the future, tigress. Now, it's been a long day, and I'm for bed—and since we've been united in unholy deadlock, I'm afraid you'll have to join me, whether you like it or not."

Indeed seeing no other choice, Hayley unwillingly climbed into the berth over the cab, Rafer following close behind her, his free hand casually cupping her backside as he boosted her into the bunk. They settled themselves as comfortably as was possible, given that both the handcuffs and the confined quarters forced them to lie closer to each other than either, all too aware of the other, would have liked. Rafer drew the blankets up about them, then flipped the light switch so only the RV's night-lights shone. In the near darkness and the silence broken only by the sounds of night in the woods, Hayley tried to ignore him lying so near beside her. But that was easier said than done, and after endless, restless shiftings of her position—which precluded sleep's coming to either of them—she finally wound up on her back, staring at the ceiling and heaving a deep sigh of annoyance and frustration.

"This is ridiculous! What if I have to go the bathroom in the night?"

"Wake me up, and I'll take you." Without warning, Rafer wrapped his free arm about her willowy waist and pulled her body up next to his own, so she lay on her left side, with him curled protectively around her. "Now, relax and go to sleep. Much as I'd like to, I'm not going to force myself on you, I swear—that is, of course, unless you want me to. Because I understand, you see, that a woman like you needs an even stronger man, that she can't respect anything less. So…would you like me to take you, Hayley, to hold you down and to make love to you? Because that's what it would be, you know…." His voice was smoky, seductive in her ear, only half-teasing; his breath was warm against her skin.

"No, I would not!" she insisted softly—and knew the words for a lie.

His low laugh sent a wild thrill shivering through her in the dimness.

"I could make you want it…want me." His hand slid up to fondle her breast through the thin cotton of her nightshirt. His thumb rotated slowly, sensuously, across her nipple until it grew rigid with excitement, strained against the fabric as waves of pleasure radiated through her. She could feel his sex stir, growing heavy and hard, pressing against her buttocks through his fatigues. "You see?"

"Please stop, Rafer." Her voice was a whisper, an entreaty—because she knew that if he continued his deliberate assault upon her senses and her body, she would relent, would yield to him in the end. Already, her heart was drumming in her breast, her blood was singing in her ears at his provocative caress. "I don't even know you!"

"Don't you? We're alike, baby, you and me—down to the bone—and you know it. We both play to win, and you're just too stubborn to admit that this is one time you lost."

"I haven't lost anything…yet—and I don't intend to! I'm going to get Dolan Pike, come hell or high water. So if you thought you could make me forget about him by seducing me, you were wrong. Now, take your hands off me!"

For a long, tense moment fraught with significance and expectation, Hayley was half afraid Rafer wouldn't do as she'd insisted. But then, at last releasing her, he turned over onto his back, shutting his eyes.

"All right…if that's the way you want it. Just remember this, baby—all's fair in love and war—so don't say I didn't warn you."

"What's that supposed to mean?"

"You'll find out in the morning. Good night, Hayley. Sweet dreams."

"Damn you, Starr!"

At that, he lifted one eyebrow devilishly and raised one eyelid to stare at her censuringly before closing it again, making it plain he wasn't going to respond. Cursing him under her breath, Hayley flopped over onto her stomach, resolutely turning her head so she wouldn't have to look at him anymore. She tried but failed to fall asleep. But after a while she became aware of Rafer's own rhythmic breathing, and moving gingerly so as not to waken him, she turned to study him in the shadowy light. Slumbering, he looked younger and not so hard as life had made him. She could only imagine what his had been like, what it had taken to belong to a Special Forces branch, to take part in the covert military operations in which she knew he must surely have participated over the course of his career in the Marines. No matter what anybody said, Hayley didn't believe that any man could come through combat unscathed, that it inevitably left wounds and scars, if not on the body, then always on the psyche. Obviously the men in his unit had been comrades, or he would not be so driven where Dolan Pike was concerned. But even knowing that Rafer's motives for wanting to capture Pike were altruistic, while her own were more selfish, Hayley still did not intend to back off. She owed her dead father, just as Rafer owed Wenona Pike's dead brother.

That thought uppermost in her mind, Hayley tentatively stretched out her left hand, inhaling sharply as she made contact with Rafer's flesh, his furry chest. He was warm, much warmer than she, his body generating more heat than hers. Briefly, she was tempted to snuggle closer to him;

she'd felt curiously safe earlier, when he'd wrapped himself around her. For the first time in a long while, she'd not gone to bed worried that she might have to use her gun in the middle of the night; she'd known that if anyone crept up to break into her RV—as sometimes happened to campers, especially in the woods—Rafer would defend her. Still, if she could obtain the key to the handcuffs, she could regain control of her situation and fate. Rafer didn't stir at her touch, so Hayley began slowly to slide her hand downward, over his belly, gasping, screaming softly when his steely hand suddenly clamped hard around her wrist.

"You know what they say, Hayley," he murmured drowsily, not even bothering to open his eyes. "Don't do the crime if you can't do the time." He turned, rolling her over onto her side, curling himself around her again, his right hand keeping hold of her left, imprisoning her. "Now, for the last time, go to sleep."

"Yes, Rafer," she replied, reluctantly and only momentarily conceding defeat.

"Hmm. I like the sound of that. I could get used to hearing you say it, to holding you in my arms, like this." His voice was low, husky in her ear.

So could she, actually, Hayley realized to her surprise, as, gradually, the heat of him pervaded her bones and, secure in his embrace, she slept.

She awoke in the morning to the smell of eggs and sausage frying on the stove. For a moment, bewildered, she thought that she was a child again, that her father was still alive and cooking breakfast. Then she spied the indentation in the down pillow Rafer had used last night, inhaled the masculine scent of him that clung to the sheets, felt the warmth of the berth, where he had lain beside her and knew that it was he, not her father, at the stove. Rafer was still shirtless, and Hayley could not help but admire his handsomely sculpted body glowing coppery in the soft morning light that streamed through the open blinds. Seeing her gazing down at him drowsily from the bunk, he smiled engagingly, in a way that made her heart turn over.

"Roust it out, Sleeping Beauty," he greeted her as he popped toast up from the toaster and arranged the slices on two plates. "Time's a-wastin'."

"People who rise and shine with the sun—and who are actually cheerful when they do so—deserve to be lined up before a firing squad and shot," Hayley grumbled as she stirred and stretched, wincing at the feel of muscles bruised and sore from her conflict with Rafer the previous evening. "Still, I can forgive a man almost anything if he cooks. Is this a going-away present?" She indicated the breakfast now on the table, at which she joined him, once he had pulled on his T-shirt and sat down.

"Is that a hopeful note I hear in your voice—or a pang of disappointment?" Rafer grinned as he slathered red plum jam onto his toast. "Personally, I like my eggs and sausage hot, so why don't we eat first and talk afterward?"

"Fine with me. It takes me a while to wake up, so I prefer quiet during my morning coffee, anyway." Picking up her brimming cup, Hayley sipped the steaming brew gratefully. It was strong and black, just as she liked it. She could fall in love with a man who had hot coffee ready and waiting for her in the morning, she thought idly, then blushed at the unwitting notion. Thank heavens, Rafer wasn't a mind reader!

Hooding her eyes so he wouldn't guess her thoughts, she hastily and hungrily applied herself to breakfast, hoping he hadn't noticed the color that had briefly stained her cheeks, since he was devilish enough to probe, and she would be at a loss for an answer. But to her relief, he was busy devouring his food, using his toast to sop up the soft-fried eggs. The meal was good, just what Hayley preferred in the morning—although, most of the time, being a night person, she rose so late that she didn't eat until noon—and the silence between her and Rafer was strangely companionable. She hadn't expected to find it so; she'd thought there would be awkwardness. They had, after all, shared the same bed last night, even if they hadn't made love in it. But it was instead as though she'd awakened after twenty years to find Rafer waiting for her; and despite herself, honesty forced her to admit that the sight of him had pleased her.

When breakfast was finished, Hayley washed and dried the dishes, observing, as she did so, that all her weapons were missing from the counter. At that realization she felt her first twinge of uneasiness and suspicion that Rafer's amiable demeanor was meant to lull her into a false sense of security. Still, she made no comment as she gathered fresh clothes, then went into the toilet stall to carry out her morning ablutions. He'd said they would talk, and clearly, they must if they were to work out anything at all between them where Dolan Pike was concerned. It was only when she emerged, clean and dressed, to be grabbed by Rafer and to have one ring of his handcuffs snapped back around her wrist that Hayley cursed herself for her stupidity. She should have known not to trust him!

"What do you…think you're…doing, Starr?" she asked between gasps for breath as she struggled furiously—futilely— against his viselike grasp.

"Settling our disagreement over Pike and the bounty," he rejoined coolly as he dragged her into the cab, then shoved her into the passenger's seat, locking the second circle of the cuffs around the shoulder portion of the seat belt and paying no heed to the invectives she hurled at him until he effectively silenced her. Before she realized what he intended, his hand caught her chin, twisting her furious face up to his, and he kissed her hard on her indignant mouth, his tongue shooting deep, taking her breath until she ceased to fight him, clung to him, trembled against him. At that, releasing her, he calmly slid into the driver's seat, opened the door and hopped out onto the ground, his combat boots scraping on rough pebbles. "That ought to keep you busy for a while." He motioned toward the handcuffs.

"Oh, so we're Mad Max instead of Rambo this morning, are we?" Hayley's voice shook with both outrage and passion. It was all she could do to hold back tears of frustration and hurt that she should prove no different to him from any other rival bounty hunter, that she should have dared to hope...what? That Rafer might actually have begun to care for her a little? How could she have been so foolish, so naive? "Are you planning to leave me a hacksaw—and to stuff a Molotov cocktail up my exhaust pipe before you go?"

"Nothing so dramatic as that." He shook his head, grinning wickedly. "You know, I think you spend too many nights all by your lonesome self here in this RV, watching too many movies, baby. You need some company, to get out more. It's not good to be alone so much."

"Speak for yourself, Max!" she retorted, incensed, embarrassed that he should have guessed so much about her solitary existence.

"Yeah, well, I've been giving my own life as a loner some thought, I'll admit. Now, the way I see your current situation is like this, Hayley. You're a strong woman. Even so, I don't think you'll be able to tear that cuff loose from that seat belt, and even if you somehow *do* manage to, you'll inevitably ruin your seat belt in the process—all for nothing, because I'll be back before you can get free, I promise you. So, it's up to you, whether you think you can make good your escape in less time than it takes me to return."

"Where are you going, Starr? How do I know that you're really planning on coming back, that you're not just going to leave me out here in the boondocks, chained to my RV? How do I know that this isn't just some rotten trick so you can get the jump on me and capture Pike before I do?"

"You don't," he said bluntly. "You'll just have to take my word for it."

With that, he slammed shut the driver's door and loped into the woods. Biting her lower lip anxiously, Hayley glowered at his disappearing back. His infamous reputation was such that how could she believe him? He was a scoundrel, a rogue—the list of names she could think of to call him was endless. Yet when she recalled the feel of his mouth upon hers, every ounce of common sense she possessed seemed to desert her. She glanced at the seat belt. With both hands, she gave it an exploratory tug. It was fastened tight to its anchor. She sat there warring with herself, debating whether she could even yank the seat belt loose, much less tear the cuff off it, and knowing that Rafer had been right, that even if she somehow *did* manage the feat, the seat belt would be destroyed—and costly to replace. Oh, surely, he had spoken the truth; surely, he planned to return, was not so unconscionable as to leave her stranded in the middle of nowhere, with little hope of escape or discovery.

No sooner had the thought occurred to her than Hayley heard the sound of an engine and, to her relief, spied a Jeep pulling up. The off-road vehicle's top was off, so she could see in the RV's big side mirror that Rafer was at the wheel. What was he doing? she wondered as he killed the ignition and swung from the Jeep, reaching back in its bed to withdraw a heavy chain. Good Lord. He was hooking the vehicle to the RV's trailer hitch! What else could that possibly mean but that he intended to take her with him? Her heart began to hammer in her breast at the realization.

"This is—this is *kidnapping*, Starr!" she sputtered as, finished with his task, he opened the RV's driver's door and climbed into the seat beside her.

"Tell it to the judge, baby," he drawled, unconcerned, flashing her another insolent grin as he fished *her* key ring from his pocket and, after jangling it before her pointedly to let her know that even if she'd somehow managed to get free, she couldn't have driven away, inserted the proper key into the ignition. The engine sprang to life. Putting the automatic gearshift into drive, Rafer carefully maneuvered the RV and Jeep from the clearing and back onto the blacktop road beyond the woods. "You wouldn't listen. You wouldn't agree to lay off Dolan Pike. You're stubborn enough to keep hounding him and me both, and I've got a sneaking suspicion, you see, that Pike'll find your face a lot more attractive than mine, that if you somehow get the jump on me, you'll sucker him into your clutches. So, I'm just going to make sure you don't get in my way."

"By abducting me? I'll have your bounty-hunting license for this, Starr!"

"I don't think so. It'll be your word against mine, Hayley. And even if the law believes you, you'll look real foolish in the business, admitting that another bounty hunter got the best of you. How's that going to help you keep your agency afloat?"

She'd no reply to that, for the simple reason that it was all too true. Of course, Rafer would have thought everything through before taking such a drastic step as this.

"Do you even have the slightest idea where Pike is, or are you just driving aimlessly?" she asked tartly. "If you'd give me the key to these cuffs, I could do some hacking with my computer, find out if he used any major credit card either last night or this morning."

To her surprise Rafer reached into the front pocket of his fatigues, withdrawing the key to the handcuffs and tossing it to her.

"Don't go getting any wild ideas, Hayley. I secured all your weapons in that closet you use as a gun safe. I've got the key to it, and I will, without a doubt, hear you if you attempt to pick the lock. Furthermore, if you attack me while I'm driving, I will most assuredly run us off the road, wrecking your RV—which I don't think you want me to do, especially since you've got money problems. How'd you afford this thing, anyway?''

"I bought it with the settlement from Dad's life insurance policy. It—it seemed the best thing to do at the time. Dad had been ill…his heart. As a result he left a lot of outstanding medical bills at his death, and I needed funds to pay for his funeral and to keep the agency solvent while I settled his affairs, besides. So I sold our house to cover everything. But that didn't matter. It was…so empty afterward, so full of memories.''

"I'm sorry. I didn't mean to hit a nerve, Hayley.''

"It's all right. I've had time to grieve, time to adjust— at least, as well as anyone ever does after losing a loved one, I guess. Dad's been gone for three years now.''

"And you've been alone all that time—no other family?''

"None other than an ex-husband, an oil man who didn't find it quite so exciting, after all, being married to a 'macho-woman' bounty hunter, as he often called me.'' Her soft, resigned tone was tinged with bitterness at the memory.

Rafer shot her a penetrating glance from beneath his lashes.

"Man was a fool. There's nothing macho about you, Hayley.'' His eyes took in her sweep of silky, honey blond hair, her porcelain skin tinted with rose, her delicate bones and her long, slender fingers with their carefully polished nails. "Strong, yes. Macho, no.''

"Yeah, well, maybe I'd do better if I actually *looked* like people seem to expect a female bounty hunter to look.'' She sighed, for the thought had occurred to her before, yet she'd always rebelled against it. Why should she be compelled to sacrifice her femininity in order to accomplish what was traditionally considered a man's job? she'd wondered—and found no good answer. "What about you? Do you have any family?''

"Nope." For a long moment Rafer was silent, and Hayley thought he wasn't going to say any more. But then he continued. "My folks are dead. My older brother stepped on a land mine in 'Nam, and my ex-wife got 'sick and tired'—or so she claimed—of my being away so much during my stint in the service. She ran off with some homebody while I was down in South America."

There was a world of explanation in those few terse sentences, Hayley reflected soberly, understanding now why he was such a loner, among other things.

"I'm sorry." Having unfastened the handcuffs, she laid them and the key aside. "South America. Is that where Wenona Pike's brother was killed? I mean, I don't want to pry, but...I heard some rumors that you'd pulled some wild stunt down there and had beaten up a fellow officer afterward for his having jeopardized men's lives on a mission, so I—I just wondered...."

"Yeah, that's where Wenona's brother bought it. He was cut down by an Uzi—not a particularly pleasant way to die, I assure you. Afterward I...went a little crazy, charged up a hill, guns blazing, inside the compound that was our target. It was a reckless, fool thing to do, actually, and just sheer, dumb luck that I survived. When it was over, I knew for sure that the officer in charge of the operation had withheld certain vital information that would have made a difference to us, saved some men's lives...so, yeah, in a blind fury after the mission, I attacked him, and we fought. I resigned my commission shortly thereafter."

Rafer didn't need to say any more. Hayley could sense, understand and sympathize with his bitterness and disillusionment. It was terrible to lose faith in what you'd believed.

"Well...I'll go see if I can turn up anything on Pike." Rising, she headed back into the body of the RV, retrieved her laptop computer and sat down at the table, starting up the internal modem. From long practice, her fingers flew deftly over the keys. Eyes glued to the screen, she scanned the information that appeared, working swiftly and competently. "Jackpot!" she exclaimed after a while, elated as she shut down her system and returned to the cab.

"What'd you find out?" Rafer asked.

"Pike used a credit card last night to pay for a long-distance telephone call placed from the Wind River Motel, which is located in a town some miles up the road." She detailed the particulars she'd discovered about Pike's call.

"Then I'm more certain than ever that he's headed for his uncle's cabin," Rafer said when she'd finished. "It's up in the mountains, way off the beaten path—Pike's bolt-hole, where he goes to hide out when things are too hot for him to handle, according to Wenona. But she gave me directions, so I can find it. You got a map of Wyoming, Hayley?"

"Yes." She was already pulling it from the map pocket in the door panel as she spoke, unfolding it, determining their shortest route as Rafer outlined what Wenona had told him.

Presently they were under way. Hayley was filled with exhilaration, despite herself, at the thought that even if Rafer *had* technically kidnapped her, they were, in reality, now more or less working together as a team.

The next few days passed without incident as Hayley and Rafer headed west toward the cabin that belonged to Dolan Pike's uncle. Even towing the Jeep, they made relatively good time in the RV, with Hayley periodically spelling Rafer at the wheel. They talked as they drove, and when there was nothing worth listening to on the radio, Hayley popped CDs into the compact-disc player. Rafer liked music as much as she did and approved of her extensive collection of jazz, blues, and rock and roll. Although she remained, technically, his prisoner, she made no attempt to escape from him, not even when they stopped for gas and groceries at convenience stores, where she might conceivably have got away from him or at least asked for help. She'd never had any real fear that Rafer would truly harm her physically, that her life was in any way threatened by him. And now that she knew he didn't intend by some devious means to rid himself of her, leaving her behind somewhere, she was perfectly content to stay with him.

They had a great deal in common; he was surprisingly good company when he chose to be—besides being a comforting presence both at night and at roadside stops, during the latter of which previously, when alone, Hayley had on numerous occasions been forced to endure not only wolf whistles and sly suggestions from local male yokels, but also actually to defend herself once or twice from jerks who'd proved overly aggressive. Although she still attracted admiring male glances, no one insulted her with Rafer at her side, his arm possessively around her slender waist, his eyes making it clear that he was not the kind of man to back down from a challenge. Still, Hayley was so accustomed to taking care of herself that it was only after incurring Rafer's growl of displeasure that she stopped automatically reaching for doors and her billfold.

"You don't have to prove anything to me, baby," he declared once, frowning. "I know you're perfectly capable of opening your own doors and paying your own way. But equality of the sexes doesn't have to preclude a man's showing a woman a little common courtesy, does it? And it is *your* RV and not my Jeep we're racking up the miles on. And I don't think you'd argue the fact that I'm eating my share of the food, either, would you? So it seems only fair that I should foot the bills for the gas and groceries."

Put that way, Hayley could hardly disagree. In fact, deep down inside, she was forced to admit that having someone look after her for a change—especially when that someone was as handsome and proficient as Rafer—was a heady experience. She didn't need a man. Still, as time passed, she grew increasingly aware that she did *want* one, wanted Rafer. When he kissed her, touched her, as he did now and then, and when he lay wrapped around her at night in the bunk over the RV's cab, she knew that the only reason she'd not yet let him make love to her was because she feared being used, rejected and hurt again. Still, the realization that Rafer was not Logan *did* cross her mind more than once as they drove along, providing food for thought.

By this time they were deep into the wooded mountains. And now the crude blacktop road they'd been following for some time ended without warning, turning into a narrow, rough dirt track, which led to the cabin where they suspected Pike was holed up. Obviously they could go no farther in the RV. After pulling off into a little clearing and switching off the ignition, Rafer just sat there silently for a long moment, drumming his fingers on the steering wheel. Then, at last, he turned to Hayley.

"I don't suppose I could talk you into staying here while I bring Pike down?"

"No—and if you're considering handcuffing me to the seat belt again, forget it! If something should happen to you, I don't want to be stranded here, at Pike's mercy. If his treatment of Wenona is any indication of his attitude toward women, I doubt he'd be above slapping me around and raping me, too, if he got the chance—especially if he learned I'm a bounty hunter after his hide."

At the thought of Pike's hands on Hayley, something wild and primal tore through Rafer. He clenched the steering wheel so tightly that he was surprised it didn't break off its shaft.

"I'd kill Pike before I'd let that happen. I hope you know that, Hayley." His voice was so grim and intent, his face so dark and murderous, that her eyes were wide as she nodded in response. This was a side of him that she'd known he must possess but that was still frightening to see, making her realize just how considerate his treatment of her these past few days had actually been, how he'd restrained himself in the face of her rebellion and obstinacy. This man could have broken her both physically and mentally had he so chosen. The fact that he had not spoke volumes. "Get changed, and get your gear," Rafer said abruptly, tossing Hayley her key ring before opening the door and sliding from his seat. "We'll take the Jeep from here."

While Rafer unhitched the Jeep, Hayley quickly changed into a T-shirt, jeans and hiking boots. Then she unlocked the closet she used as a gun safe, slipping on the shoulder holster in which she carried her Glock 19 when she didn't need her handbag. Withdrawing her sturdy backpack, she filled it with essential food, bottled water, clothing and equipment, at the last moment including, despite its weight, her Kevlar vest. It might have been only the dreariness of the day, the sullen grey sky from which spring rain drizzled, but her sixth sense had begun to prickle warningly, and Hayley had learned from experience always to trust her gut instinct. She closed the backpack, setting it and also her sleeping bag to one side, then stood debating whether to take her shotgun or her assault rifle. At last she selected the latter.

"I prefer the AR-15 myself," Rafer said as he rejoined her, his glance swiftly taking in with approval her appearance, her preparations.

"Of course. It shoots straight and fires more rounds per minute. But you know what they say…straight or not, this baby—" she indicated her Kalashnikov AK-47 "—always at least shoots, and unfortunately, the same can't be said of the AR-15."

"Unfortunately," he agreed dryly.

Hayley pulled on her long, drab green rain poncho she'd bought at an Army surplus store, then hoisted her backpack onto her shoulders and picked up her rifle and sleeping bag.

"So…what do you think?" She flashed Rafer a flirtatious smile that made his pulse race as she teasingly strutted like a model before him.

"I think it's too bad the Marines were only looking for a few good men." His eyes roamed over her slowly, smoldering like twin coals, making her heart thud wildly in her breast. "Come on. Let's go before I forget why we're really out here all alone in the woods."

Together, after locking the RV, they loaded the Jeep, to which Rafer had thoughtfully fastened the loose vinyl top—for her sake, Hayley knew, sensing that he wouldn't have bothered otherwise, despite the drizzle. He turned on the heater, too. For although the top kept out the rain, the cool, damp spring wind slithered through every crevice where the top's flaps joined the vehicle. Muddy, the narrow, wending track they followed was such that the going was slow and rough. Occasionally Hayley was compelled to hold on to the roll bar above her head to keep from being jolted too severely. They'd got a late-afternoon start; twilight fell swiftly in the woods. At dark, Rafer insisted that they stop and camp for the night. There was no point in plowing on and becoming lost. It was not likely that Pike, if he were indeed at his uncle's cabin, would venture from it tonight.

They pitched the small tent Rafer carried in the Jeep. But such kindling as they might have found would have been too wet to burn. So, foregoing a poor, smoky fire, it was by the soft, glowing light of Rafer's Coleman lantern that they consumed supper straight out of cans—a meal that Hayley somehow still found the most romantic she'd ever eaten. It was peaceful in the woods; the rain that now fell harder beat a soothing tattoo upon the tent in which she and Rafer huddled, one flap open so they could see out into the darkness. The rich, earthy scents of the rain and woods filled the night air; the boughs of evergreens and the greening leaves on the deciduous trees rustled in the soughing wind. It was as though she and Rafer were alone in all the world. Yet, unlike the previous nights they'd spent together, he was strangely silent, brooding. Hayley didn't know what he was thinking, but she was wise enough not to ask. People had a right to their privacy, she'd always believed. If a man chose to share his thoughts, she was glad to listen; if he didn't, she wasn't the kind of woman to press. So she said little, not even bothering to protest when Rafer handcuffed her wrist to his to ensure that she wouldn't sneak off in his Jeep, like a thief in the night, leaving him behind, as, after a while, they zipped their sleeping bags together to share their bodies' warmth and, extinguishing the lantern's flame, crawled inside the makeshift double bed, Hayley instinctively settling into the now familiar curve of Rafer's strong arms.

After a time it came to her gently, sweetly, as she lay there listening to the drumming rain, that somehow, despite everything, she'd fallen in love with this solitary man who held her so close and secure in the darkness.

Chapter Four

The Mountains
Wyoming

It was Rafer's disjointed, muttered ravings, followed by his hoarse cries and violent thrashing that wakened her abruptly. Disoriented in the darkness and her unfamiliar surroundings, Hayley didn't at first know where she was, and erroneously assumed she was in her RV, under assault. It was only when she tried to bring her right fist up to defend herself that, after a moment, she realized she was handcuffed to Rafer and that he was suffering a nightmare undoubtedly born of his time spent in combat. Her father, a veteran of World War II, had continued in his dreams to relive past battles more than forty years after his service to his country had ended, so she was not unfamiliar with such episodes. With the greatest of difficulty, she finally managed with her left hand to light the Coleman lantern so its soft glow dimly illuminated the tent. Then, keeping her voice low, she spoke to Rafer, careful not to touch him, knowing from experience that he might inadvertently mistake her for an enemy and attempt to kill her in his sleep. Once, when, hearing her father's terrible shouts, she'd run urgently into his room to waken him, he had, deep in the throes of one of his own nightmares, tried to throttle her, unutterably stricken when he'd roused to find his hands at her throat. Knowing what war did to people was why Hayley hated it, why any rational person did. Only madmen and fools started wars; only wackos, mercenaries, and young Turks gloried in them—and it was always women who grieved and tried to pick up the pieces afterward.

"Rafer, it's Hayley. Wake up. You're having a nightmare. Rafer, do you hear me?" Like a litany she repeated the words until, at last, her soothing voice pierced the veil of his subconscious and he suddenly sat bolt upright, glancing about the shadowy tent wildly before, with a growl, he grabbed her roughly, flung her down and pinned her to the ground. He was big and strong; his dark visage was hard with murderous intent in the half-light, frightening her. Still, Hayley forced herself to swallow her fear, to remain calm. Gently she laid her hand against his cheek. "Rafer, it's me, Hayley."

After a long, tense moment his eyes filled with recognition and remorse.

"Hayley. Oh, baby, I'm sorry. I didn't hurt you, did I?"

"No. I've been through this before...with Dad. You were having a nightmare—about South America, I think."

"Yeah, these woods...this rain...it was like being down there in the jungle all over again tonight—" He broke off abruptly, his face bleak, his eyes shadowed before he hooded them so she couldn't read his thoughts.

"It's all right. I understand."

Her heart, so full of her newfound love for him, ached unendurably as she realized then why he'd been so brooding and withdrawn earlier. Instinctively she wanted to heal his wounds, to salve his scars, to make the world and his pain go away. He'd been right: they were alike, he and she, Hayley thought in some distant chasm of her mind. And now, they lay together like two chrysalids, cocooned in the woodland tent beneath the still-falling rain, with only each other for strength, for sustenance, each yearning to feed the desperate hunger of the body and soul, to break free of the restraints that bound them, to metamorphose into something finer, to create life—despite how fleeting—in the face of death, which had haunted them both and perhaps waited for them tomorrow.

Perhaps her eyes revealed her thoughts, Hayley reflected, for no man had ever looked at her as Rafer did then, as though he knew that, in moments, he would possess her intimately, utterly, and that afterward, she would belong to him irrevocably for the rest of her days. In that instant her world contracted sharply to the tent's interior, as though some unknown force had indeed magically woven it into a cocoon, hushing the night, the woods, the wind and the rain, although it was only that her senses shut them out. She became so keenly attuned to Rafer that she and he breathed as one. He wanted her; she could see it in his eyes. His nostrils flared as, slowly reaching up, she wrapped her hand in his glossy mane of dark brown hair, faintly surprised by its softness as she drew him down to meet her moist, parted lips. She hadn't expected that, although his mouth was as starving as her own, he would permit himself only a taste of her before he suddenly tore himself away, swearing softly, shaking with the force of his emotions, his arousal, the aftermath of his nightmare.

"I don't want pity, Hayley—especially not from you!" he grated.

"I'm not offering you any...only myself, if you want me...if you'll have me," she said quietly. "I know about pain, Rafer—and that it's easier shared."

"No. I won't be...any good for you like this. You deserve better than to be dragged down into my hell."

Another woman might have misunderstood, but Hayley didn't. She knew Rafer meant that his current mood precluded slowness and tenderness, that he would use her as he willed to assuage the feral feelings, the urgent desire, the driving need his nightmare had unleashed inside him.

Still, he was not so hard and brutal as he thought if he feared to hurt her—and she wasn't afraid.

"I don't care!" she whispered fiercely. "I don't care. Take me to where you are...."

There was between them then an interminable moment as highly charged as a night sky alive with heat lightning, the silence broken only by the gentle rhythm of the rain, the faint cadence of the wind, the harsh raggedness of their indrawn breaths. Rafer's glittering eyes evidenced his brief, internal struggle before they darkened with defeat and desire, and with a low groan he fell upon Hayley blindly, his lips swooping to capture hers savagely, a devouring kiss that was hot and hard, purely primal. Intuitively she acquiesced to his wild, possessive onslaught, her mouth yielding softly for the invasion of his demanding tongue that scalded her own, taking her breath, shattering and scattering her senses as surely and strongly as though she'd suddenly been swept up by some unbridled, atavistic storm, whirled away to a dark, mindless place where she was oblivious of all but sensation. In its wake, reason fled, and instinct prevailed. She knew nothing but Rafer, his lips and tongue and hands, rough, restless, ravaging, covetously claiming her, binding her to him as inescapably as his handcuffs that chained the two of them together.

She was only dimly aware of his impatiently tearing away their clothes, of his muttered imprecation when both their T-shirts and her lacy bra caught and tangled on the cuffs, of the knife that gleamed momentarily in his hand before he ruthlessly cut the garments free, then flung them aside, driving the blade into the ground. Slick with sweat, his naked body slid across her own, dark flesh covering pale as he rolled slightly on his side, one corded leg riding between her thighs, opening her. With his imprisoned hand, he caught her free one, pinioning her wrists above her head. Then he drew back a little to look at her, his eyes like twin flames, scorching her soft, bare skin as his gaze raked her slowly, lingering on her breasts and the vulnerably exposed juncture of her inner thighs. Gratification curved his carnal mouth as, of their own volition, Hayley's rosy nipples grew as hard and taut as tightly furled buds from the wild thrill of mingled fear and excitement that shot through her at his appraising glance, at the tantalizing thought that, soon, he would be a part of her.

Watching her all the while, he deliberately cupped and squeezed her breast, pressing it high. His thumb rotated around her nipple before he inexorably lowered his head, and his tongue rasped across the peak, making her gasp from the potent waves of pleasure that radiated through her. She longed fervently to touch him, to run her hands over his beautiful, muscular body, the sheeny, coppery skin, the scars from old wounds that marked it, a mute testament to his will to survive. But Rafer held her fast, silently making her understand that this was a quintessential male act of dominance, of conquering, of possession—as he'd obliquely warned her that it would be, such was the dark mood that gripped him—and that he reveled in not only her strength, but also, as a perverse result, her helplessness against his own greater power. His sex, hard and heavy, nudged with heated promise against her belly as his mouth fastened upon her nipple, sucking greedily, his tongue laving and teasing it until Hayley moaned and strained irrepressibly against him, wordlessly begging for more. Feverishly his lips and free hand moved everywhere upon her then. He kissed her wildly, fiercely—her mouth, her temples, her throat, and then her breasts, burying his face between them, licking away the sweat that moistened their valley. His fingers tangled roughly in the strands of her damp, tousled hair before following the trail his searing lips had blazed, then slipping down her belly and the curve of her hip to roam along her inner thighs, compelling them even wider apart.

His hand sought and found her downy softness, cupped

her mound, stroked the moist petals that trembled and unfolded of their own needy accord at his bold exploration. His thumb flicked and taunted the key to her delight until Hayley was frantic, whimpering with desire, bucking against him in a silent plea for assuagement of the hollow, burning ache that had seized her, setting her afire with its atavistic flame. With two fingers, Rafer momentarily eased her desperate yearning, probed her slowly, deeply, only to withdraw them, spreading quicksilver heat before sliding them into her again, harder, faster, his mouth claiming hers, his tongue plunging between her lips, mimicking the exquisitely torturous movements of his hand until Hayley gasped for breath, thought she could endure no more, would go mad with wanting.

"Please," she whispered imploringly. "Please, Rafer."

"Tell me that you want me, baby," he demanded huskily against her mouth.

"I want you! I want you, Rafer...."

With a rasp, a groan, a calling of her name, his body urgently covering hers, his hand burrowing beneath her back, lifting her hips to receive him, he drove down into her then, a single, sudden, hard, deep thrust that pierced her to the very core, making her cry out softly, her breath catch raggedly in her throat at the mingled pain and pleasure of his forceful entry.

"God, you're tight," he muttered thickly, his own breath harsh, hot against her flesh. And such was the note of triumph and satisfaction in his low voice that she knew that he recognized that he was the only man she'd had in a long while, and that he was glad of it. "Tight and wet and hot for me, just as I've wanted you. Damn, how I've wanted you! From the moment I first saw you, I've ached to be inside you, like this...." His eyes sought their joining, then riveted on her flushed face again, mesmerizing her. "You're mine, Hayley...mine...."

He kissed her mouth and breasts again as he lay atop

her, his weight pressing her down, his sex pulsing within her, filling her to overflowing, molding and stretching her to accommodate him before, slowly, he began to move against her, driving in and out of her in a rhythm as old as time and that grew increasingly stronger and swifter as what little control he'd had deserted him. Hayley's blood roared in her ears as she writhed against him, wrapping her long legs around him and arching her hips to meet each savage thrust. His hand was upon her mound, kneading her as he plunged into her, bringing her rapidly to a gloriously explosive climax. Her head thrashed; she cried out, bucking wildly against him, then straining, tensing as wave after wave of unbearable pleasure erupted inside her, swept through her, blinding her to everything as the world spun away in a burst of dazzling brilliance. Her muscles clenched uncontrollably around Rafer's sex, maddening him, so he knew nothing any longer but the vibrant throbbing of her body around his, spurring his own exigent, primal need for release. His hands grasped and tightened bruisingly around her wrists, holding her down. He buried his head against her shoulder, his breathing labored, his own low cry ringing in her ears as he abruptly shuddered violently against her, long and hard, spilling himself inside her.

When it was over, he eased himself from her slowly, reluctantly, then searched for the key to the handcuffs and impatiently unlocked them and cast them aside before pulling her into his strong arms, kissing her deeply as he cradled her sweating body against his own. Her head rested against his broad, furry chest; she could feel his heart pounding as furiously as hers. His hand stroked her hair gently as they lay still together in the quiet afterglow, each marveling at the chemistry that had ignited so rapidly and explosively between them.

"I'm sorry, Hayley," Rafer murmured after a long while in the silence.

"Don't be. I wanted it as much as you did."

"It was too quick, too rough. I knew that it would be...I tried to warn you—"

"It doesn't matter. I understood."

"I know that you did. That was the beauty of it. You gave me what I wanted, what I needed, Hayley. Now, let me do the same for you."

Rafer was already aroused, ready for her again; her very nearness intoxicated him so. But this time when he took her, he was so infinitely patient, so incredibly tender that when it was done and he'd extinguished the lantern, Hayley lay with tears on her cheeks in the darkness at the thought that she was nearly forty years old and she had only just learned what it meant to be made love to by a man.

She awoke in the morning to the feel of Rafer's mouth and hands upon her, once more taking her to paradise before he rose, drew on his clothes and went outside to start loading their gear into the Jeep. Mist cloaked the mountains, and it had begun to drizzle again, so the spring air was chilly, and Hayley was grateful she'd thought to bring along a long-sleeved flannel shirt. She shrugged it on over her T-shirt, leaving it unbuttoned, ends trailing. Once she'd finished dressing, she brushed her hair, then double-checked the spare magazines she'd packed for both her pistol and rifle, stuffing the fully loaded clips into the ammo vest she wore. Then, pulling on her poncho, she stepped from the tent to help Rafer dismantle it.

She knew that her eyes shone when they met his, but Hayley couldn't help it. Not even reminding herself that he'd not spoken of loving her, either last night or this morning, dimmed what she felt in her heart for him. He was a man to whom such words would not come easily; she understood that. Still, she thought he must care for her, wouldn't, *couldn't* have made love to her as he had that second time, otherwise. But she was too proud to ask him,

too afraid of being rejected and hurt again. She didn't want
to know just yet if their relationship didn't mean to him
what it did to her. She wanted to hold on to what they
shared, for just as long as she could.

That her thoughts were Rafer's own, she was unaware.
He'd never before known a woman like her, had never
dreamed he'd find her like in all the world. She was everything he'd ever wanted, needed in a woman—a beguiling
mixture of femininity, strength, intelligence, wit, sensitivity
and vulnerability. He felt that last night her luminous eyes
had looked into the harshest, darkest corners of his soul
and that, instead of shrinking in fear as other women had,
she'd responded with sweetness and light, opening herself
to him unequivocally, trusting him not to hurt her any more
than he had. She had not made such a commitment lightly,
Rafer knew; nor had he taken it so. He would always be
moody and brooding—and, where Hayley was concerned,
jealously possessive and zealously protective, stronger than
she. But all that, too, she would somehow understand, he
sensed instinctively. The thought of losing her was more
painful than any wound he'd ever suffered in combat. Still,
he could not humble her pride, either, to keep her safe and
secure.

"I may be *your* baby, Rafer, but I'm not *a* baby," she'd
uttered fiercely when, his mind filled with worry for her,
for what they might face this morning if they indeed found
Dolan Pike at his uncle's isolated cabin, Rafer had again
suggested that she stay behind, wait for him to bring down
Pike alone.

Now, as they climbed in the Jeep and started down the
track, Rafer bit back the anxious words that sprang to his
tongue. Hayley had trusted him; now, he must trust her,
must have faith that she knew her job as well as he, that
she was indeed his equal in all things that mattered, because deep down inside, he knew he wouldn't want her
any other way.

They drove through the mist in silence, not even playing the radio; not only because the sound might carry to the cabin, but also because they needed the quiet mentally to psych themselves up for the expected confrontation with Pike. Despite the light rain, they had the top off the Jeep now, so they could without hindrance scan their surroundings. Now and then, Hayley raised to her eyes a pair of high-powered binoculars to look through the trees for the cabin.

Presently she said, "There's the cabin. I see it. Your hunch was right—Pike's Dually is parked out front."

Wordlessly Rafer maneuvered the Jeep so it blocked the track, then switched off the ignition, cutting off Pike's main escape route.

"We'll go the rest of the way on foot. I don't want him to hear the engine. Hayley, you've got to promise me that you'll stick close behind me—and I mean it. Pike's a woodsman. He's probably got all kinds of traps, snares, pits and maybe even *pungee* sticks rigged up out here. I know I sure as hell would." His voice was grim, and she shivered, both at the thought of what Pike might have waiting in store for them and that Rafer knew how to set such devices himself and doubtless had in the past, maybe had even killed people with them.

Wide-eyed, she nodded, hoping she didn't have to worry about snakes, too. Although Rafer hadn't said as much, she knew he was the expert on this terrain, and that was a whole lot different from his just arbitrarily giving her orders. That being the case, as they hiked through the woods, carefully skirting the occasional trap they indeed discovered, she followed hard on his heels until, from where they stood, they could without their field glasses spy the cabin that sat in a little clearing: a crude, ramshackle affair built of logs and having a corrugated tin roof. From the fieldstone chimney, smoke drifted, permeating the air with a scent Hayley had always loved. Since Pike had made no attempt to conceal the black Dually parked out in front of the porch, when a rundown barn was handy, he clearly thought himself safe from pursuit at his uncle's cabin, had no idea that his miserable, terrified ex-wife had finally worked up gumption enough to dare to give away the secret of his hiding place to Rafer.

"I'll take the front." Rafer kept his voice low so the sound wouldn't carry on the wind and alert Pike of their presence. "You go around back."

Nodding again to show she understood, Hayley withdrew her automatic from the shoulder holster beneath her poncho and checked to ensure there was a round in the chamber. Then she turned to go, startled when Rafer suddenly grabbed her, his eyes searching her face intently, as though to memorize its every detail, before he kissed her, hard and deep.

"Hayley, for God's sake, be careful," he muttered urgently as he released her. "It's only a short step from rape and armed robbery to murder—and Pike's poised to take it."

"I know. I will. Rafer, I—" She broke off abruptly, biting her lower lip. *I love you,* she'd wanted to say. "You take care, too."

Then quickly, tears stinging her eyes, Hayley turned and began to make her way furtively through the thin woods at the edge of the clearing to the rear of the cabin, her heart racing, her adrenaline pumping as it inevitably did when she closed in on a bounty. Only a fool was never afraid, her father had always told her, warning her that if she ever lost that edge born of fear and caution, she would most likely lose her life, as well. But it'd been three long years since she'd had to worry about someone else's life, too; that of a man she loved. That thought was uppermost in her mind as she crept near to the cabin, using the trees for cover until she was able to sprint across the weed-grown yard to where a rusted old pickup perched on cinder blocks out back, not far from the cabin. Crouching down low behind the junked vehicle, Hayley flattened herself against its side and started to inch her way along its length toward the mangled front bumper, from where she'd have a clear shot at Pike should he come barreling out the cabin's back door. Finally reaching her vantage point, she hunkered there for what seemed like hours, waiting for Rafer's move, her mouth dry despite the rain that drizzled down her face in the gray morning light.

At last when it felt as though her limbs had petrified from immobility, she heard Rafer kick in the cabin's front door and then shouts, followed by a frightening exchange of shots.

"Rafer!" Hayley cried softly, her heart leaping to her throat. "*Rafer!*" And cursing the slippery wet ground, she began to run.

She expected Pike, if he'd survived, to come out the back door. Instead, just seconds later, he crashed through one of the cabin's rear windows, sending shards of glass and wood splinters from the frame flying in every direction, before, with a thud, he hit the muddy earth, rolling. Skidding to an abrupt halt some yards away, Hayley took up a firing stance and, both hands wrapped around its grip, leveled her pistol.

"Freeze, Pike!" she yelled.

But wild-eyed, appearing suddenly, strangely, to move in slow motion, he sprang to his feet, discharging the gun in his hands even as he rose. The bullet took only seconds to strike her, seconds in which Hayley realized instinctively that she was going to be hit, that her body couldn't respond in time to her brain's frantic signals to her legs. Then, suddenly, the slug exploded against her chest, the violent impact knocking her flat, ripping the air from her lungs and leaving her feeling as though they were on fire as incredible, searing pain erupted inside her.

Desperately, feeling as though she were suffocating, she gasped for breath, some dark, faraway corner of her stunned mind dimly recognizing that Pike, his weaselly face cold, merciless, now towered over her, that he was fixing to shoot her again. It seemed an eternity that she stared in to the long, blued barrel of his .22-caliber Ruger aimed at her head, knowing with certainty that the next bullet had death written on it, that this was what it was to die, and silently cursing fate that it should claim her now, when she was so newly in love, had everything for which to live, everything she'd never thought to find.

"Nooooo!" Rafer's hoarse, stricken cry echoed through the woods as he jerked open the cabin's back door, nearly tearing it from its hinges, and bounded through the doorframe, his shotgun in his hands.

Pike turned to confront this new threat—and Hayley knew nothing then except that he was going to kill Rafer and then her, that Rafer was going to lose his life because of her. At the realization, she somehow miraculously found the strength from someplace deep inside her to raise her automatic, still clutched in her right hand, and to depress the trigger even as Pike pulled his own. Pike was taken off guard when her first slug bored into his leg, staggering him, the wound spurting blood, spraying her all over before her second bullet slammed into his shoulder, sending him sprawling as, at last, her pistol slid weakly from her grasp and she began trying to crawl toward Rafer, knowing only that he'd been hit, that blood dripped down his arm.

"Hayley! Oh, God, Hayley!" His voice seemed to be coming at her from a distance as, running to her side, pausing only just long enough to kick Pike's gun away, Rafer knelt over her, distraught at the sight of the blood, pinkened by the drizzle, that spattered and trickled down her poncho. He laid aside his shotgun, his hands yanking frantically at the long, twisted garment, its hem caught between her legs. She was dully aware that all the while he tore madly at her clothing, he was alternately muttering, shouting, swearing, threatening to murder Pike, who still lay moaning, writhing and bleeding on the ground. "If she dies, I'll kill you, you bastard!"

"V-v-vest," Hayley managed to rasp faintly, her eyes fluttering from the dizziness that assailed her.

"Don't try to talk, sweetheart." Rafer's expression was grim as, having hauled off her poncho, his fingers now fumbled with the lacings of her ammo vest. He was shaking so badly that he couldn't pull the wide strips from their metal loops. Snatching his knife from the leather sheath at his waist, he quickly sliced through the troublesome lacings, staring down at her chest, dumbfounded by the sight of the now misshapen bullet lodged in the Kevlar vest she wore beneath, over her flannel shirt and T-shirt. Understanding dawned; overwhelming relief pervaded his body. The blood was not hers; it was Pike's. Overcome with emotion, Rafer gathered her into his arms, rocking her, stroking her damp hair, kissing her face and mouth feverishly and murmuring, "Oh, Hayley, Hayley, my brave, beautiful, intelligent woman! You wore a vest. Thank God, you wore a vest! I couldn't have borne to lose you! I love you! I love you...."

She'd never before known such joy as she knew in that moment. Her heart soared. It was, she thought dazedly, actually worth being shot to hear him speak those words—although she knew he wouldn't have agreed.

"Love you...too...Rafer," she croaked as her labored breathing finally began to ease, the pain in her chest growing less agonizing.

After a long while, he drew away, brushing the dripping strands of her hair from her face and kissing her brow gently before he rose and went to attend to Pike, tearing away strips of Pike's T-shirt to staunch his bleeding and bandage his wounds until the first aid kit in the Jeep could be accessed. To Hayley's relief, Rafer's own injury was only a flesh wound; Pike's bullet had just nicked Rafer's arm. Hayley's shots had spoiled Pike's aim, had saved Rafer's life, just as he'd saved her own by appearing in the cabin's doorway when he had. When Rafer had finished his makeshift ministering, he handcuffed Pike's wrists behind his back and roughly hauled him to his feet, nudging him forward with the shotgun.

"I heard you always worked alone," Pike grumbled as he glared at Rafer angrily.

"Not anymore. I think you've met my partner, Hayley Harper," Rafer's reply was spoken coolly, casually, as he turned to help her up, his arm around her waist to keep her from falling when her legs trembled weakly beneath her—and not solely from her ordeal, either.

"Yeah, some angel she turned out to be!" Pike sneered.

"Dolan, that's probably the one and only thing you're ever going to get right in your entire life," Rafer observed, his eyes unmistakably alight with love as he gazed tenderly at Hayley by his side before, together, they started down the mountain.

She was now both poorer and richer than she'd ever been in her life, Hayley thought with a sigh as, her eyes closed, she leaned back in the passenger's seat, grateful to be resting, while Rafer wheeled the RV, towing the Jeep behind, down the dirt road that led away from Wenona Pike's shack. For capturing Dolan Pike and turning him into the local sheriff's office, all Hayley had to show was a massive, ugly, black-and-blue bruise tinged with yellow on her chest—and the memory of a tearfully overjoyed Wenona with a $25,000 check clutched in her hand and three suddenly hopeful, wide-eyed children hugging their mother excitedly.

"Rafer, I sure hope you meant what you said about our being partners, because after agreeing to your good deed, I am flat broke."

"That's all right, baby. I think you've got other, equally

as valuable and coveted assets to bring to our merger." His voice, while teasing, nevertheless held a note she'd come to recognize. And when she opened her eyes, it was to see that his own glittered with desire as he slowly appraised the "assets" to which he'd referred. Remembering how he'd inventoried them at quite some length last night, she blushed.

"Harper-Starr, Incorporated. I like the sound of that," she drawled impudently.

"Shooting Starr, Incorporated," he corrected just as insolently.

"Starr-Harper?" she ventured, ignoring the sound of her father's voice in her head, telling her that Shooting Star, Incorporated was an established, respected name, one he'd have been proud and glad to have put on their own agency's letterhead if he'd thought he could have got Rafer Starr to join them that way. *Good for business, and good for you, Hayley. Go for it, puddin'!*

"Shooting Starr," Rafer repeated stubbornly, his voice firm.

"Well, I don't think that's fair at all!" Hayley snapped tartly in protest, sitting up and beginning to bristle defiantly, despite how happy she knew that her father would have been for her, how he'd not only wholeheartedly approved of Rafer, but also had thought him the man for her. "Wyoming's the Equality State—and what's equal about that?"

"A moot point, since we're leaving this state."

"We are?" Her eyebrows lifted faintly with surprise. "Where are we going?"

"Nevada."

"Why? Oh, of course…the new Wanted posters we picked up in the sheriff's office. Well, who's in Nevada?"

"Not who…what."

"What? What do you mean…what? Oh, all right, then," she conceded, frowning at the penetrating glance Rafer shot her wryly from beneath his lashes. "*What's* in Nevada?"

"Wedding chapels…lots of wedding chapels."

Hayley sat there dumbly for a moment, her heart starting to jerk erratically in her breast.

"Is this—is this a marriage proposal?" she asked faintly.

"The only one you're gonna get from me," Rafer declared, the hint of a smile now playing about the corners of his mouth.

"Obstinate, arrogant man! Still, I can think of something else I'd rather you do on your knees," she teased provocatively, suddenly filled to bursting with joy.

"Hmm. So can I." His gleaming eyes traveled over her body slowly, significantly. "Reciprocation would be nice, too."

Color flooded Hayley's cheeks again at the images evoked in her mind by their banter.

"What about children?" she inquired hastily—then held her breath as she awaited his response, because, despite her lighthearted tone, she wanted kids.

"Oh, yeah. We'll definitely make some of those, too, while we're at it—at least a couple." Rafer's eyes danced with deviltry. "I hear you have to work at that day and night to ensure success—and personally, I never have liked the thought of failure."

"But—but…what would we do with them…our children? I mean…how would we take care of them after we got them, being on the road all the time and all? I'm not going to have to give up being a bounty hunter, am I?" Hayley queried suspiciously, thinking that somehow, this sounded be too good to be true.

"Nope. After all, we *do* own an RV—and we could always buy a bigger one. We could hire a nanny, too, even a tutor, if need be. There are lots of options nowadays. Somehow, we'll work things out together—I promise you that." All touch of humor was suddenly gone from Rafer's face and tone. Earnestly he continued. "Look—I know that we're two strong-minded, independent people, Hayley.

There'll be times when we'll be bound to argue, times when one of us will have to give. But I'm not afraid of commitment or compromise, either one. And no matter what, I'll never let you down as Logan did, but do everything in my power to make you happy. Is that enough for you?''

"Almost." Even though she smiled, Hayley was fighting back tears born of the love that welled in her heart for him, knowing that those last words hadn't come easily, but that he'd meant every single one of them.

"What do you mean…almost?" Anxiety at the thought that he'd laid himself emotionally bare before her, only to be rejected and hurt flickered briefly in Rafer's uncertain eyes until he saw the smile that trembled on Hayley's lips, the poignant tears she dashed away. She would sit there and sob through every heartbreaking movie they were ever going to watch together in the RV, he knew. But that was all right. Still, he was without a doubt going to burn that nightshirt of hers, the one that read *Hard-hearted Woman,* buy her something small and black and lacy….

"Just what I said," she responded to his question, oblivious of the current direction of his thoughts. "Almost…because I still have two more questions," she announced with feigned loftiness, recovering her composure.

"Fire away, then. Fire away…and fall back." The humor returned to Rafer's voice as he spoke the old military saying.

"Can I at least have Hayley Harper-Starr on our letterhead?"

"Of course. That's one. Now, what's the other?"

"Are you planning to handcuff me to you every single night for the rest of our lives?"

"If that's what it takes to hang on to you forever, baby, then I most certainly am!"

He was just rogue enough to do it, too, Hayley thought, tantalized, despite herself, at the notion. Still, he was *her* rogue, and she loved him. They might not have been right for others, but somehow, they were perfectly right for each other. That was the real bounty, all that counted—and besides, she'd grown rather fond of those handcuffs, actually!

"Hayley, I've answered all your questions, but you've yet to do the same for my one and only one." Rafer reminded her of his marriage proposal, a trifle impatiently, nudging her from her reverie—although the smug, arrogant note in his voice told her that he was already sure of her reply. "Well, damn it, woman!" he growled when—from pure orneriness, because he was so certain—she didn't respond, drawing out the suspense a little while longer and doing her best to restrain the laughter that bubbled in her throat at the expression on his face. "Hayley, so help me, I'm gonna cuff you to the bed in our honeymoon suite for days if you keep on! Now, answer me or else! Am I on the right road or not?"

Still taking her own sweet time, Hayley glanced deliberately, pointedly, at the passing road sign that indicated Interstate Highway 80, which she knew led to Nevada, to Reno—and to all those wedding chapels. Then at last, relenting, she looked back at Rafer, and the smile she gave him made his heart turn over, his pulse race. A teddy…he would buy her a small black lace teddy; she could wear it on their wedding night—for a few minutes, at least!

"Yes, you are definitely on the right road," she confirmed.

They had the radio on and tuned to an oldies station. Now, as though on cue, the opening strains of the Temptations' "My Girl" filled the cab. Flashing her a wicked, insolent, I-*knew*-I-was-right grin, Rafer cranked up the volume and put the pedal to the metal.

* * * * *

A LITTLE TEXAS TWO-STEP

Peggy Moreland

* * *

To Jean Brashear, the quintessential friend.
And a special thanks to Snuffy's of Hutto, Texas,
for inspiration in creating The End of the Road bar!

Dear Reader,

It all started in the orthodontist's office. I was thumbing through a magazine while waiting for my daughter to have her braces tightened, and I found an article about a town with a man-to-woman ratio of two to one and a dwindling population. The town leaders had advertised for women to move there, in order to avoid becoming a ghost town. Several romances and a couple of marriages resulted from the publicity the advertisement received.

The concept intrigued me, and I began to ask myself, "What if?" What if the town were in Texas? What if the town sheriff was the one who came up with the suggestion to advertise for women? What if three of the women who responded to the advertisement were friends? From all the "what ifs," my TROUBLE IN TEXAS series was born. *A Little Texas Two-Step* is a part of that series.

I hope you enjoy this peek into life in a small Texas town, as well as the romance!

All the best,

Peggy Moreland

Prologue

The minute she opened the door of her apartment, Leighanna smelled him. Polo. That spicy, sexy scent that her ex couldn't afford but always somehow managed to find the money to purchase.

She stopped, her key cutting into the palm of one hand, her suitcase cinched tight in the other. He can't be here, she told herself in growing panic. He didn't have a key any longer, and there was no way in hell that Reggie, her friend and the owner of the apartment complex, would ever let him inside.

Yet the scent of him continued to taunt her.

Her legs trembled in fear, but she forced them into motion, taking one cautious step, then another, until she stood in the center of her small living room.

"Roger?" she called hesitantly. "Are you here?"

She waited a moment, listening, but only the muted click of her mantel clock as it ticked off each second disturbed the quiet. If he wasn't here, she knew he *had* been. The scent of his cologne still hung thick in the air. But how did he get in? she asked herself in growing dread. She'd changed the locks after she'd kicked him out more than a year before.

The handle of her suitcase slipped from her fingers, and she drew her shaking fingers to her lips. Her key ring! She'd given him her key ring over a month ago when he'd offered to take her car in for repairs.

Her fingers closed into a fist against her lips as she remembered the incident. Of course, he *hadn't* had her car repaired. Instead, he'd paid some shady mechanic a pittance of what she'd given him and instructed the man to do what he could without replacing the transmission, then pocketed the rest of the money for himself. Naturally, Roger hadn't told her about his clever little scheme. She'd discovered it on her own, weeks later, when the transmission had gone out on her in the middle of Houston's five-o'clock traffic.

She was sure that at the same time Roger had been having her car repaired, he'd probably had a duplicate set of keys made to every key on her ring...including the one to her apartment.

Anger burned through her. She knew better than to trust her ex-husband. Hadn't she learned anything during the four years of their marriage? He was the master of lies and deception. And she knew without a doubt that he wouldn't think twice about stealing from her. He'd done it often enough in the past. A twenty here, a hundred there, missing from her purse. After their divorce, he'd even taken her wedding ring from her jewelry box and pawned it, spending the money on some new scam.

Money! Her fingers curled around the key ring as a new fear rose. With her heart thundering against her chest, she ran to the kitchen and jerked a canister from those that lined the counter beside the sink...and listened to the sick clink of loose coins. She knew even before she opened it that it was gone. All that she'd managed to save toward the purchase of a new car. She tipped the canister upside down, and pennies rained onto the floor.

Tears swelled and the canister blurred before her eyes. Raising the container above her head, she screamed, "Damn you, Roger!" and hurled it against the far wall where it shattered into a hundred jagged pieces right along with her dreams for a new car.

Reggie Giles frowned at the open apartment door then stepped inside, knocking on the door as she passed. "Leighanna?" she called as she stopped in the living room. "Leighanna, where are you?"

"I'm back here," came Leighanna's muffled reply. "In my room."

Anxious to hear about Leighanna's visit with their friend Mary Claire in her new home in Temptation, Reggie headed down the short hall.

"Did you know you left your front door open?" she scolded. "Anybody could come in and—"

At the door to Leighanna's bedroom, Reggie stopped cold. A suitcase lay on the bed, a tangle of clothes and shoes tumbled over its side, wire hangers were scattered over the floor. Leighanna stood in front of the dresser, jerking handfuls of lingerie and socks from the drawers.

Reggie let out a slow, long breath, unsure of what was happening. "Are you coming or going?" she asked uneasily.

Leighanna whirled. Her eyes were red, her cheeks mottled by anger. "Going!" She marched past Reggie and dumped the load she carried into the suitcase.

"Where?" Reggie asked.

"I'm moving out."

Fear knotted in Reggie's stomach. Leighanna was like family to her, as was Mary Claire, and she'd already lost Mary Claire and her children when they'd moved to Temptation. She couldn't bear the thought of losing Leighanna, too.

When Leighanna brushed past her again, headed for the dresser, Reggie grabbed her arm. "Wait a second," she said, hoping to slow Leighanna down long enough to find out what was behind this quick exodus. "Why are you moving out?"

Leighanna jerked free of Reggie's hold. "Roger!" she snapped, and marched on to the dresser. She snatched an armful of clothing from the bottom drawer, then kicked it closed with her foot.

Reggie could only stare. She had never seen Leighanna like this before. Always calm, soft-spoken, Leighanna seldom lost her temper. She was generous and loving and giving…even to that scumball of an ex-husband of hers, Roger.

And that's exactly what he was, too, Reggie thought angrily. Leighanna might have been blinded to his faults, but Reggie had never been. She had leased Roger the apartment four years ago when he'd first married Leighanna and would have kicked the loser out years ago when his first rent check had bounced if she hadn't felt sorry for his poor wife. She'd held Leighanna's hand throughout the divorce, had even tried to open Leighanna's eyes to his scheming ways when he would drop by periodically after their divorce, trying to borrow money from her. But Leighanna was naive and totally trusting, and never saw through his deceit until it was too late.

That he was behind this fit of temper didn't surprise her. What worried her was what Roger had done to provoke it.

"What does he have to do with your moving out?" she asked uneasily.

Leighanna turned on Reggie, her hands filled with clothes, her blue eyes wild with anger. "You'd think it would be enough for him that he ruined my life right along with my credit, wouldn't you?" she raged. "But, no! Not Roger! He's like that damn bunny in the battery commercial, pounding his drum. He just keeps going and going and going!"

Reggie sank to the edge of the bed, her shoulders slumping. "What has he done now?" she asked in resignation.

Leighanna threw the armload of clothes into the suitcase and planted her hands on her hips as she whirled to face Reggie. "He came into my apartment while I was gone to visit Mary Claire and stole all my money from the cookie jar."

Reggie was on her feet in a flash. "He did what?" she cried.

"He stole my money! All that I had saved to buy a new car."

Angry now herself, Reggie paced away, fisting her hands at her sides. "Well, he won't get away with it this time. Not if I have any say in the matter." Always ready to take charge, Reggie mentally listed what would need to be done. "We're calling the police. We'll file charges for breaking and entering and for burglary. When they find him, they'll throw his lousy butt in jail, and this time we'll see that they throw away the key." She stopped and wheeled, thrusting a warning finger at Leighanna. "Don't touch another thing," she ordered. "The police will need to dust the apartment for prints."

Leighanna went right on throwing clothes into the suitcase. "Forget it, Reggie. The police can't do anything."

"And why not?" she asked incredulously. "He broke into your apartment and stole your money. Last I remember, that's still a crime."

"He didn't break in. He used a key."

"A key!" Reggie all but screamed. "For God's sake, Leighanna, you gave him a key?"

"No, I didn't *give* him a key." The fight suddenly went out of Leighanna and she dropped down on the edge of the bed and covered her face with her hands. "He must have had a duplicate made last month when he took my car to have it repaired."

"Repaired?" Reggie repeated sarcastically. "You mean when he fleeced you of the repair money, don't you?'' She dropped down on the bed beside Leighanna in frustration. "Geez, Leighanna! When will you ever learn? The man can't be trusted.''

Leighanna dragged her hands down her face then tipped her face to the ceiling. "I know. I know,'' she said miserably. "But he said he knew somebody who could replace the transmission cheaper, and that he wanted to do it for me to make up for all the money he owed me.''

Reggie just rolled her eyes. It would be just like Leighanna to fall for a line like that. "Well, there's still the burglary charge,'' Reggie reminded her. "We can nail him with that.''

Leighanna turned to look at Reggie, her expression one of defeat. "And you think the police will believe me? I can't prove that the money was there and I certainly can't prove that Roger took it.'' She pushed to her feet and straightened. "Forget it, Reggie. There's only one thing left for me to do and that is to move.''

Reggie jumped from the bed. "And what will you solve by moving?''

"I'll be away from him. Far away. Somewhere where he'll never think to look for me.''

"And where would that be?''

"Temptation. I'm moving in with Mary Claire and her kids.''

One

Hank caught a movement out of the corner of his eye and glanced toward the entrance to his bar. A woman stood before the front window, bent at the waist, her chin thrust forward as she peered through its dirty glass.

Hank muttered a curse. He was sick and damn tired of people sticking their noses in his window at all hours of the day. The sign on the door clearly read Closed, but that little fact didn't seem to bother the throng of people who'd made their way to Temptation.

And it's all Cody's fault, he grumped silently, thinking of his friend and Temptation's sheriff. If he hadn't come up with the fool notion to advertise for women to save Temptation from becoming a ghost town, all these folks wouldn't have converged on their town.

He watched, frowning, as the sun panned gold from the woman's shoulder-length blond hair while the wind whipped it across her face. She caught the long tresses that curtained one cheek in long, delicately boned fingers to hold it back from her face.

Scrawny little thing, he told himself as he watched her. Probably didn't weigh more than a hundred pounds dripping wet. He stepped around the bar to get a better look. Yep, he confirmed, she was scrawny all right. Her arms were thin as reeds, her shoulders narrow, and if she had any boobs at all beneath that baggy silk blouse, she was hiding them well.

Hank snorted and shook his head. Personally, he liked his women with a little more flesh on them. Full hips made for a man to ride, breasts big enough to fill his hands, lips thick enough to wrap around his—

At that moment, she glanced up and caught sight of him through the window and offered him a tentative smile.

Well, she had the lips, he admitted reluctantly. And the pearliest white teeth he'd ever seen. While he watched, she snagged the sign from the window he'd put there three days before. She disappeared for a moment, only to reappear on the other side of the locked front door. She tapped on the glass then pointed to the sign she held.

Hank groaned. "Damn," he muttered under his breath, knowing full well that she was wanting to apply for the waitress position he'd advertised for. And Hank knew damn good and well this was going to be a waste of his time. She couldn't handle the job. The work was back-breaking, the hours long, his customers rowdy at best. A slip of a woman like her wouldn't last one shift as a waitress in a bar like The End of the Road.

Muttering curses under his breath, he crossed to the door and unlocked it. "Can I help you?"

Leighanna took a step back and pressed the sign to her breasts, startled by the intimidating size and the gruffness of the man who stood opposite her. Tall, broad-shouldered, slim-hipped, he had the face of an angel but the eyes and the mouth of the devil himself. "I hope so," she said, then nervously wet her lips.

The dart of that pink tongue made Hank think of other things he'd like that tongue to do. Before he had time to follow that train of thought, though, she extended her hand.

"I'm Leighanna Farrow," she said by way of introduction. "Are you the owner?"

Hank scowled. "Yeah, I'm the owner." Reluctantly, he took her hand in his. "Hank Braden."

Her hand was smooth as silk against his callused palm and soft as butter, further proof that she wasn't fit for the job.

She pushed a smile to her lips as she withdrew her hand…but he could see the fear in her eyes, could almost smell it over the scent of her perfume. His customers would eat a woman like her alive.

"I'd like to apply for the waitress position," she said politely, and offered him the sign.

Hank took it and stuck it right back in the window. "Sorry. You're not what I had in mind."

Her mouth dropped open. "But—"

"Lady," he growled. "This is a bar, not some damn

tearoom. You wouldn't last five minutes in a place like this.''

Her chin came up, her blue eyes as sharp as tempered steel. ''And how would you know?''

Hank snorted, then took his gaze on a slow journey from the top of her blond head to the tips of her high-heeled mules. She looked like one of those damn Dreamsicle ice cream bars, standing there in those peach-colored leggings and that baggy, watered silk blouse, looking all soft and creamy and temptingly sweet. And though he was tempted to offer her something other than a job, he knew sampling her would only bring him grief. By the regal lift of her chin and the cut of the clothes she wore, he figured she was a little classy for his taste, as well as that of his bar.

A sardonic smile tipped one corner of his mouth as his eyes met hers again. ''Trust me,'' he said. ''I just know.'' He turned his back on her and walked away.

Leighanna watched him and felt her last chance for employment slipping from her fingers. She needed this job, she told herself. She'd already walked the main street of Temptation, seeking employment in every possible establishment, but there wasn't a job to be had…other than this one.

Squaring her shoulders in determination, she yanked the sign from the window and hurried to catch up with him, her mules slapping against her heels and clicking loudly against the scarred linoleum floor. ''Mr. Braden—''

Hank wheeled and she skidded to a stop to keep from bumping into the wall of his chest. The woman was as pesky as a fly that just wouldn't shoo. "The name's Hank," he snapped. "And I said no."

If his size wasn't enough to send her running for her car, the threatening look in his eye should have done the trick. But it didn't. Leighanna was that desperate. Her creditors were already breathing down her neck. "Hank, then," she said, and fought to hide the tremble in her lips. "Look. I really need this job."

Hank heaved a sigh, then folded his arms across his chest. "Have you ever worked as a waitress before?"

"No," she replied reluctantly.

"Well, what makes you think you can do the work?"

"I managed a clothing boutique in Houston before I moved here, so I'm accustomed to dealing with the public. And I'm a fast learner," she was quick to add. "Plus, I'm willing to do whatever work is required."

He curled his mouth in disgust. "You don't even know what the job entails."

"No," she agreed in a voice as soft as her skin. "But perhaps you could enlighten me."

Deciding the best way to get rid of her might be to tell her exactly what he expected of her, Hank grabbed a chair from the top of the table and plopped it onto the floor. He hiked a boot on the seat of the chair, folded his arms across his knee and narrowed an eye at her. "In the past, I've worked the place by myself, but with all these damn strangers that keep pouring into town as a result of the media attention Temptation's received, business has picked up and I need help.

"I work the bar and the grill myself, and I'd expect

you to take the orders and deliver them. That means carrying trays loaded down with beer and food and clearing the tables when they're dirty. You'll do all the dishwashing, too. And you'll have to scrub out the toilets and mop the floors every night after we close.''

He paused, measuring her response, but she didn't appear fazed one whit by what he'd described so far. He decided to shovel it on a little thicker.

''The men outnumber the women in this town about eight to one, and they're a rough lot. They spend most of their time alone on their ranches and farms and come in here on Friday and Saturday nights to blow off a little steam and have a good time. They'll probably find a woman like you hard to resist. But I expect you to keep your mind on your job and your skirt on…at least while you're on duty,'' he added with a wink.

Though she paled a little, she didn't turn tail and run as Hank had expected. He heaved a deep breath, wondering what it was going to take to get rid of her. ''After they have a few drinks, the boys tend to get a little testy. If a fight breaks out, it's your job to bust it up.'' Her eyes widened a little and Hank decided he'd finally hit on the right vein. ''When they're drunk enough to fight, they're usually drunk enough to puke. If they do, you'll be the one to clean it up.''

Convinced by the sick look on her face that he'd painted the bleakest picture possible and there was no way in hell she'd want the waitressing job now, Hank dragged his boot from the chair. ''Well, what do you think? You still interested?''

Leighanna swallowed hard. "How much does it pay?" she asked weakly.

"Minimum wage, but you can keep your tips…if you earn any," he added, sure that she would say thanks but no thanks.

He nearly keeled over when instead she said, "When do I start?"

"I found a job," Leighanna sang cheerfully as she stepped through the back door of Mary Claire's house.

Mary Claire turned from the sink. "You did?" she asked in surprise. A smile built when she saw the excited flush on Leighanna's cheeks. She quickly snatched up a cloth to dry her hands and hugged Leighanna to her. "That's wonderful!" she cried, then pushed Leighanna to arm's length. "Where?"

"The End of the Road."

Mary Claire's smile wilted as quickly as it had formed. "The End of the Road? You mean that seedy little bar on the edge of town?"

Leighanna struggled to keep her smile in place. "Yes, that's the place. I start today at five." Ignoring Mary Claire's stricken expression, she ducked from beneath her arm and headed for the refrigerator. "Is there anything cold to drink? My car's air conditioner is still on the blink and it must be a hundred degrees outside."

"Yes," Mary Claire murmured, already wringing her hands. "I just made a pitcher of lemonade for the kids. Leighanna?" she asked nervously. "Are you sure you want to work in a place like that?"

"A place like what?" Leighanna asked innocently,

though she knew full well what Mary Claire meant. The place was nothing but a glorified beer joint, but a job was a job, and beggars couldn't be choosers. Not in a town the size of Temptation.

Mary Claire forced her hands apart to pluck two glasses from the cupboard and trailed Leighanna to the table. "Well...I haven't been there myself, but I've heard that it gets pretty rough in there. Mrs. Martin over at the Mercantile told me that the sheriff is always having to go over there and break up fights on Saturday nights."

Leighanna silently cursed Hank Braden. Oh, he'd told her about the fights all right, but he hadn't said anything about the sheriff being the one to bust them up. She specifically remembered him saying that it would be up to *her* to settle any disputes. She wondered what else he had lied about.

Sighing, she filled the two glasses. It didn't matter whether he'd lied or not. She needed the money too much to complain. "It's the only job I could find," she said, and pushed a glass across the table before picking up her own.

Mary Claire shoved aside the offered drink and fisted her hands in a white-knuckled knot on the table. "If you need money that badly, I'll loan you some until something better comes along."

Leighanna shook her head. "You're already providing me room and board. I won't take your money."

Mary Claire heaved a sigh. "But, Leighanna—"

Leighanna leaned forward, covering Mary Claire's hand with hers, and squeezed, grateful to her friend for offering, but knowing she had to do this by herself.

When she'd left Houston, she'd been on the run, hoping to escape the power her ex-husband still held over her. But she knew that putting distance between herself and Roger wouldn't solve all her problems. She'd been a mouse where men were concerned, a doormat who had continually accepted whatever dirt the men in her life scraped her way in exchange for a little of their affection.

But not any longer. Leighanna was determined to change her ways. She'd already made a large step toward achieving this goal by standing up to Hank Braden and insisting that he give her the job. And though the thought of working for such a disagreeable man frightened her, she was determined to fend for herself, relying on no one and nothing other than her own abilities to pay her way.

"No, Mary Claire," she said firmly. "I won't take your money, though I do appreciate the offer."

When Leighanna arrived at five o'clock, Hank was already behind the bar, shoving long-neck beer bottles into an insulated box filled with ice. His hair was wet and slicked to one side, and though it was obvious he'd just shaved, his jaw still carried a five-o'clock shadow. "You're late," he grumped.

Leighanna glanced at her watch. "It's not even five," she said in surprise.

Hank jerked his head toward a clock behind the bar. The clock, like the rest of the bar's decor, had obviously been supplied by the beer distributor. A fake waterfall on the clock's face spilled over a mountain stream, and neon lights above it blinked on and off, advertising Coors beer.

The hands on the clock pointed to 5:03.

Leighanna knew darn good and well that her watch was accurate because she'd set it by the radio that very morning, but she also knew it wouldn't do any good to argue the point with Hank. Swallowing her retort, she quickly stored her purse on a shelf behind the bar. "I'm sorry. It won't happen again."

"It better not."

Though tempted to tell the man where he could shove his precious job, Leighanna bit her tongue and tied a towel around her waist. "What do you want me to do?" she asked.

Hank nodded toward the open room. "Take the chairs down and situate 'em around the tables, then check the salt and pepper shakers and make sure they're full. After you're done with that, you can chop lettuce and slice up enough tomatoes and onions to fill the bins there by the grill."

Sure that there was more to her job then the tasks he'd named, Leighanna frowned in puzzlement. "Is that all?"

"Nope," he said, and stopped long enough to shoot her a lazy grin. "But I know how you blondes are. I don't want to send your brain into overload by giving you too much to remember."

She knew he was baiting her, looking for any excuse to fire her before she ever started, and Leighanna refused to give him the pleasure. But that didn't stop the sweep of anger that burned her cheeks. Marching across the room, she started jerking chairs from the tops of the tables and shoving them up underneath.

Though Hank continued to stuff beer bottles into the cooler, he watched her out of the corner of his eye. Damn fool woman, he cursed silently. Didn't she know that silk didn't belong in a place like his? The slacks and matching blouse she wore looked as out of place in The End of the Road as she did. And those shoes she had on! Nothing but a handful of thin leather straps. Her feet would be killing her by closing time…if she lasted that long. As he watched, one of the baggy sleeves on her silk blouse caught on a splintered rung of the chair she was struggling to pull down. With a cry of dismay, she dropped the chair and it fell to the floor with a clatter as she lifted the sleeve to examine the snagged fabric. A soft, pitiful moan slipped from her lips.

Hank's blood heated in anger. He wouldn't feel sorry for her, he told himself. Any fool would know not to wear something like that to work as a waitress.

"Careful with the furniture," he snapped. "You break, you pay."

Her head came up, her chin jutting imperiously as her gaze met his and held. He saw the anger, the frustration in those blue depths, but ignored it. He'd tried to tell her she couldn't handle the job, but she wouldn't listen. So now she'd just have to learn it the hard way.

He waved a hand toward the tables. "Better get moving. You've still got those shakers to refill."

Leighanna dropped the sleeve with an indignant huff and stooped to turn the chair upright. Shoving it under the table with a little more force than necessary, she started snatching shakers from the centers of the tables. By the time she'd gathered them all, she'd calmed somewhat. She tried to lift the tray...and realized too late that she'd overloaded it.

She stole a glance at the bar and saw Hank watching her. She could tell by the measuring look in his eyes that this was all some kind of ridiculous test, and he was just waiting for her to fail. Determined to prove that she could handle the job, she set her jaw and lifted the tray. Straining under its weight, she staggered across the room, then had to hitch the tray's edge against her breasts for added leverage to raise it high enough to shove it onto the bar's high, scarred surface.

"Better be careful," Hank warned from the other side. "Or you'll smash what little bit God blessed you with."

Leighanna dropped the tray to the bar, her cheeks flaming, while salt and pepper shakers rolled crazily across its surface. Grabbing one before it toppled over the edge, she slammed it back down on the tray. "How much or how little God blessed me with is certainly no concern of yours," she said indignantly.

Hank arched a brow, his gaze dropping to her breasts. "No, but I've got eyes," he said, and grinned wickedly as he looked back up at her.

"Well, you can just keep your eyes to yourself," she snapped, and marched behind the bar. Not wanting to ask the aggravating man where he kept his supplies, she searched beneath the counter until she found the commercial-size containers of salt and pepper. Dragging them out to the bar, she started refilling the shakers.

Hank decided that this new waitress of his looked pretty cute when her feathers were all ruffled. Unable to resist ruffling them a little more, he eased up beside her, not close enough to touch, just close enough to let her know he was there. He heard her huff of breath and bit back a grin as he picked up a salt shaker and slowly unscrewed its top.

"No need to get your panties in a twist," he said mildly. "Some men like women with small breasts...I just don't happen to be one of them."

"Thank heaven for that," she muttered under her breath.

Acting as if he hadn't heard her, he poured salt into the shaker. "But some of the men who'll be coming in tonight aren't as selective as me. You might consider buttoning that blouse of yours up a little higher. You wouldn't want them to think you're advertising...unless you are, of course."

Frowning, Leighanna dipped her chin to look down at her blouse. Her eyes flew wide when she saw that the tray had pulled one of the buttons from its hole, exposing a generous view of a lace covered breast, a view she knew Hank had already taken advantage of. Quickly she grabbed the plackets together and forced the button back into place. "Thank you," she murmured in embarrassment, unable to look Hank in the eye.

Hank just chuckled and screwed the lid back on the shaker. "Don't mention it."

Leighanna was sure that he was doing it purposefully, just to fluster her, because everywhere she turned he was there, in her way, all but breathing down her neck.

"Don't you have anything to do?" she finally asked in frustration as she pushed a knife through a plump, red tomato.

He just grinned. "Am I bothering you?"

Juice dripped from her fingers as she tossed the thinly sliced tomato into the bin…and their shoulders bumped…again. "Yes," she said, and dug her shoulder into his and gave him an impatient shove.

"What am I doing that's bothering you?"

"You're—you're—"

"What?" he prodded.

Fighting for patience, she rested her wrists on the cutting board and turned, angling her body just enough to frown at him. But looking at him was a mistake. His eyes were filled with mischief, and his mouth was quirked in that teasing grin he'd worn ever since he'd warned her about her blouse.

Scowling, she twisted back around and grabbed an onion. "You're in my way," she muttered and slashed the knife through the onion, cutting it in half and sending its sharp aroma spiraling beneath her nose.

"Really?" he asked innocently and purposefully pressed his shoulder against hers again. "I don't mean to be. I'm just watching to make sure you know what you're doing."

The onion's odor was strong, burning her nose and filling her eyes with tears, but it was the heat from his body where their shoulders touched that she was most aware of. "I know what I'm doing," she replied, sniffing. "Any fool can slice vegetables." She lifted her hand to swipe a tear from her eye.

Hank caught her wrist in the width of one wide hand. Startled, she glanced up at him.

"I wouldn't do that if I were you," he warned. "You're liable to get onion juice in your eye, and it'll make it sting that much more." He caught up a towel. "Here, let me." He dabbed at the tears beneath her eyes, his touch gentle, his knuckles rough where they scraped against her cheek…and Leighanna wondered what he was up to. He'd already made it clear that he didn't want her in his bar, which made her suspicious of his kindness now.

He took his good easy time blotting her tears, then bent his knees and put his face level with hers. "How's that?"

She'd purposely avoided making eye contact with him all afternoon, but with him this close, she could do little else. The eyes that met hers were a dark brown, almost black, and his mouth less than a breath away. His features were almost too perfect, his forehead wide, his jaw square and shadowed, his cheekbones carved if by a sculptor's knife. His hair, thick and black, just brushed his collar and seemed to cry for a woman's hands. That he was aware of his sexual appeal was obvious in the cocky slant of his lips and the teasing glint in his eye.

Leighanna had known another man whose sex appeal equaled Hank's…and was still paying the price for falling prey to his charm. Determined not to fall again, she twisted back around and sniffed again. "Better, thank you."

Hank's grin broadened into a smile. "Good. I like to keep my employees satisfied."

"I'll just bet you do," she muttered under her breath.

Hank watched Leighanna from his spot behind the bar and grudgingly admitted that he might just have been wrong about her ability to handle this job. She sashayed between the tables, a tray propped on her open palm, smiling while she set mugs of beer in front of his customers. She made change, toted food, wiped up spills...and dodged the occasional straying hand.

He chuckled as he watched old Jack Barlow sneak an arm around her waist. Smooth as silk, she removed his hand, smiling sweetly enough not to offend the man before she headed back to the bar.

She shoved the empty tray onto the bar and sagged against it, mopping her damp brow with the back of her hand. At some point during the evening, she'd rolled her billowy sleeves to her elbows, revealing slender arms and even slimmer wrists. Her fingers were long and delicate and her almond-shaped nails were painted a light pink, almost the exact same shade as her blouse. A ketchup stain just above her right breast blotted the blouse's once perfect pink color.

"Two beers and a whiskey chaser," she said, raising her voice to be heard over the blaring jukebox.

Hank couldn't help but notice the weary slump of her shoulders. He stuck two frosted mugs under the tap. "Tired?" he asked.

Leighanna immediately straightened, not wanting to admit to her exhaustion. "No. Just hot."

Hank nodded sagely. "Yep. It's hot all right." He set the mugs on her tray and picked up a bottle of Jack Daniels. "You can take a break, if you want. I can keep an eye on things for a few minutes."

A break sounded wonderful after being on her feet for over six hours, but Leighanna quickly shook her head. She was determined not to give him any reason to doubt her abilities to handle the job. "No, I'm fine." She glanced at the clock behind the bar. "We'll be closing in less than an hour, anyway. I can wait until then."

Hank glanced at the clock, too, before adding the jigger of whiskey to the tray. "Your call, but remember we'll still have some work to do after they all clear out."

Leighanna stifled a groan, thinking of the toilets that would need scrubbing and the floor that would need mopping. She forced a perky smile. "Don't worry. I can handle it."

"Hey, Hank!" a man called from a corner of the room.

"Yo, what'cha need?" Hank called back.

"Has that little barrel racer from over Marble Falls way been back?"

Hank's chest swelled, and a gleam of what Leighanna could only describe as cockiness shown in his eyes.

"You mean Betty Jo?" Hank asked, trying hard not to smile as he curved his hands through the air, tracing a rather top-heavy hourglass shape.

The guy tossed back his head and laughed. "Yeah, that's the one."

"Nah, haven't seen her," Hank replied. "But she'll

be back,'' he added, shooting the man a knowing
wink. "They always do.''

Leighanna snatched the tray from the bar and rolled
her eyes as she turned away to deliver the drinks.
"Men,'' she muttered under her breath.

Leighanna dropped the toilet brush into the bucket,
then used her wrist to push her hair from her face.
Lord, but she was tired. Her feet felt as if they were
swollen twice their size, the leather bands of her san-
dals cutting viciously across her instep, and her calf
muscles ached from all the walking...and she still had
the floor to mop.

Groaning, she snagged the bucket's handle and
limped from the bathroom and back out into the bar.
Hank stood at the cash register, his lips moving silently as he slowly counted the night's proceeds. He
glanced up, his gaze hitting hers and holding just long
enough to make her want to squirm, before he non-
chalantly went back to his counting.

The clock behind him read 12:45.

Stifling a moan, Leighanna trudged to the small
kitchen and mixed up mop water, then hauled the
bucket and mop back out front. With a scowl at Hank
who hadn't done anything in the last half hour more
strenuous than lift a handful of change from the cash
drawer, she slapped the mop to the floor and began
scrubbing. Back and forth, round and round, she
swished the mop across the floor, the ache in her back
growing until it was all she could do not to cry.

By the time she'd made her way back to the bar,
the clock read 1:15. She'd put in over eight hours and

it felt like eighteen. With no strength left in her arms, she dragged the bucket back to the kitchen and dumped the murky water down the drain.

Tugging the towel from her waist, she tossed it onto the bar, then ducked under it to retrieve her purse. "I'll be going now."

"Would you do me a favor before you leave?"

Already headed for the door, Leighanna stopped and wearily turned. "What?"

Hank gestured to the money stacked on the bar, then scratched his head. "I can't make the totals match. Would you mind recounting the money for me while I run the tickets again? It shouldn't take you more than a minute or two."

She doubted that, since he'd been counting the money the entire time she'd been scrubbing toilets and mopping floors. But it wouldn't hurt to prove to him that she could do more than scullery work. She tossed her purse onto the bar, climbed up onto a stool in front of it and grabbed a stack of bills. She quickly separated them into stacks of ones, fives, tens and twenties, then began to count, recording the totals of each stack on the back of an order blank.

Unaware that Hank had even moved, she suddenly realized that he had rounded the bar and stood beside her, his head tipped close to hers. She craned her neck to look at him. "What are you doing?" she asked, frowning.

He grinned. "Watching you."

"Well, don't!" she huffed impatiently, and snatched up another stack of bills.

"Why? Do I make you nervous?"

"Yes!" she said, and went back to her counting.

His nose bumped her neck and nuzzled. "You sure do smell nice."

She tried her best to ignore him, even managed to continue to slap down bills, silently counting, but heat raced through her as his nose traced the curve of her neck.

"What scent is that you're wearing?"

She dropped the money to the counter. "Do you want me to count this money, or not?" she asked in frustration.

"I think I'd rather you kissed me."

Her eyes widened and she jumped to her feet. "Kiss you!" she repeated, incensed that he would suggest such a thing.

"Yeah, you know. Press your lips against mine."

Leighanna snatched her purse from the counter and slung its strap across her shoulder. She stabbed a finger at his chest. "Let's get one thing straight, buster. You hired me to work as a waitress, not to service your more basic needs!"

Hank hooked his hands at his hips and whistled low through his teeth as he rocked back on the heels of his boots. "Man, oh man, but you sure are pretty when you're riled." Leaning forward, he crooked a finger and pressed its knuckle beneath her chin, forcing her face up to his. "But, honey, we need to get one more thing straight. Us kissing has absolutely nothing to do with you working for me. It's inevitable, that's all." He let his hand drop and shot her a wink. "But I'm a patient man."

* * *

Hank poked the key into the front door and turned it, glancing, as he did, out the window into the darkness beyond. Leighanna limped across the gravel parking lot, her shoulders stooped, as she headed for a shadowed car parked at the far end. He wanted to laugh at her sorry state, but couldn't quite work up the enthusiasm required for the task.

He supposed he should feel guilty for working her so hard, especially considering he'd shoved more than half his workload onto her slim shoulders...but he didn't. Hell, she was the one who'd wanted the job, he told himself, all but forcing him to hire her when he knew damn good and well she didn't have any business working in a place like The End of the Road.

His eyes went unerringly to the gentle sway of her hips. Even tired, the woman knew how to move. He blew out a slow breath. He didn't want to be attracted to her. Didn't even know why'd he'd bothered to tease her. He supposed it was just a natural reflex. Her being a woman, and all, and him being...well, him being just Hank.

A grin slowly built on his face. And Hank did love women. The feel of them, the taste of them, the feminine smell of them. Hell, he just liked women. And the fact that this one didn't seem interested in him only increased the challenge. For, as much as he liked women, Hank liked a challenge.

While he continued to watch, she opened the door to her car. The accompanying screech of metal made him wince. Squinting against the darkness, Hank looked at the car. It was a junker. Even from a distance, he could see that the windshield was cracked, the front bumper was missing, and the car's body had more rust than paint.

He heard the engine turn with a dragging *waaaa, waaa, waaa* before it finally sparked to life, smoke pouring from the tailpipe at the rear. The headlights popped on, one a little brighter than the other, and he listened to the grinding of gears before the car finally chugged off.

What is a classy lady like her doing, driving a piece of crap like that? he wondered. Better yet, he asked himself, what was a classy lady like her doing in a two-bit town like Temptation?

Shaking his head, he pulled down the shade and headed for his room at the rear of the bar. Didn't matter why she was in Temptation, he told himself. She wouldn't be back at The End of the Road. Not after what he'd put her through tonight.

Two

"I swear, the man thinks he's God's gift to women!"

Mary Claire couldn't help but laugh as she set a pan of hot, steaming water on the stoop at Leighanna's feet. "From what I hear, he is."

Leighanna scowled, remembering the barrel racer mentioned the night before, and levered a heaping tablespoon of Epsom salts into the pan of hot water and stirred. She didn't want to ask, but couldn't resist. "What have you heard?"

Mary Claire sat down on the porch beside Leighanna and propped a bowl of peas on her lap. "Nothing specific, really. Just that he has quite a way with the women."

"He could have fooled me," Leighanna said dryly.

She eased her swollen feet into the hot water and had to bite her lower lip to keep from crying.

Chuckling, Mary Claire patted her arm. "They'll feel better after you've soaked them for a while." She picked up a pea pod and broke off its end. "Did you make much in tips last night?"

"A little over forty dollars."

"That's good, isn't it?"

"I suppose. But it doesn't come anywhere near matching the salary I made as manager of the boutique." She threw up a hand, stopping Mary Claire before she could even offer. "And, no, I won't accept a loan from you."

Mary Claire pressed her lips together and went back to her shelling. "I still don't understand why you got stuck with all of Roger's debt."

Leighanna heaved a sigh. "Because we were married. Because the debts were in both our names. Because Texas is a community property state. And because Roger is a jerk and refuses to pay them."

"Couldn't you just declare bankruptcy?"

"I could...but I won't. It's bad enough that I have to suffer because of Roger's shortcomings. I won't allow anyone else to suffer, too."

"So, you're just going to work your fingers to the bone until they're all paid off?"

"If it takes that. But the bonus at the end is that my name will be clear and my credit standing will be good again. That makes all the hard work worthwhile."

Not wanting to think about her debts anymore, it was much too pretty a day for such morbid thoughts,

Leighanna closed her eyes and lifted her face to the sun. "I see why you love it here so much. The air is clean, the sky is clear—"

"And there's not a traffic jam in sight," Mary Claire finished for her. "Heaven, isn't it?"

"What's heaven?"

Mary Claire and Leighanna both looked up to see Harley, Mary Claire's fiancé, strolling down the brick walk toward them. Leighanna could see the love in the man's eyes as he looked at Mary Claire and felt just the tiniest stab of envy. She'd met Harley on her first visit to Temptation and had immediately liked the man. Beyond the fact that he was drop-dead handsome, he seemed to adore Mary Claire and her children, and that alone was enough to win Leighanna's approval of him.

Smiling, Mary Claire lifted her face for Harley's kiss. "Temptation." She patted the spot next to her on the step. "Join us. Leighanna was just singing the praises of her new home."

Harley chuckled as he dropped down beside Mary Claire. "Tough night at work?" he asked, gesturing to the pan of water where Leighanna soaked.

Leighanna frowned. "In more ways than one."

Mary Claire bit back a smile. "I think your friend Hank made a bad impression with Leighanna."

Harley reared back, looking at Leighanna in surprise. "Hank?"

"Yes, Hank," Leighanna said sourly. "Do you know that he had the audacity to ask me to kiss him?"

"Did you?" Harley and Mary Claire asked at the same time.

Leighanna reared back, looking at them in surprise. "Well, of course I didn't! The man's a lecher!"

Mary Claire bit back a smile and Harley nearly choked on a laugh, but both remained silent.

"Well, he is!" Leighanna cried indignantly. "Every time I turned around, he was there, touching me or brushing up against me." She shuddered, remembering.

"Most women would kill to have Hank pay 'em that much attention," Harley offered quietly.

Leighanna rolled her eyes. "Well, as far as I'm concerned, they can have him. The man has a one-track mind. Sex!"

Leighanna tried the door and found it unlocked. "Hank?" she called hesitantly as she pushed open the door. "Are you here?" When he didn't answer, she hesitated a moment, then with a shrug, stepped inside and closed the door behind her.

Heading straight for the bar, she tossed her purse behind it and grabbed a clean towel to tuck into her jeans. If she'd learned anything from her first night at work, it was the proper apparel for a waitress in a place like The End of the Road. Today she'd worn jeans and a *washable* cotton shirt. She'd already ruined one silk blouse at The End of the Road and wasn't anxious to sacrifice another.

She caught a glimpse of herself in the mirror behind the bar and fought back a shudder. Always a woman who took pride in her appearance, her current state of dress was somewhat depressing. As the manager of the clothing boutique in Houston, the image she had projected had been important. Since the owners of the boutique had included a generous discount on all the clothes she purchased there, doing so had been easy.

Glancing down at her feet, she frowned. The running shoes were certainly not a fashion statement, that was for sure, but hopefully, with their help, she wouldn't need to soak her feet again.

With a sigh, she glanced at the clock behind the bar...and smiled. Four-thirty. She'd purposefully arrived early, just to spite Hank. Too bad he wasn't around so that she could gloat.

Humming softly, she dragged the chairs from the tables, then refilled the salt and pepper shakers, just as she'd done the night before. When Hank still hadn't appeared by the time she'd finished, she glanced around, trying to decide what she should do next. One look at the filthy front windows gave her the answer she needed. Taking the bucket, she filled it with water and a heavy dose of vinegar, grabbed a couple of clean rags and headed for the front door.

Once outside, she parked the bucket beneath a window and stepped back, folding her arms beneath her breasts as she studied the building. The structure itself was old, probably built more than fifty years before, and was constructed of native limestone. Only two windows faced the front of the narrow structure, but the double doors situated between them each sported a glass. A faded sign stretched above the door. The End of the Road, she silently read.

It was certainly that, she admitted, glancing around at its remote location. Situated at the edge of town, the building stood over two hundred feet from the

main road. Fronted by a gravel parking lot, and pro-
tected on three sides by thick stands of cedar, the bar
seemed to have sprouted from the rocky ground itself.
Thick clumps of cactus cropped up here and there
along the fence line bordering the parking lot, and a
tangle of weeds and vines grew in the narrow strip of
ground between the gravel lot and the building itself.

The place could use a face-lift in the worst sort of
way, she thought, frowning. The eaves needed painting, the front doors could definitely use a new coat of
varnish, and those weeds should be replaced with a
strip of hedge. A spot or two of color wouldn't hurt,
either, she mused, thinking a pot of geraniums at either
side of the entrance would certainly add charm. And
charm would bring in more customers, increasing the
bar's business, and hopefully her tips.

Sighing, Leighanna stooped and picked up a rag.
She knew without asking that even if she found the
courage to suggest the improvements to Hank, he'd
never implement them. The man obviously had a problem accepting change. His comments to her about all
the strangers who'd flocked to Temptation proved that.

Sighing again, Leighanna dipped the rag into the
bucket. Washing the windows wouldn't help the bar's
appearance much, but at least it was a start. Besides,
she told herself, it would pass the time while she
waited for Hank to show up, and maybe even impress
him with her resourcefulness.

Enjoying the feel of the sun on her back, she put
her hand in motion on the door's window and her
elbow behind her work. When she'd cleaned them
both, she went back inside and dragged out a bar stool

to stand on in order to reach the high windows that flanked the doors.

Leighanna finished the first and stepped down to admire her work. The transformation was staggering. The window gleamed like new glass, catching the sun's rays and reflecting it back. Motivated by her accomplishment, she dragged the bucket and stool beneath the second window.

Just as she made the last satisfying swipe, she heard tires spitting gravel behind her and glanced over her shoulder to see a truck speeding across the lot straight for her. Her movement made the tall stool rock beneath her, and she slapped a hand against the window to brace herself.

The truck slid to a stop, shooting up a cloud of white dust, and Leighanna frowned, thinking of the windows she'd just cleaned. Hank swung down from the truck and charged for her, his face twisted in a scowl.

"What in the hell do you think you're doing?" he asked, grinding to a stop at the side of her stool.

"I'm cleaning the windows," she said, surprised by his anger.

He grabbed her by the waist and hauled her down. Caught off guard, Leighanna planted her hands against his chest to keep from crumpling when her feet slammed against solid ground.

"I didn't ask you to clean the damn windows," he snarled.

His mouth was set in a thin tight line, his eyes dark and threatening. For the life of her, Leighanna couldn't imagine what she'd done to anger him so.

"No, you didn't," she said nervously. "But you weren't here and I'd already done everything else and the windows needed cleaning, so I cleaned them."

His jaw tightened and a muscle twitched beneath his eye. When his fingers continued to cut into her waist, she decided she'd had enough of his rotten attitude. "If you don't mind," she said, and gave his chest a shove. "I'd appreciate it if you'd let me go."

His fingers cut a little deeper and his eyes narrowed to dangerous slits. "And what if I do mind?" he asked.

Leighanna's eyes flipped wide. Hank saw the fear in them, and it shamed him to think he had put it there. He'd never frightened a woman before, had never used force on one, either, for that matter, had never needed to. But there was something about this woman that seemed to bring out the worst in him.

"It doesn't matter if *you* mind or not," she cried indignantly, "because *I* do!" She pushed a little more insistently. "Now let me go, I've got work to do before customers start arriving."

But Hank wasn't ready to let her go just yet. He hadn't expected her to show up for work again, not after what he'd put her through the night before. Then to find her there, swaying like a suction cup, dashboard ornament on that damn rickety stool, washing windows…well, it had just about given him a heart attack. All he could think about was that fragile body of hers lying in a crumpled heap on the ground, those delicate bones shattered beyond repair, and not a soul within a three-mile radius of the bar to hear her calls for help.

Knowing that she was safe didn't loosen his hold

on her, though, for now with her close like this, with her womanly scent teasing his senses and the feel of her soft flesh curving beneath his palms, the fear slowly subsided, leaving in its place nothing but a keen awareness.

"There's time, yet," he murmured, and enjoyed watching the indignant thrust of her chin. He forced himself to soften his hold on her until his hands merely rested in the curve of her waist. He dipped his face a hair lower, just close enough to warm her lips with his breath. "You've got dirt on your cheek," he said, his voice husky.

Leighanna immediately lifted a fist to her cheek and scrubbed. "Where?"

He caught her hand and forced it back to his chest. "Right here." He lifted a finger to her cheek and whisked softly, his face drifting closer, then closer still, until it was his lips that brushed her cheek instead of his fingers. His mouth opened and his tongue arced out, sweeping like wet velvet across her cheek.

Leighanna sucked in a sharp breath, fisting her hands in the fabric of his shirt as her knees turned the consistency of wet noodles. Now she understood why Harley had said most women would kill to have Hank pay attention to them. The man was a master at seduction.

She could feel herself weakening, falling deeper and deeper under his spell as his tongue and lips teased. "Please," she begged, her voice little more than a whimper.

"Please, what?" he murmured huskily.

But before she could ask him to stop, his mouth

slipped to cover hers. Leighanna almost wept at the feel of those lips on hers. Strong and commanding, they moved against hers in a most satisfying way, while his thumbs stroked persuasively at her lower ribs.

She knew she was weak, spineless, susceptible when confronted with a man's seductive charm. Her years with Roger had certainly proven that.

How many times had Roger come to her, whispering sweet nothings in her ear and cuddling up to her while he tried to wheedle money out of her? She'd always been a sucker for affection. Raised by a father who didn't have a clue about the needs of a young girl, she'd never received any. Roger had known her weakness, knew just the right buttons to push to get what he wanted from her.

The thought of Roger's manipulations dragged her from beneath Hank's spell. She set her jaw and firmed her lips beneath his. He might not want money from her as Roger had, but he wanted something. That was obvious in the seductive prodding of his tongue against her lips...and she wouldn't, no matter how strong the temptation to remain in his arms, allow herself to fall prey to a man's charm again.

Lifting her foot, she brought it down hard across his instep. He released her with a yelp of pain and hopped around on one foot while he cradled in his hands the one she'd stomped.

"Why in the hell'd you do that for?" he asked incredulously. "You could've broken my damn foot!"

Leighanna folded her arms beneath her breasts. "You're lucky I didn't aim a little higher."

Hank's eyes widened in surprise while his grip on his foot loosened. "Why, you little hellcat," he murmured.

He couldn't have called her anything that would have pleased her more. Leighanna Farrow would never again be any man's doormat! She snatched up the bucket. "If you're smart, you'll remember that before you try to make another pass at me." She jerked open the door. "Get the stool," she ordered firmly, pointing a stiff finger at the stool beneath the window. "We've got work to do."

Hank's chest swelled in anger. "I think you're forgetting who's the boss around here."

Leighanna refused to bend under his threatening look. She'd done enough bending in her life. "No, I haven't forgotten, but it appears one of us needs to keep an eye on the business. You obviously don't care." With that she stepped through the door with a deliberate toss of her blond hair and let the door slam closed behind her.

Didn't care about his business! Hank snatched up the stool and jerked open the door, following her into the bar. "And just exactly what is that supposed to mean?" he asked, slamming the stool down on four legs as he stomped after her toward the kitchen.

Leighanna calmly tipped over the bucket and emptied its contents down the drain. "Exactly what I said. You don't care about your business."

"That's a damn lie!"

She set the bucket on the floor by the sink and brushed past him on her way to the bar. "It isn't. If you did, you'd take better care of the place."

Hank followed her. "I take care of my business!"

She wheeled, and he fell back a step to keep from slamming into her. "Do you?" she asked, arching a neatly shaped brow.

"Well, hell, yes!"

"Then why are you letting this place fall down around you?"

Hank looked at her in dismay. "It's not falling down!"

"Sure it is." She stepped to the wall and tapped a manicured nail at a spot of chipped plaster. "This for instance. How long has this been this way?"

Hank frowned. "The walls look the same as when I bought the place."

"And how long has that been?"

"Six years."

She dipped her chin and looked at him from beneath her eyebrows, the smirk on her mouth telling him that his answer only proved her point.

"Well, I sure as hell don't hear my customers complaining," he said defensively.

"That's because they don't have a choice. Yours is the only bar in town. But if another opened," she quickly added, before he could interrupt, "which is a strong possibility with all the people who keep swarming through Temptation, then you might very well lose your customers."

Her statement momentarily stripped Hank's tongue of the scathing remark he'd been about to make. He'd never thought about the possibility of competition. The End of the Road had been the only bar in Temptation for as long as he could remember.

Before he could gather his wits enough to respond, the door opened and Cody Fipes, Temptation's sheriff, strolled in.

"Hey!" Cody called, hooking a thumb over his shoulder. "Who cleaned the windows? Had to put on my sunglasses to kill the glare."

Leighanna turned to Hank, folding her arms beneath her breasts. "See?" she said, smiling sweetly. "Someone did notice."

It rankled more than Hank wanted to admit, but Cody wasn't the only one who commented on the clean windows that night at the bar. Even old Will Miller, Temptation's one-and-only barber and the crankiest SOB in town, noticed the change and even found a smile for Leighanna when he'd learned she was responsible for the work.

Hank bit back an oath. Wasn't nothin' wrong with the looks of The End of the Road, he told himself as he scooped coins from the cash register drawer onto his open palm. Hell, business was good, always had been, and nobody'd ever complained about the appearance of the place before...at least not before Leighanna had taken it upon herself to clean those damned windows.

It was all her fault, he told himself as he started sorting the coins into piles by denomination. He'd never thought twice about what his bar looked like. He'd been too damn busy serving drinks and slapping hamburgers on a grill to pay it any mind...at least not until Leighanna had shot off her sassy mouth.

But as a result of her comments, earlier, when the

sunshine had been gleaming through those windows she'd cleaned, the plaster on the old interior walls had appeared to him a little more crusty and duller than they had before. Even the mirror behind the bar seemed intent on rubbing Hank's nose in his neglect by reflecting the chipped plaster back at him when his back was turned to the open room.

Angrily, he scraped a handful of quarters into his hand to count. "What else do you think is wrong with the place?" he muttered disagreeably.

Startled by the unexpected question, Leighanna straightened from her mopping and used her wrist to push her hair from her face as she turned to look at him. His head was bent over the coins, but she could tell by the way one side of his mouth curled down that he was still irritated by all the attention the clean windows had drawn.

And that is just too bad, she thought peevishly. Because she was right. He *had* neglected the building.

"The eaves need painting, the doors need revarnishing and it wouldn't hurt to freshen up the sign." She started to mention the pots of geraniums, but decided she'd better not push her luck. "And that's just on the outside," she said before going back to her mopping.

His head snapped up. "And what's wrong with the inside? Other than the plaster," he quickly added before she could rub his nose in that again.

Leighanna sighed and drew the mop up, folding her hands over the top of its handle. "Well, for starters, the tabletops are a disgrace. They've been scrubbed so much there is nothing left of their finish but raw wood. It's all but impossible to get the stains off them.''

He hunched his shoulders defensively. ''I can't afford to replace every damn table in the place.''

''You wouldn't have to. You could either refinish them, or maybe even use tablecloths to cover them. A bit of color certainly wouldn't hurt.''

''Tablecloths!'' He snorted and slapped a ten dollar stack of quarters onto the bar. ''If you had your way, you'd turn this place into a damn tearoom.''

''Tables in a tearoom are covered with linen and lace. I was thinking more in the line of checkered oil-cloths.''

Hank cocked his head to look at her in disgust. ''Checkered?''

''Yes,'' she said, hoping she could hold his interest long enough to convince him. ''Preferably red and white. It would carry out your country motif.''

''What the hell's a motif?''

''You know,'' she said, fluttering her hand at him. ''Theme.''

It was all Hank could do to keep from rolling his eyes. A country motif, for God's sake! As if he'd actually had a theme in mind when he'd opened The End of the Road for business.

But then he remembered the compliments the clean windows had drawn and Leighanna's warning that somebody might move into Temptation and open a new bar to compete against him. He'd already heard the rumors about a couple who were moving to town to open a clothing store. For all he knew, someone could very well be planning to open a bar. Hank knew he was stubborn, but he certainly wasn't a fool.

He levered a pile of dimes into a stack. "I suppose if a person were of a mind," he muttered, "they could pick up something like that over at Carter's Mercantile."

Surprised that he'd even consider her suggestion, Leighanna took a hesitant step toward him. "I could do it for you. In fact, I could measure the tables and cut the cloth myself."

He hesitated only a second. "All right, do it then. But I don't want anything checkered. Stick with a solid color, something that won't show dirt. You can tell Mrs. Martin over at the Mercantile to charge it to my account."

The man was so bullheaded, Leighanna thought in frustration. Checkered cloth would look a hundred times better than any solid. But at least he was willing to make a change. "I'll go first thing in the morning and have the cloths on the table by tomorrow night."

He waved a negligent hand, then went back to his counting. "Whatever."

Bracing herself for an explosion, she squared her shoulders. "I will expect to be paid for my time."

He didn't look up, but kept sifting through the coins on the bar. "Fine. Keep up with the time you spend and turn it in Saturday with your regular hours."

Since he didn't balk at the idea of paying her for extra work, Leighanna decided to go for broke. "I can paint, too."

His head jerked up, his brown eyes slamming into hers. "Paint?"

Leighanna swallowed hard. "Yes. I could revarnish the front doors and paint the building's eaves for you, if you like."

Hank dropped his gaze to the delicate manicured hands that still clutched the mop handle, then back to her face. "You're kidding, right?"

Leighanna stiffened her spine. "I assure you I can handle the job. My father was a paint contractor. I know what work is required."

He just shook his head, chuckling. "And when would you find the time? You're already putting in a forty-hour week here as a waitress."

"We're closed on Sundays. I could do the work then."

Hank sobered, slowly becoming aware of the earnestness in her expression...and remembered the desperation in her voice when she'd first asked for the waitressing job. At the time she'd told him she needed the money. Since she was willing to work seven days a week, and at a job most men avoided, he figured she must need it pretty damn bad.

Frowning, he gave his head a brisk nod, telling himself that he wasn't doing her any favors. She'd more than earn the hourly wage he would pay her. "All right. The job's yours. I've got an account at the hardware store. Charge whatever supplies you need and tell 'em to send me a bill." He shifted to lift up the tray in the cash drawer and scooped out a key. He tossed it to her and she caught it between her palms. "You'll need a key. And don't lose it," he warned. "There are a couple of ladders in the shed out back. The key opens that door, as well. Use whatever you need. And for God's sake, brace the ladder so you don't fall and break your neck.''

"Can I help you?"

Leighanna glanced up to find a gray-haired bear of a woman, chugging down the cluttered aisle toward her and knew she had to be the owner of the Mercantile, Mrs. Martin. She offered the woman a tentative smile. ''Well, yes, as a matter of fact you can. I was looking for oilcloth.''

Mrs. Martin tilted her head back, peering at Leighanna through smudged reading glasses perched on the end of her nose. ''You're Leighanna, aren't you? Mary Claire's friend?''

"Yes. I am.''

''Thought so.'' She gestured for Leighanna to follow her as she shuffled down the aisle toward the back of the store. ''Did you find yourself a job?''

Leighanna bit back a smile. It seemed Mary Claire was right about Mrs. Martin. She kept track of all of Temptation's goings on. ''Yes, ma'am, I did. I'm working as a waitress at The End of the Road.''

The woman stopped and whirled, her walruslike brows arching high on her wrinkled forehead while her glasses slipped even further down her nose. ''You?'' she asked in amazement. ''Waitressing at The End of the Road?''

Leighanna firmed her lips in irritation. She was a little tired of everyone thinking she was incapable of handling the job at The End of the Road. ''Yes, me.''

''Well, I'll be...'' The woman let the words drift off before she started shaking her head and wagging a finger beneath Leighanna's nose. "You be careful around that old Hank Braden. He's a rounder, that one, and wouldn't know how to treat a well-bred lady like yourself."

Leighanna had to catch herself before she laughed. Not that she doubted Hank was a womanizer. She'd seen enough proof of that for herself. But as to her being well-bred? Now that was worth a laugh. Her father was nothing but a mean-spirited paint contractor from the wrong side of Houston, with a heart as cold as a block of ice. And her mother had been such a mouse she had died in order to escape a marriage she didn't have the courage to end.

Leighanna liked to believe she'd inherited nothing from her father. Her heart, she thought, if anything, was too warm and full of feeling. But from her mother? Well, maybe she'd inherited one or two of the mouse genes. But that certainly didn't mean she was as weak as her mother! She'd proved that when she'd found the courage to divorce Roger, thus removing herself from a disastrous marriage, and had proved it even more so when she'd left Houston for Temptation.

But Mrs. Martin didn't have to know any of that. Leighanna was determined to put her past behind her.

"Thank you for the warning," she said instead. "But I can handle Hank Braden. Now about that oilcloth," she said, hoping to refocus Mrs. Martin's attention on the task at hand. "I'm making tablecloths for the bar, and I'll need about forty-two yards."

"Tablecloths for The End of the Road?" Mrs. Martin parroted.

"Yes, tablecloths," Leighanna replied firmly.

Mrs. Martin eyed her for a moment, then surprised Leighanna by tossing back her head and cackling like a chicken that had just laid a prize egg. "Well, I'll be hog-tied!" she said, her breath wheezing out of her. "Tablecloths at The End of the Road. Who'd have ever thought?" She slapped Leighanna on the back, nearly sending her to her knees. "I believe you might just be able to handle old Hank, after all." Still chortling, she gave Leighanna a push toward the back of the store.

"That Hank's a wild one," she said, wagging her head. "Always was. Had to be, I guess, in order to survive, what with him not having a daddy to keep him in line."

"His father is deceased?" Leighanna asked, unable to suppress her curiosity.

"Wouldn't know whether he's deceased or not. Hank's mother never knew who fathered the boy. She was too busy slipping out of one bed and into another to notice, I guess. After Hank was born, half the time she'd even forget to take him with her when she made the shift." She made a clucking sound with her tongue. "Poor little fellow. Fended for himself for the most part. Amazing, really, that he turned out as well as he did."

Leighanna felt a pang of sympathy for the little boy Hank had once been…then just as quickly, pushed it back. She wouldn't feel sorry for a man like Hank Braden. He was a womanizer, stubborn as a mule and a little too good-looking for his own good. He didn't deserve her pity.

Mrs. Martin stopped before a rack of shelves that climbed all the way to the ceiling. She waved a hand at the bolts of fabric neatly stacked on one of the upper shelves, sending the loose skin on her under arm flapping. Solids in white, black and a dull navy sat propped against each other. ''Keep all my bolts of fabrics and notions and such back here in the corner out of the way of grimy fingers. What color will you be needin'?''

Leighanna eyed them a moment, remembering Hank's instructions to select something dark that wouldn't show stains. That certainly ruled out the white. But she knew that the black and navy would do nothing but add more gloom to the already dreary bar.

Impulsively, she swung her finger to point at a bolt of red-and-white-checkered cloth tucked almost out of sight. She drew in a deep, fortifying breath. ''That one.''

Three

Leighanna knelt in the shade of the old live oak in Mary Claire's backyard with her knees buried in cool grass, her head bent over the bolt of red-and-white checkered cloth spread out in front of her, while she painstakingly cut another square. A neat stack of folded squares, already cut from the bolt, lay on the grass at her side. Behind her, propped on an old board balanced between two sawhorses, a line of red, spray-painted tuna cans dried in the sun. In a box beneath the sawhorses, fifteen lantern globes nested in shredded newspaper, sharing the space with fifteen long, tapered white candles. A five-pound bag of sand rested against the side of the box.

Leighanna made the last snip in the oilcloth and sank back on her heels, pressing a hand at the ache in her lower back. Cutting the cloth on Mary Claire's kitchen table would have been easier, she knew, but being outdoors certainly outweighed whatever inconveniences she'd endured. While living in Houston, the closest she had come to enjoying the outdoors had been in lying by the pool at the apartment complex where she'd lived.

She tipped back her head, letting the sunshine—dappled by the lacework of leaves overhead—warm her skin. God, how she loved it here! She'd never lived in a real house, not even as a child. She'd always lived in apartment buildings or duplexes, where trees were simply ornaments and the only flowers in sight swung from baskets suspended from high balconies or eaves.

She let her chin drop slowly until her gaze rested on the picket fence surrounding Mary Claire's house…and her heart squeezed in her chest. She'd always dreamed of living in a house, a real house, with trees in the yard big enough to offer shade on a sunny afternoon, where a profusion of flowers that changed with the seasons filled the beds…and all of it framed by a white picket fence.

With a sigh, she pushed to her feet. Someday, she promised herself, she'd live that dream, but for now she had work to do and debts to pay off. She crossed to the sawhorses and placed a tentative finger to one of the cans and found the paint dry. All that was left for her to do now was to cart her supplies to the bar and set it all up.

At the thought, she caught her lower lip between her teeth. What would Hank do when he discovered what she had done? she wondered. Would he be angry enough to fire her?

She gave herself a firm shake. He wouldn't fire her, she told herself. It wasn't as if she'd bought all these things just to spite him. The idea to make the center-pieces had been an inspiration, coming to her when she'd found the lantern globes on a discount table at Mrs. Martin's store. She knew that she had over-stepped her bounds in purchasing the globes. After all, Hank had only given her permission to buy the oil-cloth. But she also knew the centerpieces would look fantastic sitting in the center of each of the red-and-white-checkered cloths. She banked on Hank realizing that, too, once he saw them in place.

Besides, she told herself, the cost in making them was hardly anything the man could quibble about. The empty tuna cans had been donated by Mary Claire. God love her, Leighanna thought with a soft laugh. Mary Claire, once a die-hard city girl, had turned into a frugal country woman after her move to Temptation, saving everything for which she thought she might one day have a use. It had taken some talking, but Leigh-anna had finally convinced Mary Claire that The End of the Road needed the cans more than she did.

The candles were the only costly item. And if Hank threw a fit when he received the bill for them from Mrs. Martin—well, he wouldn't, she told herself. Once he saw the tables covered with the red-and-white-checkered cloths and the candles glowing inside the lantern globes, he'd see for himself what a difference the centerpieces made.

The sound of an engine's roar interrupted her

thoughts. Shielding her eyes against the sun, she turned toward the sound and saw a tractor bumping across the pasture toward the fence. Smiling, she lifted a hand in a wave, knowing that it was Harley coming to Mary Claire's for lunch.

Anxious to get to the bar and get everything set up, she quickly tossed the scissors into the box, then stooped and gathered the cut cloths into her arms.

"Hey, Leighanna!" Harley called as he swung down from his tractor. "What're you doing, getting ready for some target practice?"

Leighanna glanced at Harley over her shoulder then followed his gaze to the line of cans perched on the board. She laughed. "No, but I might need some if—" She was about to say she might need a little target practice if Hank came gunning for her when he found out what she'd done, but her explanation died on her lips when she saw a second man climb down from the tractor's cab.

Hank! All her self-assurances that he would approve of what she'd done suddenly vanished when confronted with the hard, disapproving lines of his face. Dressed in worn jeans and a cotton T-shirt that hugged his muscled chest and arms, he cut an imposing, if breathtaking figure as he strode toward her.

Harley didn't seem to notice her sudden uneasiness. "Mary Claire in the kitchen?" he asked as he paused at the makeshift table.

Leighanna tightened her arms around the tablecloths, hoping to disguise their color from Hank as he came to a stop alongside Harley. "Y-yes," she stammered. "Lunch should be just about ready."

"Good. I'm starving." Harley swung around and headed for the house, leaving Hank and Leighanna to follow.

Hank hitched his hands at his hips and frowned at Leighanna. "What are you doing here?"

Leighanna nervously wet her lips. "I live here. Mary Claire is a friend of mine." Disgusted at her nervousness and a little irritated that he would question her presence there, she tossed his question back at him. "What are *you* doing here?"

He lifted a shoulder in a shrug. "Harley needed help with his hay. I've been raking while he baled." Still wearing the frown, he nodded toward the cloths she held. "Are those the tablecloths for the bar?"

"Yes," she replied, and hugged them protectively against her breasts.

His frown deepened. "Thought I told you to buy a solid color?"

"You did, but the selection at the Mercantile was limited. Mrs. Martin only had white, black and a dull navy. I thought the checkered fabric the best choice."

He merely grunted, then gestured toward the cans. "What's all this?"

Here it comes, Leighanna thought. The moment of reckoning. She took a deep breath, her nerves beginning to dance again beneath her skin. "Bases for centerpieces. I found these lantern globes on the discount table at the Mercantile and thought how wonderful they'd look on the tables with a candle lit inside. They cost almost nothing to make," she hurried to explain as Hank hunkered down to examine the contents of the box at her feet. "Mary Claire donated the cans and the paint, and the cost of the sand was minimal. The candles were the only true expense. I'm sorry I didn't ask you first, and if you want to dock my pay for the expense—''

Hank glanced up at her, his eyes narrowed against the sun at her back. Dust powdered his face and darkened the grooves at the corners of his eyes. He stood, his gaze still on hers, aligning his body almost flush with hers. He brought with him the mingling scents of sweat and sunshine and the sweet scent of freshly mown hay. Bits of it still clung to his hair and his T-shirt.

Cleaned up, he was mouthwateringly handsome. Drenched in sweat, and with dirt streaking those perfect features, he was even more ruggedly so. The sight of him, the very smell of him, robbed Leighanna of her guilt over the purchases she'd made and left her with only the memory of those muscled arms wrapped around her, the devastating power of that frowning mouth pressed over hers.

It was crazy. She knew it was. Especially since she was the one who had ended that last kiss. But she had the most insane urge to close the distance between them, to offer herself to him, to feel again that muscled wall of chest pressed seductively against her breasts. To feel those work-roughened hands of his moving against her skin. To taste the sweat that beaded his upper lip and to savor the salt from it on her tongue.

Horrified by her own thoughts, she fell back a step before she could give in to the urge.

Hank brought his hands to his hips as she moved away, his lips twisting into a scowl. ''What is it with you?'' he asked in frustration. ''Every time I get near you, you start doing this little nervous two-step. Are you afraid of me or something?''

''N-no,'' she said, and stopped herself before she could take another step in retreat.

''Well, what is it then?''

Leighanna struggled to think of an excuse for her actions. ''I…I just don't want to give you the wrong impression,'' she finally said.

His forehead furrowed. ''What wrong impression?''

''That I'm…w-well, that I'm leading you on, or something.''

''Leading me on!'' he echoed, choking back a laugh. ''And how, in the name of God, would I get an idea like that with you dancing away from me every time I get within ten feet of you?'' When she didn't say anything, his eyes narrowed in suspicion. ''You are afraid of me, aren't you?''

''No!'' She immediately regretted the speed and force of her response, knowing by the satisfied purse of his lips that he knew she lied. ''Well, maybe a little,'' she amended reluctantly.

He took a step toward her, robbing her of the space she'd managed to place between them. ''I don't usually frighten women.''

Leighanna stiffened, refusing to let him see her fear. ''Perhaps that's because you treat them differently than you do me.''

''And how do I treat you?''

''You frown at me all the time, and nothing I do ever seems to please you.''

His left eyebrow arched appraisingly as he took his

gaze on a slow journey down her front. He returned his gaze to hers. "Oh, you please me all right," he replied, a teasing grin chipping at the corner of his mouth.

"That's exactly what I'm talking about," she said, her chin coming up in that regal lift that tended to drive Hank a little crazy. "You take unfair advantage of your role as my employer."

"Unfair advantage?" he repeated, trying not to laugh at her prim tone.

That he would find this discussion amusing made Leighanna's chest swell in indignation. "Yes, unfair advantage," she repeated firmly.

He studied her a moment, then lifted a hand to her cheek and caught a stray tendril of hair. Lazily he tucked it behind her ear, leaving his fingers to curl at her ear's delicate shell.

"And how do I do that?" he asked, his voice taking on a low, seductive drawl.

His touch was gentle, almost tender, but burned like fire against Leighanna's skin, weakening her ability to keep her mind on the point she was trying to make. "You...you...you kissed me," she finally managed to say, and felt her cheeks burn in humiliation when his lips curved into a full-blown smile.

"A kiss isn't supposed to frighten. It's supposed to please." He took a step closer, slipping his hand from her ear to cup the back of her neck, and sent shivers chasing down her spine. "Here, let me show you."

Her eyes widened in alarm as his face lowered to hers. She would have stopped him, she knew she would, but just before his lips reached hers, he veered, catching her totally off guard as he captured instead the tender lobe of her ear. His teeth nipped, his lips soothed, and she felt her knees weakening, her breath growing shorter by the second.

"See?" he murmured, his breath blowing warm against her neck where he nuzzled. "That isn't anything to be afraid of, now is it?"

"No, but—"

Before she could finish that *but,* Hank shifted again, bringing his lips to hers. At the first contact, Leighanna tensed and willed herself to remain unmoved, remembering the devastation and the seductive power of his last kiss. But though her resolve remained steadfast, it seemed her body had a mind of its own. Slowly, muscle by muscle, she melted against him as his lips moved like magic across hers. The tablecloths she held pressed against her breasts slipped from her grasp, and her arms dropped bonelessly to hang slack at her sides.

Quickly closing the space the tablecloths had once filled, Hank gathered her waist in the curve of his arm and pulled her hard against him. He knew that she was right, that he didn't treat her like he did other women. But she wasn't like any other woman he'd ever known. She was a paradox: classy as a New York model with her slender figure and delicate features, yet she worked like a mule at whatever menial tasks he tossed her way. Half the time she looked as if she'd jump out of her skin if he so much as said "boo" to her, while the other half she was all temper and sass.

So maybe he did treat her differently. But damned if he took unfair advantage of her. She'd wanted that first kiss as badly as he.... She just didn't want to admit it. And that was what he wanted to prove.

But something happened when her body met his, when the nipples of her small breasts stabbed against his sweat-dampened chest, when that soft whimper escaped her lips as he'd thrust his tongue into the sweetness of her mouth. A knot had formed in his stomach and an ache had grown in his groin...and his heart had done a slow three-sixty-degree turn. Even as he drew the kiss out, deepening it, he felt his heart right itself and slam against his chest into a pounding beat.

He wanted her. And for more than just a kiss. He wanted her naked on the ground beneath him, right here, right now, writhing, her legs wrapped around his waist, his manhood buried so deep inside her that it would take hours for them to separate. He wanted to hear her cries as he drove her over the edge. He wanted to feel the pulsations of her body around him as she lost control.

He wanted to hold her and never let her go.

And that's what scared him.

Oh, not that he wanted her. He'd wanted women before. Had never had a problem finding a willing one to bed. But none of those women had ever aroused him the way this one did. He'd never been tempted to hold on to one too long, not like he wanted to do with Leighanna. In the past, he'd always been more likely to just give and take a little pleasure with a woman then give her an affectionate pat on the butt when they went their separate ways.

And that's what scared him more than anything else.

He didn't think that one night of sex was going to be enough. Not with Leighanna.

Knowing this and not liking it one damn bit, he purposefully softened the kiss, then slowly withdrew, careful to keep his expression blank as he let his gaze meet hers. The blue eyes that met his were glazed with passion, the cheeks flushed, the lips swollen…and he was tempted to drag her into his arms again.

Fighting the desire to do something he'd more than likely regret, he took a step back and forced a teasing grin to his mouth. "See?" he said, lifting his hands palms up. "That wasn't so bad, was it?"

Bad? It was anything but bad, Leighanna thought numbly, her blood still racing like fire through her veins. *Tempting, seductive, world shattering* all seemed much more appropriate terms for what she had just experienced. But Hank's casual, almost offhand remark about something that left her wanting nothing but more of the same infuriated Leighanna. She sucked in a raw breath and opened her hand at her side.

His indifferent stance made Hank vulnerable to the force of the hand that suddenly streaked out and slapped the side of his face. Reeling, he staggered back a step, covering the already reddening cheek with his palm as he stared at Leighanna in openmouthed surprise. Her lips were still swollen from his bruising kiss, her cheeks still flushed, but the passion that had glazed her eyes before had disappeared, leaving those blue depths the color of fired steel.

"What was that for?" he asked incredulously.

Her hand still stinging from the force of the slap, Leighanna glared at him. "I warned you once," she said, fighting to keep the tremble from her voice as she stooped and scraped the dropped cloths back into her arms. "Next time you better think twice before kissing me." Straightening, she glanced up and the anger drained out of her at the sight of the angry red handprint she'd left on his face.

She'd never struck anyone before. The thought that she had done so now, and to her boss no less, set her insides quivering. She swallowed hard and raised her gaze higher until her eyes met his. Fear stabbed through at her at the lethal look she found in those brown depths. "I suppose you're going to fire me now," she said, trying to keep the tears that threatened at bay.

His gaze continued to bore through her. "I could," he agreed slowly. "You've certainly given me cause. But I'm not," he added, surprising her. "Like I told you before, us kissing has nothing to do with you working for me." He continued to stare at her, his expression turning thoughtful. "You know what?" he said slowly. "I don't think it's me you're afraid of at all. I think it's what my kiss does to you that scares you." He lifted a hand to run a thumb along her bottom lip. "But don't worry," he promised softly. "I'll take heed of your warning. Next time it'll be *you* kissing me."

With that, he turned on his heel and strode for the house, whistling merrily under his breath.

"Sure smells good," Hank said as he stepped into Mary Claire's kitchen. "Did y'all leave anything for the hired help?"

Sitting across from the door, Mary Claire waved a hand toward the opposite side of the table. "There's plenty." She pushed from her chair to greet him. "You must be—"

"Hank," he said, grinning. "And you must be Mary Claire."

"Yes," she murmured, unable to keep from staring at the red mark on his face. "What happened to you?"

Hank chuckled ruefully as he touched three fingers to his still-smarting cheek. "I ran into Leighanna's hand."

Mary Claire's mouth dropped open. "She slapped you?"

Hank shrugged. "I guess you could call it that."

Mary Claire wagged her head, unable to believe her friend capable of such a violent act. "You're teasing me, aren't you? Leighanna would never lift a hand against anyone. She's much too gentle a person for that."

Hank snorted as he dropped down in a chair opposite Harley and pulled a napkin across his lap. "Are we talking about the same person, here? The Leighanna I know is a little hellcat. The last time I crossed her she nearly broke my damn foot."

"Leighanna?" Mary Claire cried in dismay.

"Yes, Leighanna."

Unable to think of anything that would push Leighanna to such lengths, Mary Claire trailed him to the table. "What did you do to cross her?"

Hank shrugged as he reached for a bowl of mashed potatoes. "Just gave her a little kiss, that's all."

"A little kiss," Mary Claire repeated, casting a furtive glance Harley's way. Harley just shrugged a shoulder and dipped his head over his plate and shoveled another forkful of chicken-fried steak into his mouth, obviously not wanting to get involved in this discussion. Knowing she was on her own on this one, Mary Claire turned her gaze back on Hank. Fully aware of his reputation around town, she narrowed an eye at him. "And did Leighanna *want* you to kiss her?"

"Sure she did," Hank replied, defensively. "Though I'm sure she'd never admit it."

"Then what makes you think she wanted you to kiss her?" Mary Claire asked pointedly.

Hank paused a minute, a heaping spoonful of potatoes suspended halfway between the bowl and his plate. "'Cause she liked it," he said after a moment's consideration. He lifted a shoulder in a careless shrug as he levered the potatoes on his plate. "A man can tell when a woman's enjoying a kiss."

"If she was enjoying it so much, then why she did try to break your foot? And why did she slap you just now?" Mary Claire persisted.

Hank just shook his head. "Beats me. Like I said, she was enjoying it just fine, then all of a sudden she does this little twister act and starts swinging and kicking and acting all insulted. If you don't believe me, ask her. If she's honest, she'll tell you the same damn thing."

Mary Claire sank down on her chair, convinced that Hank was telling the truth, at least the part about the slap. The evidence was there right before her, staining his left cheek. She knew that Leighanna had changed since she'd moved to Temptation. She'd seen a new strength in her friend, a confidence that she'd never exhibited while living in Houston. But to physically attack someone? Mary Claire dropped her face in her hands.

Thinking he'd somehow upset her and she was about to cry, Hank nearly choked on a mouthful of potatoes when Mary Claire started laughing.

He dropped his fork to his plate in disgust. "And what, may I ask, is so damn funny?"

Unable to stop laughing, Mary Claire flapped a weak hand at him. "It's not you. It's Leighanna. I can't believe she had the nerve to really hit you."

Hank rubbed a hand across his cheek, working his jaw to make sure it was still intact. "Trust me. She had the nerve, all right." He dropped his hand and reached for the platter of steak. "Scared her, though," he said, chuckling as he remembered the fear in her eyes. "Once she cooled off enough to realize what she'd done, she was worried that I was going to fire her."

Mary Claire instantly sobered, knowing how much Leighanna needed this job. "Are you?" she asked nervously.

"Don't see why I should," Hank replied as he stabbed his fork into a steak and levered it onto his plate. "She does what work I assign her. Even volunteers for extra." He frowned, glancing Mary Claire's way. "She even volunteered to paint The End of the Road. Is she really that desperate for money?"

Since it was obvious Leighanna hadn't shared her financial problems with Hank, Mary Claire didn't consider it appropriate for her to discuss them with him now. "You'll have to ask Leighanna that question," she replied. "It's not my place to say."

The tables were beautiful, the flickering candles beneath the globes adding just the right touch of ambience that Leighanna had hoped for. She fussed around the tables, smoothing the cloths and straightening the occasional leaning globe...but the kinks of tension Hank's kiss had put in her stomach weren't as easily dealt with.

Sighing, she dragged out a chair and dropped down on it, propping her elbows on the checkered cloth and covering her face with her hands. Hank was right, she thought miserably. She was afraid of him, afraid of what his kisses did to her.

But how could something as simple as a kiss be so devastating? she asked herself for the hundredth time since arriving at the bar.

Because it wasn't simple, came her conscience's reply...and Leighanna had to agree. There had been nothing, not from the first touch of his lips on hers to the last moment when he'd stepped away, that was simple. It had been world shattering. Bone melting. Heart wrenching.

Roger's kisses had never made her feel that way. In comparison Roger's kisses had been teasing, almost playful. Hank's had been anything but. He drew at a primitiveness within her that she hadn't even known existed. Sexual, she thought on a trembling sigh. Purely sexual. His kiss had promised sex, hot and satisfying...and she'd been more than ready to cash in on that promise.

But then he'd stopped, withdrawing from her a little too easily as if the kiss had meant nothing to him, when it had meant everything to her. That, more than the kiss itself, was what had made her slap him. More than he'd angered her, he'd insulted her with his casual disregard for something that affected her so strongly.

She opened her palm, staring at it, able, even now, to feel the sting of the slap.

But I'll take heed of the warning, she remembered him saying. *Next time it'll be you kissing me.*

Leighanna dropped her hands to her lap and squeezed them into a tight ball. Next time? Would there be a next time?

Before she could pursue that thought, a noise came from outside. Knowing it was probably Hank returning to the bar, she rocketed to her feet. In her haste, her chair toppled over backward, crashing to the floor behind her. Through the front windows, she watched as his truck flashed past and disappeared around the corner of the building.

Her heart kicked into a rib-rattling beat. Already yearning for that next time, she placed her hand over her breast to keep her heart from pounding right out of her chest. She forced herself to take long, deep breaths, strengthening her resolve.

There won't be a next time, she told herself firmly. She wouldn't, couldn't let herself get involved with another man.

Especially not one like Hank Braden, who probably notched his bedpost with every new conquest.

Dreading seeing him again so soon, she quickly grabbed the chair and righted it just before the back door slammed shut and Hank appeared in the opening that led to the kitchen.

"I'm gonna take a shower," he called to her. "Can you handle things alone until I get cleaned up?"

If she had expected anger or a cold shoulder directed her way for the slap she'd given him, she would have been disappointed. His expression was free of any sign of condemnation, his tone neutral at the very worst.

Determined to appear as unaffected as he by what had passed between them, Leighanna cinched her fingers tight around the chair's back for support and forced a smile to her lips. "Yes, I'll be fine."

Hank started to turn away, then turned back, bracing a hand on either side of the door frame. A frown furrowed his forehead. "While I was at Mary Claire's eating lunch, I asked her why you were so desperate for money."

Leighanna's fingers tightened on the chair. "What did she tell you?"

"She said I'd have to ask you."

Leighanna's fingers relaxed, but only a little. "Why do you want to know?"

He lifted a shoulder in a shrug. "Just curious."

Turning her back on him, Leighanna kneed the chair back into place under the table. "I have debts to pay off."

Hank snorted. "I swear. You women and your credit cards."

Leighanna whirled to face him. "They aren't *my* debts," she said furiously.

"Then why the hell are you paying them?"

"Because—" She stopped, embarrassed to admit her own naiveté in allowing Roger to sink her so deeply in debt. "Because, in a sense, they are mine," she murmured.

Hank tossed up his hands. "Damnation! They either are, or they aren't. Which is it?"

Leighanna's cheek burned in both anger and humiliation. "They're mine, because they were incurred by my husband."

Hank's eyes widened. *Husband?* It had never occurred to him that Leighanna might have a husband. "You're married?"

She quickly shook her head. "No. Divorced."

Hank almost sighed in relief. He might like women, but he made it a rule to never fool around with another man's wife. "Then why isn't *he* paying the debts?" he asked, still confused.

"Because he won't...or he can't." She waved the explanation away as if it didn't matter. "Either way, I have to repay them or my credit rating is ruined."

Hank studied her, his arms folded across his chest, mentally adding integrity to the growing list of character traits he'd discovered in Leighanna. "So why didn't you stay in Houston? Surely the job market is better there than here?"

There was no way Leighanna would admit to Hank that she'd left Houston on the run because she was so weak that she couldn't say no to Roger. "I needed a change," she replied, somewhat vaguely, hoping he would drop the subject.

"What kind of change?"

Leighanna rolled her eyes in frustration. "A change! You know, new town, new people, new job."

"New husband?"

Leighanna stiffened her spine defensively. "I don't recall mentioning wanting a husband."

"No, but that's what the media's pushing for with all their talk about the man-to-woman ratio here in Temptation. Half the folks that have trooped through here to check out the place are single women looking for a husband. Just figured maybe you were, too."

"I assure you, my reasons for moving to Temptation did *not* include seeking a husband."

Though he doubted her motives for moving to Temptation, Hank gave his shoulder a whatever-you-say shrug. "Do you like it here better than you did Houston?"

Relieved to have his inquisition take a different slant, Leighanna's shoulders relaxed. "Yes, I do."

"Why?"

"Because the pace is slower, the people are friendly and the town has a charm all its own."

Hank chuckled. "Careful. Cody'll be using you for one of his advertisements to lure people to Temptation."

Leighanna smiled in spite of herself. "I seriously doubt my opinion would sway anyone in this direction."

"Maybe. Maybe not." Hank started to turn away again, then turned back. "By the way, the tables look good," he said, and shot her a wink before turning toward his apartment again.

Four

The front door to The End of the Road opened and slammed shut.

Startled by the unexpected noise, Leighanna glanced up and was startled even more to see Mrs. Martin standing just inside the entrance, her hands fisted on her wide hips. In the week Leighanna had worked at the bar, Mrs. Martin was the first female of Temptation's population to pass the threshold.

"Had to see it for myself to believe it!" Mrs. Martin exclaimed as she gaped openly at the covered tables. "But dang if you didn't go and put cloths on the table, just like you said you were going to do!"

Leighanna smiled as she rounded the bar to greet Mrs. Martin, pleased by the woman's praise as much as she was by her presence there. "Lovely, aren't they?"

Mrs. Martin gave a curt nod as she shuffled into the room. "They're sure that." She dragged a chair from beneath a table near the bar and settled her wide girth onto its seat. "What have you got other than beer to wet a person's throat?" she asked brusquely.

"Soft drinks. Tea. What would you like?"

"A soda will do, doesn't matter what flavor, just so it's wet and cold." She pulled a wrinkled handkerchief from her dress's pocket and mopped her sweaty brow. "Where's that scoundrel Hank?" she asked as she leaned to poke a gnarled finger at the centerpieces Leighanna had made.

Leighanna bit back a smile at the woman's impertinence. "He's in his apartment."

"Tell that good-for-nothing so-and-so that he's got himself a customer out here."

Not sure whether Hank had had the time to shower and dress, Leighanna hesitated.

"Well? What are you waiting for?" Mrs. Martin huffed impatiently. "Go and get him!"

With a sigh Leighanna turned to do her bidding, but before she took a step in that direction, Hank strode from the kitchen, bare from the waist up and rubbing a towel over his wet hair. The sight of that bare chest had Leighanna reeling.

He stopped short when he saw Mrs. Martin sitting at the table. His lips curved into a welcoming smile as he dropped the towel around his neck. "Well if it isn't the queen of Main Street!" he exclaimed and headed straight for her table. Catching her hand, he pulled her up, then wrapped his arms around her in a bear hug and swung her off her feet, dancing her in a fast dizzying circle.

Leighanna could do nothing but stare.

"Unhand me, you beast," Mrs. Martin sputtered as she struggled to tug his arms from around her waist. Hank settled her on her feet and dipped his head to give her a smack full on the lips. The woman's face reddened, but Leighanna thought she caught a glint of pleasure in the old woman's eyes as she tussled her dress back in place over her hips.

"You'll never change," Mrs. Martin muttered disagreeably. "Always hustlin' a woman, no matter what her age."

Hank just grinned that woman-killing grin of his and angled the chair and held it so that Mrs. Martin could sit back down. He surprised Leighanna by pulling out another chair, and taking a seat beside her.

"And what brings you to The End of the Road?" he asked, teasing her with a smile.

"Humph! Had to see for myself what all changes were going on over here. Couldn't believe it when Leighanna came in and bought that cloth for the tables." She smoothed an age-freckled hand across the checkered cloth. "Looks real nice," she added, giving a nod of approval. "Though I'm sure Jedidiah is turning over in his grave."

Jedidiah? Unable to stem her curiosity, Leighanna took a step toward them. "Who's Jedidiah?"

Mrs. Martin twisted her head around to frown at Leighanna as if she thought Leighanna should have known the man. "He ran this place right up until his death. God rest his soul," she murmured, quickly crossing herself. Frowning again, she leaned back in her chair and folded her hands in her lap. "He was meaner than sin, but always had a soft spot for Hank, here," she added, pursing her lips at him and appraising him in a skeptical way. "God knows why. Jedidiah refused to sell the place to anybody but him, even though there were others who'd have gladly paid a bigger price."

"I'm sure that it was my charm and keen business sense that attracted him," Hank returned, grinning.

"Pshaw! You don't have a lick of charm, except for the ladies, and the only good business sense you've ever shown was in hiring Leighanna."

Leighanna winced at the praise, remembering well Hank's irritation over all the attention the clean windows had drawn. She was sure that Mrs. Martin's comments would anger him just as much. But when Hank glanced Leighanna's way, his gaze was more assessing than judgmental, and it was all she could do to keep her mouth from dropping open.

Mrs. Martin either didn't see the exchange or chose to ignore it. "Personally," she continued, "I've always wondered if Jedidiah might have done it to alleviate his guilt because he thought he was the one who fathered you." She narrowed her eyes, peering at Hank intently. "You've got his eyes, and that's a fact."

Leighanna saw Hank's face redden and a vein at his temple begin to pulse. Knowing that he probably wasn't enjoying having his illegitimacy discussed in front of her, she turned away and headed for the bar to fill Mrs. Martin's request for a soda. But their voices carried, and Leighanna couldn't help but hear the rest of their conversation.

"My eyes are my own," Hank muttered defensively. "And you know as well as I do that any one of a hundred or more men could have fathered me."

"Can't argue that." Mrs. Martin's ample breasts rose and fell on a heavyhearted sigh. "Just seems a shame that no one stepped up and claimed you as their own, especially after your mother passed on. Everybody needs family."

Hank shoved back his chair and stood. "Not me," he said, catching the towel's ends in his hands. "I get along just fine on my own." In spite of the anger that still stained his cheeks, he dipped his head and pressed a kiss on Mrs. Martin's cheek, then gave her shoulder an affectionate pat. "But thanks for the concern."

Flustered, she waved him away. "Go get yourself some clothes on before I call Cody and have him arrest you for indecent exposure."

Behind the bar, Leighanna let out a shuddery sigh as she watched Hank stroll past her and disappear into the kitchen once again. She waited for the sound of his apartment door at the back opening and closing before picking up Mrs. Martin's soda and rounding the bar.

Though her heart was breaking at the false bravado she'd detected in Hank's voice when he'd claimed he got along just fine without family, she forced a smile to her face as she set the glass in front of Mrs. Martin. "Here you go," she said pleasantly. "Would you like anything else?"

Mrs. Martin gave the chair Hank had just vacated a nod. "A little company's all," she replied.

Leighanna sank down on the chair, instantly aware of the heat it still held from Hank's body.

Mrs. Martin picked up her drink and eyed Leighanna over its rim. "Are you sleeping with him yet?" she asked bluntly.

Leighanna's mouth dropped open in surprise. "I beg your pardon?"

"I said, are you sleeping with him yet? You've been working here, what, a week?"

"Yes," Leighanna whispered, then quickly corrected any misconceptions Mrs. Martin might entertain by adding, "I mean that, yes, I've been working here a week."

"Most women would have fallen for his charm by then."

"I'm not most women."

Mrs. Martin tilted her head, frowning as she studied Leighanna's face. "No," she said slowly. "I can see that you're not. But you're not immune to him, either," she added. "I can see that, as well."

Leighanna felt color rise up her neck to stain her cheeks.

Mrs. Martin nodded sagely. "I figured as much." She surprised Leighanna by chuckling. "Mark my word. He'll have you in his bed 'fore the month's up." She chuckled again, wagging her head. "You oughta sell tickets. Watching your fall would be well worth the price, no matter what the cost."

Leighanna parked in front of the hardware store and stepped from her car, dabbing at the perspiration on her forehead. She was going to have to get that air conditioner repaired and soon, she told herself. Otherwise, she'd melt before the summer was over.

"Hey, Leighanna! How you doin'?"

Leighanna glanced up to see Cody strolling down the sidewalk toward her. She waved a greeting. A frequent customer at The End of the Road, Cody had endeared himself to her the day he'd commented on the clean windows. "Fine, thanks," she replied, smiling. "How about you?"

"Can't complain. Though we could stand a little rain. Would cool things down a bit." He stopped and waited for her to climb the two steps that led from the street to the hardware store. "What brings you to town?"

"Supplies. I'm doing some painting at The End of the Road tomorrow."

"Really?" Cody tossed a friendly arm across her shoulders and walked with her into the store. "That's quite a job to take on in this heat."

"I'm planning on getting an early start."

With a nod at the store's owner, Cody trailed Leighanna down the aisle. "How are you and Hank getting along?"

Leighanna tensed at the mention of Hank, remembering Mrs. Martin's prediction that before the month ended she'd be in his bed. She wondered if everyone in town thought she was sleeping with Hank.

She forced her shoulders to relax. "Fine." She reached for a sample card of paint colors and pretended to study it. "He does his work, I do mine."

Cody nodded his head. "Sounds like a fair deal." He hooked an arm along the edge of an upper shelf. "Is painting part of your job description as a waitress?"

Leighanna stuck the card back in the rack and chose another. "No. This is in addition to my normal duties. I need the money."

"Who doesn't?" Cody dipped his head and thoughtfully rubbed a finger beneath his nose. "If you're interested in making a little more, you might talk to Mayor Acres. He's looking for someone to head up a committee to plan a little celebration he's putting on at the end of the month."

The prospect of increasing her income making her instantly alert, Leighanna turned to him. "Really?"

Cody nodded his head. "Yep. He's hoping to fill the town's coffers from all the media attention that's come Temptation's way." He lifted his shoulder in a shrug. "The job probably won't pay much, but if you're interested, I could put a bug in Acres's ear for you."

She laid a hand on his arm, her eyes bright with excitement. "Would you? Oh, Cody, I'd be grateful."

"No trouble," he mumbled, obviously embarrassed by her gratitude.

Her mind already racing, Leighanna caught her lower lip between her teeth. "My shift at The End of the Road is from five until closing time, but I suppose I can work around that. If it's all right with Mayor Acres, I could work for him in the morning and in the early afternoon, then for Hank at night."

"I'm sure Acres would agree to that."

"Oh, Cody," she said, unable to contain her excitement. "I really appreciate your telling me about this job."

Cody just shook his head and chuckled. "You might not be so grateful after you've worked with Acres for a while. He can be cantankerous at times. His moods swing faster than the price of grain."

Leighanna arched a brow, thinking of her current employer and his wild mood swings. "He couldn't be any worse than Hank Braden."

By seven a.m. Sunday morning, the sun was already making its presence known. Its rays reflected off the tin roof of The End of the Road and heat radiated from its surface, turning the tin the color of polished silver. Having already worked nearly an hour gathering and setting up her supplies, Leighanna paused at the side of the building, already bone tired, and rested a shoulder against the rough stone.

It had been almost two when she'd arrived home from work the night before, but it was well after four before she'd finally drifted off to sleep. And it was all Hank's fault, she thought on a weary sigh. Ever since that afternoon at Mary Claire's when he'd kissed her, he had haunted her sleep. And he was messing with her mind. She just knew he was. For some unknown reason, he was being nicer to her, even helping her with the duties that he'd originally assigned to her. The night before he had even insisted on mopping the floor while she counted the night's proceeds. And why? she asked herself.

The why behind his sudden change of nature didn't

matter, she told herself. She had more important things to concern herself with. And painting Hank's building was at the top of the list. With the prospect of a new job on the horizon, she wanted to have the painting completed so she would be free to take advantage of Mayor Acres's job if he offered it to her. Still, it took all her willpower to step from the shade created by the building and out into the bright sunlight.

After adjusting the six-foot metal ladder she'd found in the shed in front of the bar's entrance, she stooped and turned on the portable radio she'd brought along to keep her company. Switching the station to one that played rhythm and blues, she cranked up the volume, then turned to the makeshift table where she'd set up her supplies. Choosing a pad of steel wool, she moved her hips in rhythm with Bonnie Raitt's voice as she attacked the peeling varnish on the front door. Working with the grain, just as her father had taught her years ago, she scrubbed, chipping away at the old varnish and baring the wood beneath.

Birds sang in a nearby tree, and Leighanna added her voice to theirs, singing lustily right along with Bonnie Raitt. The words were familiar, the beat fast, pumping up the speed of Leighanna's hand as she pushed the stiff wool up and down over the wood.

Unaware of anything but the pulsing sound of the music around her and the door beneath her hand, Leighanna suddenly found herself flat on her face when the door was jerked open from the inside.

"What in the hell are you trying to do? Wake the dead?"

Warily, she lifted her head a fraction to find a pair

of bare feet planted an inch from her nose. Slowly she lifted her gaze higher, skimming up denim-clad legs, hesitating only slightly at the three buttons left open at the jean's fly, but coming to a shocking halt when her gaze hit on the bare skin created by the jeans' opening. A little higher and muscled pecs, tensed in anger, swelled beneath a fur of thick black hair. Swallowing hard, she forced her gaze higher until she stared unblinkingly into the face of Hank Braden.

His hair still tousled from sleep, he towered over her, his hands on his hips, while a muscle twitched dangerously on his jaw.

Slowly pushing herself to her feet, she bent to dust off her knees. "I'm sorry. It didn't occur to me that you would still be asleep or I would have—" She winced when her fingers hit a raw spot on her knee. Bending at the waist, she saw that blood oozed from the scrape.

"Now look what you've done," she said, fighting back tears. "You've bloodied my knee."

"*I've* bloodied your knee! You're the one who fell!"

She snapped up her head to glare at him. "I wouldn't have if you hadn't opened the door so unexpectedly." Tucking her chin, she examined the scrape.

Hank dipped his head over hers to look, as well. "Ah, hell. It's just a little scratch," he muttered.

"It's bleeding, isn't it?" she cried indignantly.

Cursing under his breath, Hank grabbed her by the wrist and wheeled, dragging her behind him.

"What do you think you're doing?" she cried as she stumbled after him.

"I'm gonna doctor that knee before you develop blood poisoning and the damn thing rots off."

With his hand cinched tightly around her wrist, Leighanna was forced to run to keep up with him. He didn't stop until he reached his apartment at the rear of the bar. At the door, he slowed only long enough to push her through the doorway ahead of him. "Take a seat there on the bed while I grab my first aid kit from the bathroom."

Stunned, Leighanna watched him disappear behind a door. *Sit on his bed?* Slowly she turned to stare at the item in question. A tangle of sheets and blankets covered the old iron bed, a heady reminder that Hank had just climbed from it. She could almost see him there, naked, stretched across its length, and wondered what it would be like to lie there with him. With a moan of frustration at her lustful thoughts, she tore her gaze away and looked for a less intimate place to sit...but discovered there wasn't one.

The apartment consisted of only one room, with a small kitchen tucked into one corner. A dresser lined the wall to her left. On its dusty surface sat a television, angled for easy viewing from the bed positioned opposite it.

Beside the bed was a small nightstand which held a dilapidated lamp and a plate smeared with dried ketchup. It seemed the bed was the center of activity, used for everything from sleeping, to eating, to relaxing while watching the tube. A shiver shook her shoulders as she wondered what else it was used for.

Before she could ponder this further, Hank stepped from the bathroom, carrying a small box and a washcloth dripping water. With a huff of impatience that she hadn't followed his instructions, he gave her a shove that sent her sprawling across the mattress.

"Prop your knee up," he ordered as he tossed the box onto the bed beside her.

Pushing herself to her elbows, Leighanna glared at him, but hooked a foot on the bed rail, presenting her knee, anxious to get this over with and out of his apartment. He stooped over her, dabbing the wet cloth at the scrape. Wincing, Leighanna jerked away. He immediately stopped and glanced up at her. "Did that hurt?"

"A little," she murmured reluctantly.

Grunting, he squatted down in front of her and reapplied the cloth, but gentler this time. With him hunkered down in front of her, Leighanna found herself confronted with an unrestricted view of his bare chest. The muscled pecs tightened and swelled with each stroke of his hand. She remembered well the feel of that chest pressed against her, but the sight of it naked was almost more than she could bear. Her breath grew shorter and shorter until she had to force herself to look away, to focus instead on his hands...though doing so didn't offer much relief.

The fingers that held the cloth were thick, the palms wide and the skin beneath the hair that dusted the back of his hand tanned a golden brown. The hands were those of a working man, callused and strong, yet his touch was painfully gentle, reminding her of other times when he'd touched her. Now, like then, heat surged through her body at the contact, and she found herself aching for an even more intimate touch.

At that moment he glanced up at her, but Leighanna's gaze never made it any higher than his lips.

Next time, it'll be you kissing me...

She caught her bottom lip between her teeth as his words came back to haunt her, wishing with all her heart that he'd ignore her warning, as he had before, and try to kiss her again. She knew without a doubt that this time she would let him. She might even beg him. She raised her gaze higher.

"I'm gonna—" Hank stopped when her eyes met his, and he rocked back on his heels, a grin chipping at the corner of his mouth. "You're thinking about that kiss, aren't you?"

Leighanna stiffened, mortified that he could read her thoughts so easily. "Don't be ridiculous!"

Hank just chuckled. "Oh, you're thinking about it, all right." He tucked his tongue in the corner of his mouth as he eyed her, then nodded knowingly. "And you're wondering if it was as good as you remember it." When her face reddened, he chuckled again. "Trust me, sweetheart," he said with a wink. "It was."

Leighanna sucked in an outraged breath. "You are undoubtedly the most egotistical man I've ever met."

Hank just shrugged. "Maybe. But it takes two to make a kiss memorable. And believe me, sweetheart, I haven't forgotten that kiss, either."

Leighanna's eyes widened in surprise. "You haven't?"

"Well, hell no." His gaze took on a considering

look. "But maybe that's because we've never really finished a kiss."

She swallowed hard, unable to fathom what the end of a kiss meant to Hank. "We haven't?"

"Not in my book." He continued to stare at her, his eyes warming and darkening in that look that both frightened and aroused her. "Maybe we should have another go at it. Just to see if what we experienced was as good as we remember it."

Leighanna knotted her fingers in the tangle of bed-covers at her sides, knowing full well that in agreeing to his suggestion she was playing with fire. "I suppose we could do that," she said nervously.

Hank rocked forward until his feet were flat on the floor again. Drawing her hitched leg from the bed rail, he guided both her legs around him, then slowly dropped to his knees until he knelt in the V he'd created with her legs.

Holding her legs snug against his hips, he leaned forward, but stopped just shy of her lips. He drew away, eyeing her suspiciously. "You're not going to slap me again, now are you?"

She shook her head, her eyes riveted on his mouth. "No." She wet her lips, already thinking of the feel of that sensuous mouth on hers. "No," she repeated. "I won't slap you."

Satisfied, he nodded and leaned toward her again. She closed her eyes, drifting to meet him...and nearly tumbled into his lap when he jerked away from her again. "What about kicking or stomping?" he asked, frowning. "You planning on doing anything like that?"

Not sure now whether she wanted to kiss him or kill him, Leighanna clapped her hands against the sides of his face. Digging her fingers into his cheeks, she glared down at him. "For God's sake, will you *please* just kiss me and get it over with?"

Chuckling, Hank scooted closer. "Yes, ma'am. I surely will. But as to getting it over with, now I can't make any promises about that." Slowly, he lifted his face and closed his mouth over hers. Catching her lower lip between his, he drew it deep into his mouth, suckling gently.

Shivers chased down Leighanna's spine while arrows of need shot straight to her feminine core. This is what had haunted her, she thought weakly as his tongue slipped into her mouth. This is what had kept her awake night after night, ruining her sleep. This is what drove her crazy each time he brushed against her when they worked side by side at the bar.

On a low moan of surrender, she looped her hands around his neck and slid bonelessly from the bed, landing with a soft plop against his thighs while her breasts melted against his chest. Giving herself up to the tastes and the textures, to the raw level of need that pulled at her, she moved her hips in rhythm with the movements of his lips on hers.

And Hank was sure he would die.

The feel of her, the pressure of her body rubbing against his, that seductive feminine scent she'd dabbed in all the right spots.... He'd never been to heaven, didn't have a prayer of ever crossing through those pearly gates, but he knew this had to be what heaven must be like and about as close to the place as a man like him could get. With her knees squeezed around him, those small, firm breasts of hers pressing hard against his chest, that tongue of hers playing a game of tag with his in her mouth...well, it was more than he'd bargained for and definitely more of a temptation than he was willing to let pass.

Loosening his hold on her legs, he dragged his hands upward, running them up the tautened muscles of her thighs to cup her denim-clad buttocks. He paused there a moment, enjoying the feel of her muscles tightening beneath his hands before he slipped his hands higher to slide under the hem of her T-shirt.

Silk and sandpaper, he thought as his callused hands skimmed her smooth back. Yet another contrast between them to explore. But later, he told himself. At the moment he had only one thing on his mind, and that was to simply give and take a little pleasure.

Drawing his hands slowly away from her spine, he shaped them around her sides, noting again the delicacy of her small frame and the fullness of her small, unencumbered breasts. His thumb grazed a nipple, and he felt the purr of a moan vibrate against his lips. His or hers? he wondered fleetingly before he took her breasts fully into his hands. This time he recognized the moan that vibrated between them as his own. He remembered well teasing her about what little God had blessed her with and telling her that some men liked women with small breasts...he just wasn't one of them. But with the weight of her breasts in his hands, with her turgid nipples stabbing at his palm, he knew that he'd been wrong.

And he knew he had to taste them.

But would she let him? he wondered. If something as innocent as a kiss had earned him a foot stomping and a face slapping, what would she do if he dared to bare her breasts? He steeled himself for whatever punishment she inflicted, knowing it would be well worth the pain.

In an action smoothed by years of practice, he had her T-shirt over her head and his mouth pressed over hers once again to smother any protest...but to his surprise, none was forthcoming. Her only response was a low whimper that originated low in her throat and slowly died there as she tightened her arms around him, pressing her naked breasts against his chest.

And now it was just skin against skin. The desire to be closer still was overpowering. Cupping her buttocks in his hands, he stood, lifting her with him. Instinctively she wrapped her legs around his waist as he dug a knee into the mattress. He laid her down on his bed, then followed, covering her body with his. Unable to stand the temptation any longer, he shifted, tearing his mouth from hers and closing it over a breast.

With a sharp cry of pleasure, Leighanna arched, thrusting herself hard against him. She'd never felt so utterly out of control before, so detached from herself. Was this like death? she wondered. If so, she welcomed it with open arms. The sensations that ripped through her robbed her of air and numbed her to everything but the feel of that hot, clever mouth against her breast. His teeth nipped, his lips soothed, his tongue laved a path from one breast to the other...and left the first aching for more. Never in her life had she throbbed like this. Never had she felt this overpowering need for a man's touch. She wanted him to do more than kiss her, she wanted, with a fervency she'd never experienced in her life, for him to make love to her.

The idea that she would even consider such a thing pushed ice through her veins. She had to stop him, she thought wildly, before she totally lost control.

She caught his face in her hands and forced his mouth back to hers. But instead of stopping him, her actions seemed to incite him even more. With a growl, he shifted again, dragging his body up the length of hers, and she nearly wept at the length of hardened maleness that pressed against her femininity. It took every fiber of will she possessed, but she pressed her hands more firmly against his cheeks and tore her mouth from his.

With her chest heaving with each drawn breath, she met his gaze. Their eyes seemed to weld together in the heat that burned between them. She saw the passion in his brown eyes, that wild unsatisfied yearning, and knew it must be mirrored in her own. It would be so easy, she thought with a stab of regret, to give in to that passion and let it carry them on. But she couldn't. She knew she couldn't. She didn't trust herself when it came to dealing with men, especially a man like Hank Braden.

Struggling to remain calm, she nervously wet her lips. "I think we're finished," she said, but was unable to keep the telltale tremble from her voice. "I need to get back to work."

For a moment he continued to stare at her, then slowly his lips curved into a smile. "Are you sure?"

Though returning to work wasn't at all what she wanted to do, she gave her chin a quick jerk. "Yes. I'm sure."

"All right then." He shifted his weight until he was stretched out beside her.

With his body no longer shielding her nakedness, Leighanna instinctively tried to cover herself, but Hank placed an arm between hers, preventing her. "We'll have none of that."

Holding her in place with nothing but the strength in his gaze, he gently forced her arms down to her sides and rested his arm across her abdomen. His hand molded the gentle curve of her waist. He lowered his face to hers and Leighanna stiffened, fearing that he was going to kiss her again and not at all certain she would have the strength to stop him this time.

"Before you go, sweetheart," he said, his breath feathering at her lips. "You need to understand one thing. We haven't even come close to finishing that kiss."

Five

A week later, Leighanna sat at Mary Claire's kitchen table with her chin cradled in her palm, staring at the oak tree outside the kitchen window, her thoughts as fleeting as the summer breeze that sent the leaves on the old oak dancing. Her checkbook, a stack of bills and a legal pad with a carefully planned budget were spread on the table in front of her. With the money Hank had paid her for painting The End of the Road, she had decisions to make...which bill to pay first.

But Leighanna couldn't concentrate on the task at hand. Hank refused to let her. He was there, if only in her mind, pushing himself to the forefront of her thoughts and making it all but impossible to focus on anything but him.

Oddly enough, it wasn't the seductive power of his

kisses that plagued her, though she had spent some
time dwelling on that. It was simply…him. In her
mind she kept seeing again his apartment, that old iron
bed with its tangle of covers, that plate sitting on the
nightstand with dried ketchup smeared across its surface. Along with the vision came the memory of what
Mrs. Martin had unwittingly revealed about his past.
No roots. No family.

And Leighanna's heart ached for him. For the child
he'd been, without a father or a mother to look out for
him, without a place to call home. And for the man
he'd become, who tried to pretend that he didn't need
any of those things.

But he did. She knew he did. At the time she might
have been momentarily blinded to everything but the
passion he drew from her, but on reflection she remembered the gentleness of his touch, the sighs of
contentment when he'd held her tight in his arms. She
remembered, too, the fondness he'd shown Mrs. Martin, a woman more than twice his age, a woman who
cared for him like a mother would.

Because Leighanna understood those needs, that
same yearning for love and affection that she herself
craved, she recognized them in Hank.

But there was a difference between Hank and herself. Leighanna had known a mother's love, the security in having a home, even if the address *had* kept
changing over the years. She wanted only to duplicate
those things, improve on what she'd experienced as a
child. She wanted to love someone, and to have that
someone love her in return. Beyond that, she wanted
a home, a spot of security and permanency that she

could call her own. And though she'd married once and failed to see that dream fulfilled, she still believed she would one day live it.

In comparison, Hank sought fulfillment for those same needs in an unending line of willing women, much like his mother had in the succession of men she'd bedded.

A part of Leighanna, a secret part that she dared not examine too closely, wanted to give him what he needed. She wanted to love him and nurture him, to fill the voids in his life, to—

"What are you daydreaming about?"

Leighanna jumped at the sound of Mary Claire's voice and guiltily began to shuffle through the stack of bills, trying to appear busy. "Nothing. Just paying bills."

Mary Claire set a basket of laundry on the opposite end of the table and plucked out a towel to fold, biting back a smile. "Never knew a bill could bring such a dreamy look to a woman's eye."

Leighanna's face warmed. "The truth is," she admitted reluctantly. "I was thinking about Hank."

Mary Claire's fingers stilled on the towel, and she glanced Leighanna's way. "Hank?"

Leighanna's forehead puckered into a thoughtful frown. "Did you know that he hasn't a clue as to who fathered him?"

"No," Mary Claire murmured hesitantly. "Though I have heard rumors that his mother…well, that his mother was rather loose."

Leighanna snorted. "Loose is putting it mildly. According to Mrs. Martin, Hank all but raised himself.

To quote her, 'Hank's mother was so busy slipping out of one bed and into another that half the time she'd even forget to take him with her when she made the shift.'"

Not having heard this before, Mary Claire set the folded towel aside and thoughtfully picked up another, her mother's heart breaking for the child Hank had once been. "Poor little fellow. He must have been pretty tough to have survived unscathed."

"I don't think he did."

Mary Claire dropped the towel she was folding to look at Leighanna in confusion. "What?"

"Think about Hank's reputation. If everything that is rumored about him is true, he is obviously trying to fill the voids in his life with all his flirting and with all the women he's supposedly bedded. Considering his past and his mother's loose ways, that's the only way that he would know how."

Mary Claire snatched the towel she'd dropped from the basket and pursed her lips as she began to fold it. "Leighanna," she warned. "Don't even think it."

"Think what?" Leighanna asked in surprise.

"That Hank Braden is some kind of wounded bird that you can adopt and heal."

Insulted, Leighanna tilted up her chin. "I wasn't thinking of adopting him."

"Well, what *are* you thinking?" Before Leighanna could answer, Mary Claire dropped down in the chair opposite her and gathered her friend's hands in hers. "I know you, Leighanna," she said gently. "Probably better than you know yourself. You have the softest heart in the world and it would be just like you to think that you could take Hank under your wing and make up to him for all the neglect he's experienced in his life.''

"Don't be ridiculous," Leighanna sputtered defensively and tried to pull her hands away. But Mary Claire refused to let her go, forcing Leighanna to meet her gaze.

"You'll only get hurt, Leighanna," she murmured. "And I don't want to see that happen."

"For heaven's sake!" Leighanna cried. "You're talking as if I was planning on marrying him!" She tugged her hands free of Mary Claire's and sat back in her chair with a huff. "I just thought that I should be nicer to him, more understanding. In fact, if it's all right with you, I'd like to invite him to have lunch with us on Sunday."

By Thursday night, Leighanna was beginning to panic. She'd been trying all week to find just the right moment to offer the invitation to Hank, but business at the bar had been crazy, at best.

The new decor had set up a furor around town and it seemed like everyone in the county was determined to drop in and see for themselves all the changes The End of the Road had undergone. Naturally, that meant more work for Leighanna and Hank, which kept them hustling all evening, with not a second to themselves so that she could invite him as she'd planned.

But she was determined that tonight before she went home, she would offer the invitation. Her arms elbow-deep in dishwater, Leighanna racked her brain, trying to think of an opening, some casual way to invite

Hank to lunch at Mary Claire's without it sounding like a date, or worse, a come-on. Unfortunately, nothing came to mind.

"Heard Mayor Acres hired you to head up the committee that's throwing that bash on Labor Day weekend."

Leighanna glanced over at Hank, who was working about ten steps away, wiping down the grill, and silently cursed herself for not already telling him about the job herself. She'd been in such a stew all evening about the lunch invitation, the new job had totally slipped her mind. "Yes, he did," she said, hoping to hide her guilt behind a smile. "In fact, I start Monday. But don't worry," she assured him as she dipped the last plate into the rinse water, then laid it on the drain with the others to dry. "The hours I work for him won't conflict with my hours here."

Hank merely grunted and picked up a cloth. He plucked a plate from the drain and began to dry. "Don't I pay you enough?"

Hearing the edge in his voice, Leighanna rested her hands on the lip of the sink and turned to look at him. "Well, of course you do. I just—"

"Need the money," he finished for her.

"Yes, I do," she replied firmly.

Hank merely shook his head as he set the plate aside and selected another to dry. "Sweetheart, you're gonna work yourself into an early grave."

Leighanna bit back a smile, knowing she had been right about Hank. There was a soft spot buried beneath that flirtatious, skirt-chasing man's skin. "A little hard work never killed anyone," she said lightly. "Besides, the job will only last until Labor Day."

Hank focused his gaze on the plate he was drying and frowned. "I suppose I could give you a raise."

Leighanna arched her brows, surprised by the offer. "A raise would be appreciated, I assure you, but I certainly don't expect one. Heavens!" she said, laughing. "I've worked here less than a month!"

"Doesn't matter how long you've been here," he argued. "The fact is, you've earned it."

Touched by his concern, Leighanna laid a hand on his arm. "Thank you. But if you're thinking a raise will discourage me from accepting the job from Mayor Acres, it won't," she warned him. "The extra money I'll make will help me pay off my debts that much sooner." She sighed softly as he continued to frown, then she turned back to the sink and pulled out the plug, wondering if this might be the very opening she needed. "Would you like to come to Mary Claire's for lunch on Sunday?"

Hank snapped up his head, his hands stilling on the half-dried plate. "Lunch?"

Leighanna turned to him and couldn't help but smile at his startled expression. Obviously he didn't receive invitations for Sunday lunch very often. "Yes, lunch," she repeated. "Mary Claire always serves a huge meal at noon on Sundays."

"Well, I suppose I could," he murmured uncertainly. "Though I promised Harley I'd help him unload some bulls he's hauling in from a sale."

"I'm sure that won't be a problem since Harley is planning to be there, too." Leighanna took the plate from him and finished drying it. ''Plan to be there by noon. And come hungry. Mary Claire always cooks enough to feed a small army.''

''Uh-oh,'' Mary Claire murmured.

Leighanna stepped to her friend's side and peered through the kitchen window above the sink to follow the line of Mary Claire's gaze. In the backyard, Hank lay on the grass beneath the old oak tree, his arms folded across his chest, his eyes closed, obviously enjoying a nap after the big lunch he'd just consumed. In the pasture beyond, she could see Harley walking the fence, checking for breaks.

''Uh-oh, what?'' Leighanna asked, not seeing anything to be concerned about.

Mary Claire lifted a hand and pointed to the side of the yard where her children, Stephie and Jimmy, were tiptoeing toward Hank with mischief in their eyes. ''Hank's about to be attacked,'' Mary Claire said, chuckling softly.

Knowing from past experience how disagreeable Hank could be when he was awakened, Leighanna lunged for the back door...but she was too late. Stephie and Jimmy had already pounced, landing on Hank's chest, and were squealing and laughing as they dug their fingers into his ribs, tickling him.

With a roar, Hank bucked, catching both kids around the waist, and flipped them over, turning their backs to the ground and kneeling over them with his knees squeezed at their waists.

Sure that he meant them harm, Leighanna cleared

the porch steps in one jump and was racing across the yard to rescue the children from his anger.

"You think you're pretty smart, don't you?" she heard him say in a threatening voice as she ran. "Well, you're not as smart as me."

She ran faster, her heart pounding against her ribs as he continued to hold them prisoner.

"Don't! Don't!" Stephie and Jimmy screamed, laughing hysterically. Shocked by the children's laughter, Leighanna stumbled to a stop behind Hank. She was even more shocked when Hank joined in.

"Say uncle," he teased, while his fingers played their rib cages like he would a piano.

"No," they screamed in unison as they twisted and turned, screeching and laughing as they tried to escape his hold on them.

"Better say uncle," he repeated, chuckling. "Or the tickle monster's going to get you."

"Never!" Jimmy yelled, then collapsed into a fit of giggles as Hank turned his fingers full force on him.

Leighanna folded her arms across her breasts, shaking her head and chuckling softly at this new glimpse of Hank's personality. She'd never seen him act like a child before. The sight softened her heart toward him a little bit more.

Spying Leighanna, Stephie cried, "Leighanna! Help us!"

Hank's fingers stilled, and he glanced over his shoulder to find Leighanna standing behind him...and that was all the diversion the children needed. They wriggled from beneath him and pounced again, wrestling Hank to the ground.

Leighanna felt a hand snake around her ankle and a yank, and before she knew what was happening, she was tumbling to land on top of them with a surprised yelp.

"Get her, kids!" Hank yelled, and suddenly it was Leighanna who was on the bottom and two sets of small hands and a set of decidedly larger and stronger ones were tickling at her ribs.

"Say uncle," Stephie demanded, obviously delighted with this new twist to their game.

"Stop! Please!" Leighanna begged, as she swatted futilely at their hands.

"You gotta say uncle first," Hank warned, grinning as he found a particularly vulnerable spot.

"Uncle, my foot," Mary Claire chided, hauling her children away from the pile. "I swear Hank Braden, you are as bad as the kids," she huffed. "Now get off Leighanna before you break her in half."

His hands stopped tickling but Hank didn't budge an inch. He gazed down at Leighanna, grinning like a fool. Though his eyes were set on Leighanna's, his words were directed to Mary Claire and her children. "She's gotta say uncle first. Right, kids?"

"Right!" Stephie and Jimmy yelled in unison. Rolling her eyes, Mary Claire turned and dragged them to the house.

Leighanna watched them leave in growing panic. Swallowing hard, she turned her gaze to Hank's. She could tell by the look in his eyes that this was a whole new game, and she wasn't at all sure she knew the rules. "Are you going to let me up?" she asked uncertainly.

Hank's knees tightened around her and his fingers found that vulnerable spot again, the one just below the fullness of her breast...but he didn't tickle this time. He stroked his thumb seductively down three ribs and back up. "Not until you say uncle."

Leighanna's eyes widened as she recognized that dark warmth that came into his eyes. She'd tried so hard throughout the meal to keep her distance from him, to make this invitation to lunch as platonic as she'd sworn to Mary Claire it was. And now he was going to kiss her again!

"Uncle!" she blurted out. "Uncle!"

"Coward," he murmured and lowered his face to hers.

Knowing how susceptible she was to his persuasive charm, Leighanna twisted her face away and bucked, trying to get out from beneath him. "I'm not a coward," she grated out.

"Sure you are. You're afraid I'm gonna kiss you again."

She stilled instantly and looked up at him. "I'm not afraid," she lied. "I just want up."

"So get up, then," he teased.

She frowned up at him. "I can't. You're on top of me."

He shrugged a shoulder. "We could shift, and you could be on top, if you like."

"Very funny, Braden," she said dryly.

"I'm not trying to be funny, just trying to get a little kiss."

Leighanna snorted. "A little kiss," she repeated in

disgust. "You don't even know the meaning of the term."

Hank just grinned. "Sure I do." Before she could argue further, his mouth was on hers, his lips brushing hers in the sweetest, most chaste way...and she closed her eyes on a defeated sigh, giving herself up to the feel of him, the taste of him. Then, to her disappointment and amazement, Hank was pushing himself up and off her. She opened her eyes to see him standing over her. The kiss had lasted only seconds, but the effects on her system lingered.

He stooped and held out a hand, grinning. "See?" he told her as he hauled her to her feet. He slung a companionable arm around her shoulder and turned her toward the house. "I told you I knew what a little kiss was."

A long, gooseneck cattle trailer was backed up to the corral at Harley's ranch. Inside, three bulls pawed and shifted, sending the trailer rocking beneath them as they rammed their horned heads against the steel bars that confined them, looking for a way of escape.

Standing alongside Mary Claire at a safe distance from the trailer, Leighanna fought back a shudder.

"They look mean," she whispered under her breath.

"They are mean," Mary Claire whispered in return as she nervously watched Harley move to the trailer's rear door. She raised her voice to yell a warning to Stephie and Jimmy who were playing King of the Mountain on a stack of hay piled high near the barn door. "You kids stay right where you are until the bulls are unloaded, you hear me?"

"We will, Mom," they called in unison.

With their eyes riveted on the men, Mary Claire and Leighanna watched as Hank swung open one of the trailer's rear doors and Harley swung open the other and quickly moved behind it. A Brahma bull, his eyes wild from the forced confinement, lowered his head and charged for the opening, catching his horn between the door's iron rails on Harley's side and tossing it back. Before Harley could react, the door slammed into him and sent him flying, his arms striking at the air. He landed flat on his back with a grunt of pain, while dust churned around him. The movement caught the bull's eye and he spun. With a target now to vent his anger on, the bull pawed the ground, then lowered his head again and charged straight for Harley.

Stunned, Leighanna could only stare while Mary Claire's scream rent the air. "Harley! Watch out!"

But Harley didn't move. Already racing for the corral, Mary Claire screamed again. "Hank! Help him!"

Already aware of the situation, Hank was swinging the trailer's rear doors closed again. He jerked the latch in place, locking the other two bulls inside, then whirled and ran for the raging bull, yelling and flapping his hat.

Just before the bull reached Harley, he spun again, fixing his eyes on Hank. While the bull's attention was diverted, Mary Claire ducked between the corral gates and grabbed Harley's arms and started tugging and pulling him toward the side of the corral.

Leighanna ran to kneel on the opposite side and the two women pulled and pushed until they had dragged Harley beneath the corral's lowest rung and to safety.

Breathing raggedly, and with sweat stinging her eyes, Leighanna glanced up just as the bull charged for Hank.

"Hank!" she screamed, scrambling to her feet. "Run!"

But Hank stood frozen in place, his face tense, his dark gaze fixed on the bull. Just as the animal reached him, Hank lunged to the side, narrowly missing being gored by the bull's deadly horns by inches. The bull whirled again with a frustrated roar, his eyes wild, mucous swinging from his mouth.

Instinctively sensing Hank's intent, Mary Claire pointed to the gate behind him. "The gate, Leighanna! Open the gate!"

Seeing the gate on the far side of the corral, Leighanna ran for it. With her fingers trembling, she fumbled at the latch, managed to pull the iron pin free and swung the gate wide.

In the center of the corral, Hank stood, his back to her, waiting for the bull's next move.

Hoping to divert the animal's attention away from Hank as Hank had done for Harley, Leighanna boldly stepped into the opening and let out a yell, waving her hands over her head.

The bull lifted his head, and for a split second Leighanna looked straight into his eyes and knew what death must look like. She hollered again, and Hank twisted his head to look over his shoulder. She saw panic slip into the dark depths of his eyes when his gaze met hers.

"Get out of the way!" he yelled.

She started to turn away, but the bull chose that moment to attack. With a powerful lunge, he ducked his head and charged straight for Hank. Leighanna felt the ground beneath her feet reverberate with each pounding of his hooves against the hard-packed dirt, and the view before her slipped into slow motion. The bull slung his head, caught Hank in the stomach on the curve of his horn and sent him arcing in the air and over his back before he raced on for the opening. With a speed she hadn't known she possessed, Leighanna jumped out of the bull's way and swung the gate closed behind him as he raced past her, bucking, into the open pasture.

Quickly she slid the pin back into place and scrambled over the corral and ran for Hank, her heart in her throat. When she reached him, she dropped down to her knees on the ground beside him. "Hank! Are you all right?" she cried. When he didn't answer, she leaned over him and pressed a cheek against his chest, listening for a heartbeat. Murmuring a prayer of thanks when she heard one, she started to lift her head…and saw the ragged tear on his shirt. With shaking fingers she lifted the torn cloth and nearly fainted when she saw the blood oozing from the torn flesh.

"Oh, Hank," she cried, blinded by her own tears. "Please don't die."

"He's a lucky man," the doctor said with a shake of his head. "You both are."

Harley nodded, testing the bandage on his forehead with a tentative finger. "How bad's he hurt?"

"I've stitched up the hole in his side, but he's got a cracked rib that's going to take some time to heal. But my biggest concern right now is his concussion."

The doctor blew out a frustrated breath. "I told him I wanted to keep him overnight for observation, but he pitched a walleyed fit. Says he's never spent a night in a hospital and doesn't intend to spend one now."

Harley chuckled. "Must not be hurtin' too bad, if he's complaining."

The doctor frowned at Harley. "He's hurting all right, he's just too damn stubborn to admit it." The doctor shook his head. "In the mood he's in, I'd be better off letting him go home. Is there anyone there to take care of him? He's going to have to be awakened on the hour for the next twenty-four and have an eye kept on him for at least another forty-eight."

Harley stole a glance at Mary Claire, who stood beside him. "No, but I guess I could take him home with me and care for him."

Squaring her shoulders, Leighanna stepped forward. "That won't be necessary. I'll take care of him."

Both Harley and Mary Claire stared at her in surprise, but Leighanna firmed her lips and stubbornly met their gazes. "It's my fault he was hurt. If he hadn't turned to look at me when I yelled, he'd never have been gored."

"Now, Leighanna," Harley murmured soothingly. "It's not your fault Hank got—"

Leighanna turned her back on Harley, ignoring him, and gave her full attention to the doctor. "If you'd be kind enough to write out your instructions, I'll see that Hank follows them to the letter."

Leighanna sat by the side of Hank's bed in a chair she'd dragged in from the bar, her back straight as a board, her gaze riveted on his face. Occasionally she'd tear her eyes away, but only long enough to check the clock she'd placed on the bedside table.

Four hours had passed since Harley, Mary Claire and the kids had left, leaving her solely responsible for Hank's care. Four long nerve-burning hours.

Thankfully, Harley had stripped Hank of his clothes and put him to bed before he'd gone, sparing Leighanna that difficult task. By the time she'd locked the doors behind them all, Hank's pain pills had kicked in and Hank was out like a light.

That first hour alone, Leighanna had used her time wisely, gathering all the supplies she thought she might need during the night. Water, ice stored in a small cooler, an alarm clock, a shallow bowl and a handful of washcloths, along with the medications and the instructions the doctor had written out for her.

For the next three hours she'd kept a vigil next to the bed, waking him each hour as she'd been instructed, alternately coaxing and bullying a response from him until she was sure he hadn't slipped into a coma as the doctor had warned he might.

Those minutes in between each wakening had been miserable for Leighanna as she stared at Hank's bruised face, reliving those nightmarish minutes in the corral, knowing that she was at least partially responsible for the injuries Hank had suffered.

He was so brave, so unselfish, stepping in front of that bull to save Harley's life. Few men would have done what Hank had done for Harley, she knew that. She remembered the look in his eyes when he'd seen her standing in the open gate, the fear, the panic. It was in that split second where he lost his concentration that he was left at the bull's mercy...and it was her fault, as surely as if she'd thrown him in the path of the raging bull. It was also in that split second, when the terror was clawing its way up her throat in a scream, that she'd known that what she felt for him wasn't platonic. Her feelings were seeded much more deeply than that.

Catching her lower lip between her teeth to stop the tears that spurted to her eyes, she leaned, catching a wisp of hair from his forehead. Tenderly she combed it back into place with her fingertips. "Oh, Hank, please be okay," she whispered. "I—" she caught herself before uttering the words of love that trembled on her lips.

Hank awakened, feeling as if someone were holding a branding iron to his side. Struggling against the darkness that sucked at him, he forced his eyes open a slit and saw a pair of dusty cowboy boots hitched on the foot of his bed. He opened his eyes a little wider and twisted his head slightly, just far enough to follow the line of crossed denim legs, to the man who sat slumped lazily in the chair beside his bed.

"What the hell are you doing here?" he grumped, fighting to bring Cody into focus.

Cody dropped his feet and lowered the chair to all four legs, grinning. "Nursing you."

Hank closed his eyes on a groan, remembering the accident with the bull and the trip to the hospital. He tensed when he remembered the gentle hands that had soothed him through the night. Opening one eye, he squinted at Cody suspiciously. "How long have you been here?"

"Oh, a couple of hours, I guess. Leighanna had to run over to Acres's office and sit through a briefing, discussing what all our fine mayor wants her to do for this shindig he's hell-bent on throwing. She said she wouldn't be gone long. She's planning on bringing all her stuff back here and working on it while she keeps an eye on you."

Hank eased out a breath of relief, thankful to know that it had been Leighanna's hands that had soothed him through the night and not Cody's.

Cody stood and poured water into a glass, then shook a pill from a bottle on the nightstand. "Leighanna said you were supposed to take this if you woke up." He held out the glass and the pill.

Hank shook his head, still feeling the effects of the last pain pill he'd taken. "Don't want any more of that stuff. It just makes me sleep."

Cody chuckled. "That's the idea." He gave Hank's hand a nudge. "Now bottoms up or Leighanna's gonna skin my ears for not following her instructions."

Hank frowned at his friend. "Tell you what. You help me get to the bathroom so I can take a leak, and I'll take the damn pill."

Cody puckered his lips, shaking his head slowly. "Leighanna specifically said that you aren't to get out of this bed. She left a jar right here," he said, leaning down to retrieve it, "for you to use when nature calls."

Hank narrowed an eye at Cody, letting him know what he could do with the jar. "Bathroom or no pill, which is it?"

Heaving a sigh, Cody offered an arm for support. "All right, but if you tell her I let you do this, I'll swear you're lying through your teeth."

Six

When Hank awakened again, he could tell by the slant of the sun against the apartment's only window that it was late afternoon. He could also tell that Leighanna had been busy.

A table from the bar had been moved into his apartment and situated in front of the west-facing window. A long phone line stretched from the kitchen counter where his phone was usually mounted to the table where it was now perched. Leighanna sat at the table with her back to him, speaking in a low voice to someone on the phone, obviously not wanting to disturb him.

Keeping still so as not to let her know he was awake, Hank watched her lift a weary hand to the back of her neck and rub.

"Yes, we can make arrangements to have electricity available in the field where you set up your carnival," he heard her say. She listened a moment, then said, "No problem. As long as you have everything set up by noon on the Friday before Labor Day weekend." Another pause, then, "Thanks. I'll expect to hear from you then."

With a sigh she replaced the receiver and fell back against the back of the chair, lifting her hair away from her neck, then pressing her hands upward in a spine-arching stretch. The curve of that back, the delicate stretch of those arms, did something to Hank's insides.

At that moment the alarm she'd positioned in the center of the table went off with an earsplitting ring. She dropped her arms and stretched across the table to hit the Off button. Twisting around in the chair, she turned a concerned eye to Hank...and found him watching her.

"It's okay," he murmured, his tongue still thickened by the drugs. "I'm already awake."

Leighanna was on her feet and scurrying to the side of the bed. "Do you need anything? Are you in pain?"

Unable to keep his eyes open any longer, Hank let them close. "No, I'm fine." He licked his dry lips. "A drink of water might be nice, though."

Leighanna picked up the pitcher she'd placed on the nightstand and quickly poured half a glass. Slipping a hand under his head, she lifted him and pressed the glass to his lips. He drank long and deep. "Thank you," he murmured, sinking back against the pillows.

"While we're at it," Leighanna said, "you might as well take your pills."

Hank shook his head. "Can't," he said, struggling to try to sit up. "Got to get to the bar."

Leighanna pressed a hand against his chest. "Don't worry about the bar. We're taking care of everything."

Too weak to argue, Hank sank back against the pillow. "Who's 'we'?" he asked, squinting to keep her in focus.

"Harley is tending the bar, Mary Claire is manning the grill, and Stephie and Jimmy are going to help me serve and clear the tables."

Hank closed his eyes, his lips curving in a wobbly smile. "Takes that many to replace me, huh?"

Leighanna chuckled. "Yes, that many." She took the bottles and shook out the required pills before replacing the tops again. "Here," she said, taking his hand in hers and pressing the pills against his palm.

Though his eyes remained closed, a soft smile tugged at one corner of his mouth. "What do I get for taking them?"

"A headache and an infection if you don't," she replied, dryly.

"But shouldn't I get some kind of reward for being a good patient?"

"Like what?" she said, smiling at his boyishness in spite of her weariness.

He sighed. "A kiss would be nice."

Chuckling, she gave his hand a nudge, relieved that he felt well enough to tease her. "Take the pill and we'll see."

Dutifully, Hank lifted his head, popped the pills into his mouth and grinned crookedly at Leighanna over the rim of the glass before washing the pills down with water.

As soon as she removed the glass, he settled back against his pillows, closed his eyes and puckered up.

Without hesitation, Leighanna leaned over and pressed her mouth to his. All the fear, all the worry she'd carried for the past few hours drained from her as his lips moved on hers. He might be hurt and he might be half out of his mind with drugs, but he still had the power to weaken her knees with something as simple as a kiss. When at last she drew away, Hank sighed again.

He opened his eyes and looked at her. "You know what I hate most about these pills?" he asked.

"What?"

"They make me sleepy."

Leighanna laughed softly, leaning close to wipe a smear of lipstick from his lips. "That's what they're supposed to do."

"I know," he said on a sigh heavy with regret. "But at the moment, there's something I'd a lot rather do than sleep."

Leighanna turned off the lights in the bar and made her way back to the apartment in the darkness, yawning. She was exhausted. After two days without sleep and with putting in a full day of work at two jobs, she was bone dead tired.

She quietly opened the door to the apartment, then tiptoed to the side of the bed. The lamp was on, and in its glow she could see that Hank slept peacefully. Sitting down on the chair beside the bed, she eased her tennis shoes off her feet and bit back a moan of relief. After checking the clock, she noted that she had another thirty minutes before it was time to wake Hank and give him his medication.

I'll just close my eyes for a minute, she told herself, and rested her forehead against her hands on the bed next to Hank.

When the alarm went off thirty minutes later, it was Hank who hit the Off button. Leighanna never moved so much as a muscle. The sight of her keeping vigil—even if she was sleeping—made Hank's heart go soft. He'd never had anyone watch over him, even as a child. The idea that Leighanna would, touched him like nothing in his life ever had before.

Pressing his hand to his stitches to keep from tearing his wound open, he shifted, turning on his side so that he could see her better. Carefully, he smoothed her hair away from her face. The toll of caring for him while holding down two jobs was evident in the dark circles beneath her eyes, in the depth of her sleep. She'd spent two nights at the side of his bed caring for him, or so he'd been told. Personally, he didn't remember much about the past forty-eight hours, though he did remember the touch of gentle hands and a soft, feminine voice that pulled him from his sleep, then soothed him back into it again.

Knowing how uncomfortable she must be, sleeping like that slumped against the side of the bed, Hank shook out his pills and quickly gulped them down with water, then turned and gave Leighanna a gentle nudge.

"Leighanna," he whispered, lowering his face close to her ear.

"Hmm?"

"Come on, sweetheart," he urged gently, slipping her hand from beneath her head and giving it a gentle tug. "Come on up here." He scooted over, making room for her on the bed, while keeping up the gentle pressure on her hand.

More asleep than awake, she let him guide her onto the bed, then immediately curled up into a ball at his side, fitting her hands beneath her cheek.

Unable to resist, Hank moved closer, laying his head next to hers, and rested his arm in the gentle curve of her waist.

Sighing, he closed his eyes and slept.

Leighanna awakened slowly to the feel of warm, moist breath blowing rhythmically against her cheek and the weight of an arm draped loosely at her waist. She opened her eyes to find Hank watching her.

"Good morning," she said sleepily.

"It is that," he replied, a slow grin curving at his mouth. "Did you sleep well?"

"Yes, I—" Suddenly her eyes flipped wide as she gained full consciousness. Panicked, she tried to sit up, but Hank kept her in place with the weight of his arm.

"Your medicine," she cried, managing to twist around far enough to glance at the clock. "I didn't hear the alarm! You've got to—"

"Relax," he soothed. "I've already taken it."

"You did?" she asked, twisting back around to look at him.

"Yep, I did."

Relieved to know that she hadn't truly failed in her

duties, that Hank had followed the doctor's instructions, she dropped her head on the pillow and let out a long sigh of relief.

And realized where she was.

Her eyes rounded as she peered at Hank, suddenly aware that she wasn't on the chair, but in the bed with Hank. "What am I doing up here?" she asked in a shocked whisper as she inched away from him.

Chuckling, he tightened his arm around her. "Don't worry," he soothed. "You only slept." He drew her next to him again, then winced slightly at the strain the movement placed on his cracked ribs.

"Oh, Hank," she said, popping up. "Did you hurt yourself?"

"Just a little," he said, and placed a hand on her cheek, forcing her head to the pillow next to his. "Want to kiss it and make it better?"

Relieved that he hadn't done any damage to his wounds, Leighanna laughed at the teasing in his voice. "You can't be hurting that much if you've got kissing on your mind."

His eyes warmed, taking on that seductive hue. "Oh, I'm hurting alright. And you know what hurts the most?"

Unable to resist touching him, she smoothed a stray lock of hair from his forehead. "What?"

"The fact that I've finally got you where I want you and I'm too banged up to do a damn thing about it."

Hank's apartment had taken on the look of a war zone. Sticky notes were stuck to every available surface, a huge map of Temptation's downtown area was tacked to the wall with different colored pins, representing God knew what, poked at strategic points across its surface. In the center of it all, Leighanna sat at the table she'd set up—a pencil stuck in the roll of hair she'd piled on her head, and the phone receiver pressed to her ear—while she flipped through the organized chaos in front of her.

From his spot on the bed, Hank had a bird's-eye view of all the goings-on, even if it was a little blurred by the medication he'd been taking. He had to give Leighanna credit, he thought with a shake of his head. The woman was an organizational whirlwind. In just three days, she'd taken all of Mayor Acres's grandiose plans for the festival and made them a reality, at least on paper. Committees had been set up, a carnival arranged and a variety of activities planned to take place throughout the downtown area during the two-day event.

"Yes," she said into the receiver, "I have that information right here." She quickly selected a card from those fanned on the corner of the desk and read the information to the party on the other end of the line.

He watched as she replaced the phone. "How can you make sense of all this stuff?" he asked with an expansive wave of his hand.

Leighanna turned to him, smiling. "Because I know exactly where everything is." She stood and walked to the side of the bed, reaching, as was her habit, to smooth a hand across his forehead, then drawing it tenderly down the side of his face. Touching him had become so natural over the past few days that she didn't give a thought to the intimacy it suggested. "How are you feeling?"

"Like a caged lion," he grumped. "I want out of this bed."

Leighanna tipped her head in sympathy. "I know you're miserable, but by tomorrow you should be strong enough to be up and around for a little while." She glanced toward the dresser, the only other substantial piece of furniture in the room. "Would you like me to turn on the television?"

Hank snorted in disgust. "There's nothing on but soaps and those damn ridiculous talk shows."

Chuckling, Leighanna took his hand in hers and squeezed. "Well, what can I do to help you pass the time?"

Hank glanced at her, arching a brow. "I could think of a thing or two."

After spending three days with him, Leighanna had grown accustomed to his constant teasing and only laughed. "I swear, you have a one-track mind."

"Yeah," he said, pulling her down beside him. "But at least I'm consistent."

Sighing, Leighanna settled in the crook of his arm, stretching her legs out beside his. "You are that."

He placed a finger beneath her chin and angled her face to his. His gaze moved over her face as he slowly traced the line of her jaw. "Has anyone ever told you how beautiful you are?"

Leighanna's cheeks burned in embarrassment, but she was secretly pleased by his compliment. "You're only saying that because I'm the only woman you've seen in the past three days."

"No. It's the truth." He twisted slightly until he faced her. "But the hell of it is, you're beautiful inside and out. I've never met a woman like you before."

"Hank, that's awfully sweet, but—"

"Shh," he said, pressing a finger at her lips. "Don't argue, just say thanks."

Smiling, she pulled his finger away. "Thanks."

He tucked his hands beneath his head and settled next to her, smiling, too. "Wanna mess around?"

Leighanna chuckled. "You wish."

He sighed, closing his eyes. "Yeah, I do."

Thinking he was going back to sleep, she started to rise, but he pressed an arm at her waist, stopping her. She twisted around to look at him, but his eyes remained closed. "Don't go just yet," he murmured.

"But you need to rest."

He tightened his arm around her, pulling her back down beside him. "So do you."

She did nap, but not nearly as long as Hank. When she awakened, he was still curled at her side, his arm slung around her waist, their heads resting on the same pillow. Unable to resist touching him, she smoothed a lock of hair from his forehead and gently finger combed it back into place. He's getting to you, she warned herself. His vulnerability due to his injuries, his constant teasing when they both knew he didn't have the strength to follow through, his care for her own welfare when he'd insisted that she rest with him the night before and again today.

One more day, she remembered with more than a little regret. One more day and Hank would be up and around and strong enough to care for himself. One more day and she'd be spending her nights at Mary Claire's again. The thought saddened her.

Easing from beneath his arm, she allowed herself one last look at his handsome face, at the muscled strength of his bare chest exposed above the sheet that covered him. Sighing, she turned away and headed back to her makeshift desk and the work that awaited her.

In the darkness Hank lay on what he'd come to think of as his prison—his bed—and listened to Leigh-anna's movements coming from the other side of the bathroom door. The sound of the shower running, the whisk of clothes as she peeled them over her head. The muffled click of the shower door as she closed it behind her. Her soft sigh of contentment as she stepped beneath the water. He could imagine her there with the water sluicing over her upturned face and streaming down between her small, taut breasts. He could almost smell the soap as she lathered it over her body.

The thoughts were so vivid, the images they drew so clear, he felt his groin tighten with desire. He wanted her, had wanted her from the first day he'd laid eyes on her. But that wanting had taken on an urgency over the last few days. Sighing, he folded his hands beneath his head. Tonight, he told himself. He'd thought about it all day and, stitches and cracked ribs or not, tonight he would make her his.

The water shut off and Hank tensed, listening as he monitored her movements. When the bathroom door at last opened, he quickly laced his hands over his chest and closed his eyes, feigning sleep. He heard her soft footsteps, smelled that utterly feminine fragrance that was so much a part of her as she drew near the bed. Then he felt the silkiness of her touch as she gently laid a hand against his forehead. He'd grown used to her touch, missed it when she wasn't near.

Moving slowly so as not to startle her, he took her hand in his and drew it to his lips. He heard her soft gasp when his lips met the sensitive center of her palm, and he smiled.

Her soft laugh wafted to him through the darkness. "I thought you were asleep," she teased gently.

"I was." He drew her to sit beside him on the bed and wished he had more than moonlight, so that he could fully see her face. "But I woke up when I heard you in the bathroom."

"And I was trying so hard to be quiet. I'm sorry."

"I'm not."

Nerves danced to life beneath her skin at the huskiness in his voice. "You're not?"

"No."

A sigh shuddered out of her as he gently guided her to lie down beside him.

"What's all this?" he asked, angling so that he could catch the folds of her silk nightgown between his fingers.

"I got tired of sleeping in my clothes. I had Mary Claire bring me a few things so that I could change."

"Ummm." He brought the fabric to his cheek and rubbed. "Soft," he murmured appreciatively. He laid a hand against the thigh he'd exposed beneath the silk fabric. "But not as soft as you."

Leighanna's breath snagged in her chest. His fingers skimmed her thigh, gradually moving higher, and she was sure she would suffocate beneath the sensations that spiraled through her and knotted her lungs. His other hand moved to mold her face.

"Leighanna," he murmured, his breath blowing warm at her lips. "I want to make love to you."

His statement didn't shock Leighanna, nor did it frighten her, for she wanted the same thing. Had wanted it for days now. "But Hank, your stitches, your ribs," she reminded him gently.

His touch on her heated flesh never once wavered. "I think I can manage if we're creative."

Trembling now, Leighanna tried to imagine what he meant by creative. But then his lips met hers, and her mind went blank, and she gave herself up to the heat that flamed to life between them. His hand slipped higher, dragging her nightgown up her legs, then higher still, until it was twisted at her waist. His hand drifted to the mound of her femininity and with a moan of pleasure, he cupped her, molding her with his strong hand.

His fingers stroked, lighting fires between her legs that caught and flamed upward, spreading throughout her abdomen. She arched against him, hungry for more than just his touch.

"Leighanna, beautiful Leighanna," he murmured, drawing back to look at her face in the soft moonlight. "I want to please you. Tell me how."

"I...I don't know," she whispered desperately,

then gasped when his finger slipped between the velvet folds and found the center of her core.

"Then I'll show you."

Releasing his hold on her, he caught her nightgown in his hands, pulled it over her head and tossed it to the floor. Before she could draw the first ragged breath, his fingers found her again in the darkness and he lowered his face to her breasts. Taking a nipple between his teeth, he suckled, slowly drawing her in, while the stubble of his beard rasped against her bare flesh. His tongue teased, his fingers probed and Leighanna was sure that she would die of frustration unless she could touch him, as well.

Reaching out, she found his chest and moaned softly in sympathy when her fingers grazed the strip of gauze that covered his wound and the wide strips of tape that bound his ribs. Careful not to hurt him, she eased past it, sliding her hand in a downward journey, enjoying the feel of the coarse hair that veed below his navel and gasping when her hands bumped against his arousal. Timidly she touched him. He shifted, giving her better access and moaned his pleasure against her breasts when her fingers instinctively wrapped around his hardness.

"Don't be shy, Leighanna," he murmured against her heated skin. "Do whatever feels natural."

Boldly she let her hand slide down until her knuckles grazed the coarse hair nesting at the base of his staff. The movement incited her as much as it did Hank, and she repeated the motion again and again, until they were both breathless.

"Leighanna," he groaned, shifting again until his body was flush against hers. "You're killing me."

Emboldened by his words, she sought his mouth, mimicking with her tongue the movements of her hands on him until he tore his mouth from hers, gasping. He'd planned this all day, lying in his bed, dreaming of a slow seduction. But now with her there, lying naked next to him on his bed, with her clever hands playing over his swollen staff, he knew he'd never last. "I want you now," he said fiercely. "Now!"

Leighanna knew a moment of uncertainty. Not that she didn't want him, too, but she wasn't at all sure how they could proceed without hurting him. She lifted her gaze, seeking his in the moonlight. "But how?"

In answer, he caught her by the waist and turned her, fitting her buttocks tight against his groin, spoon fashion. With his lips at her ear, murmuring to her, he guided her until his manhood pressed at the moist folds of her femininity. Gathering her in his arms and holding her tight against him, he pressed a hand at her abdomen and eased inside.

She gasped at the first feel of him and arched against him, unconsciously drawing him further inside. "That's right, baby," he murmured against her ear. "That's the way." Then he began to move against her, slowly at first, but gradually increasing the speed and the rhythm, guiding her with his body until she raced along with him.

The heat increased, blinding Leighanna to everything but the feel of him inside her. Colors pressed against her closed lids, flashing sharper and sharper, gathering into a tight ball until they exploded into shattering white. Crying out his name, she arched hard against him, thrusting her hips in the curve of his groin...then bonelessly melted against him, absorbing the shudders of release that tore through him, as well.

His hand came around to cup her breasts and his nose nuzzled at the smooth column of her neck. Never in her life had Leighanna felt so utterly weak, yet so sated.

"Oh, Hank," she whispered, covering his hand with her own. "I never knew it would be like this."

His breath moved her hair in a sigh. "Neither did I," he murmured. Gathering her even closer, he said again, "Neither did I."

Thursday afternoon Leighanna glanced up from her work at the grill to see Hank leaning against the door frame, watching her. For the first time since his accident, he was standing upright and fully dressed.

Catching up a dishcloth, she quickly dried her hands, smiling as she crossed to him. "Just look at you," she teased, carrying a hand to his cheek. "You've even shaved."

A grin chipped at one corner of Hank's mouth as he covered her hand with his own. "For you," he murmured. "I was afraid if I rubbed you raw with my stubble, you wouldn't let me near you."

She laughed softly, smoothing her hand down his cleanly shaven jaw. "Oh, I don't know. There's something to be said for a man with a beard."

"Then I'll grow it back," he promised, lowering his face toward hers.

Leighanna stretched to her tiptoes to accommodate him, wondering how, with the night they'd spent, she could thirst for him so. But the touch of his lips on hers reminded her of just exactly how. Wrapping her arms around his neck, she gave herself up to the heat that pulled at her.

The front door banged open. "Hey, you two! Cut that out. There are innocent children approaching."

With her arms still looped around Hank's neck, Leighanna tore her mouth from Hank's and turned to see Harley, standing just inside the entrance to the bar and wearing a broad smile. Her cheeks burning in embarrassment, she quickly dropped her arms and tugged her shirt back in place just as Mary Claire and her children stepped around Harley.

At the shocked look on Mary Claire's face, Leighanna struggled to think of an explanation. "We were just—"

"Kissing," Hank finished for her, and slipped an arm around her shoulders, not in the least embarrassed to be caught in what he considered such a natural act. "Don't tell me these kids have never seen anyone kiss before."

Stephie looked up at Harley, her future stepfather, and beamed a smile. "'Course we have. Harley kisses Mama all the time."

"Gross," Jimmy muttered, and headed for the jukebox.

Hank tossed back his head and laughed. "The day'll come," he warned, "when you'll be wanting to kiss a girl."

Jimmy made a gagging sound and slipped a quarter

into the jukebox. "I'd rather kiss a pig," he muttered, studying the selections.

"You'd have to catch it first," Stephie sassed as she skipped across the room to join her brother. Before Jimmy could stop her, she punched in a number.

The slow, seductive thrum of guitars wafted across the room before Clay Walker added his voice to the music, singing, "Hypnotize the Moon."

Jimmy rolled his eyes. "Jeez, Stephie. Why'd you pick that sappy song? You know that's Mama's and Harley's favorite?" Without waiting for a reply, he stuffed his hands in his pockets and trudged off with Stephie trailing close behind. The back door slammed once, then quickly opened and slammed again as Stephie kept up a fast pursuit.

A man accustomed to taking advantage of an opportunity when it presented itself, Harley caught Mary Claire's hand in his. "How about a dance?"

Smiling lovingly up at him, she stepped into his waiting arms. She closed her eyes as she rested her head in the crook of his neck, losing herself in the music and the lyrics as he slowly danced her around the room.

On a wistful sigh, Leighanna folded her arms at her breasts and watched them. Seeing the dreaminess in her expression, Hank shifted, turning her into his arms. "Do you dance?" he asked softly.

Immediately, she tensed and lifted her gaze to his. "Yes, but I've never danced to Country music. I—"

Before she could refuse him, Hank guided her arm around his waist and caught her other hand up in his.

"It's not that much different," he instructed gently. "Just follow my lead."

And she did, just as she'd done the night before when he'd led her in an entirely different dance. She let him draw her close until the length of her body pressed close against his, the pressure of his thigh squeezed between her legs. Laying her head against his chest, she felt the familiar thud of his heart against her cheek and knew that she'd follow him anywhere. He danced her around the perimeter of the long, narrow room, adroitly dodging tables and occasionally Harley and Mary Claire's blended forms while Clay Walker seduced them all with the words of his song.

Hank tipped her face to his without missing a step. "You're like her, you know," he said, his voice husky as he gazed down at her.

"Who?" Leighanna murmured, lost in the depths of those dark brown eyes that looked so deeply into her own.

"The lady in the song. You, too, can charm the stars and hypnotize the moon just by walking into a room."

And Leighanna lost a little more of her heart to him.

Seven

The bar had been unusually crowded for a Thursday night, a result of a rodeo being held in nearby Bandera. Though only a few customers remained, Leighanna worried about Hank holding up to the unaccustomed pace after lying flat on his back for the past three days.

Mary Claire had already gone home, taking the children with her, but, thankfully, Harley had insisted on staying until closing time, obviously not wanting Hank to overdo things on his first day back at work. For that Leighanna would always be grateful, because she knew that without Harley there, Hank would have insisted on carrying his share of the workload and probably ended up suffering a relapse.

As she glanced Hank's way again, she noticed that his face seemed a little more pale that it had before.

Picking up the tray of dirty glasses she'd just gathered, she headed his way, determined to make him go to his apartment and rest.

Setting the tray on the corner of the bar, she moved to stand beside him. Without a thought to the customers still in the bar who might be watching, she lifted a hand to his cheek and angled his face to hers. Her heart nearly broke at the sight of the fine lines of weariness that fanned from the corners of his eyes.

"Hank, darling," she murmured in concern. "You've done enough for one night. You need to be in bed."

His smile softened as he hitched a hip against the counter and turned to her, closing his hand over hers. "Only if you're there with me."

Leighanna huffed out a breath, then laughed, shaking her head. "If I thought you'd truly rest, I would."

"Hank Braden!" a woman's voice called. "Is it true what I've heard, that you've taken up bullfighting?"

Leighanna thought she felt Hank's fingers tense over hers, but then his hand was gone and he was turning away.

"Well, hello, Betty Jo," he said, and planted his hands on the bar. "What are you doing in our part of the world?"

Betty Jo? Leighanna's heart stopped, then kicked against her ribs as she recalled why the name sounded familiar. The barrel racer from Marble Falls, whom the men in the bar had teased Hank about when Leighanna had first started working at The End of the Road.

Swallowing hard, she turned to look at the woman

standing just inside the entrance to the bar. A mane of wild, red hair corkscrewed from beneath a wide-rimmed black hat, and a breast-enhancing vest showed a generous view of cleavage, while she stood with her hands fisted on hips cemented beneath skin-tight jeans. Her eyes fixed on Hank, a huge smile on her face, Betty Jo headed for the bar.

"Rode barrels over at Bandera tonight," she said, her hips rocking suggestively with every step she took. "Thought I'd stop in here before I headed my trailer for home and see if you might need some cheering up after the run-in you had with the bull."

When she came to a stop opposite Hank, she leaned across the bar, offering an even more alarming view of her breasts. With a sultry smile, she took his cheeks between her hands, drew his face slowly to hers and covered his mouth with her full lips.

Sucking in a shocked breath, Leighanna took a step back, then another, and bumped into Harley who stood at the grill, watching, too. Whirling, she braced her hands on his arms to keep from stumbling and lifted her horrified gaze to his. In his eyes she saw not the shock that she felt, but only pity. Her cheeks flamed in embarrassment as she remembered that only hours before, Harley had caught Hank kissing her. Whirling again, she ran for the kitchen.

Once there, she pressed her palms to her hot face, willing away the tears that threatened. She wouldn't cry, she told herself fiercely. She'd known what Hank was like. She'd heard the rumors about his reputation, had even experienced his captivating charm firsthand. He was a rounder, a man who thought nothing of drifting from one woman to another without a thought to the one he left behind. Unfortunately, during the days alone with him in his apartment, she'd forgotten that well-known fact and allowed herself to fall prey to his seductive tactics.

But not any longer, she vowed.

Forcing herself into action, she stabbed the stopper into the sink and turned on the water, squeezing a liberal dose of dishwashing liquid beneath its spray. Grabbing a trayful of dirty glasses, she propped it on the edge of the sink and started sinking glasses beneath the growing mountain of bubbles.

By the time she'd washed her way through three trays of dirty dishes, she'd calmed somewhat and felt more in control of her emotions. At least she knew she wouldn't cry.

"Leighanna?"

She heard Hank's voice behind her, but refused to turn around. "Yes?"

"Are you okay?"

She rammed the dishrag into a beer mug and swirled furiously, but forced a tone of indifference in her reply. "Why shouldn't I be?"

Hank noted the tenseness in her shoulders, the angry jabbing of her arms into the dishwater. He knew she was angry, and knew what had brought on the mood, but didn't have a clue what to do or say to make things better between them. Damn Betty Jo, he cursed silently. Why'd she have to show up tonight of all nights?

"Leighanna, Betty Jo is—"

"A very striking woman, isn't she?" Leighanna finished for him.

Hank stepped up behind her and laid a hand on her shoulder. "Not as pretty as you," he murmured, dipping his lips to her neck.

Leighanna lifted her shoulder to shrug off the meaningless caress. "And what a figure!" she continued as if he hadn't spoken, then stretched to place the mug on the drain board. "Did you get a load of those breasts? I remember you saying you preferred a woman with large breasts. I'd say she's just about the perfect size for you."

"Leighanna..."

She dragged the stopper from the sink and snatched up the towel to dry her hands. Hoping to escape him before she humiliated herself further by allowing him to see her cry, she brushed past him. "If you'll excuse me," she said. "I need to mop the floor."

Hank caught her before she'd taken a full step. Whirling her around, he clamped his hands on her shoulders, and, using his thumbs beneath her chin, forced her face to his.

He saw the glimmer of tears and knew he'd hurt her. "Leighanna, I'm sorry."

"Sorry?" she repeated, forcing a laugh. "Whatever for?" Ducking beneath his arms, she grabbed for the mop bucket.

Angry now himself, Hank snatched it from her hands. "For God's sake, Leighanna, the floor can wait until tomorrow."

"Fine," she said, and headed for his apartment

door. "I'll just get my things and get out of your way."

Hank stared at her back, panic tightening his chest. With a frustrated growl, he tossed aside the bucket and stomped after her into the apartment. "Where do you think you're going?"

She snatched her nightgown from the bedpost where she'd tossed it earlier that morning and stuffed it into a bag, trying her best to avoid his gaze. "Mary Claire's. There's no reason for me to spend the night any longer. You're more than capable of taking care of yourself."

"But, Leighanna, I want you to stay."

Angry that he would think she was that easy, that free with her affection, she whirled, her eyes blazing. "Three's a crowd, Hank."

"If you're talking about Betty Jo," he said hesitantly, "she's gone."

Leighanna tore her gaze from his and marched to the bathroom, raking her toiletries from the countertop and into the bag. "Well, I'm sure that if you feel the need for more *company,* there are other women that you can call."

Hank grabbed her as she brushed past him again and spun her around, sinking his fingers into her shoulders. He gave her a hard shake. "What is wrong with you? There isn't anyone else that I want to call. I want you!"

Leighanna pressed her hands over her ears, unwilling to listen to his lies. The tears that had threatened broke through, streaming down her cheeks.

At the sight of them, Hank hauled her into his arms,

but before he could offer any comfort, Leighanna was bracing her hands against his chest and shoving for all she was worth.

"No!" she cried, backing away from him as she dragged her hands to her eyes. Before she could disgrace herself any more, she snatched up her bag and all but ran for the door.

Leighanna sat at the kitchen table with her hands pressed against her face, wishing with all her heart that she'd never been born.

"I hate him," she mumbled against her fingers. "I hate him, I hate him, I hate him."

"You don't mean that," Mary Claire scolded. "You're just upset right now."

Leighanna tore her hands from her face and slammed them into fists against the top of the table, making Mary Claire jump. "You're darn right I'm upset," she cried as she pushed herself from the chair to pace Mary Claire's kitchen. "You should have seen her. She had these jeans that were so tight I'm sure she had to lie down on the bed just to get them zipped. And her boobs," she raged on, holding out her hands a good foot in front of her chest. "They stuck out to here and you *know* how much Hank likes boobs!"

Mary Claire bit back a smile. "No, I'm afraid I don't."

Leighanna whirled on her. "Well, he does. Trust me." She paced away again, tossing her hands in the air. "And then she kisses him! Right there in front of God and everybody, she lays this lip-locker on him that had his eyes bulging out of his head and smoke coming out his ears!''

Mary Claire had already heard this story, or at least she'd heard Harley's version of the story, and was having difficulty making the tales mesh. ''And this made you angry?''

Leighanna spun to look at Mary Claire, her eyes sparking in righteous indignation. ''Well, of course it made me angry! Wouldn't it you?''

''That would depend on how I felt about the man being kissed.''

Leighanna felt heat crawl up her neck, and she quickly turned, pacing away again.

''You're in love with him, aren't you?''

Leighanna stumbled to a stop, her spine arching as if she'd just suffered a blow there. Slowly, her shoulders slumped in defeat. ''Yes,'' she murmured pitifully. ''And I hate him.''

Mary Claire nodded sagely, her heart going out to her friend. ''The two emotions can sometimes be confused.''

Leighanna crossed back to the table and dropped onto the chair opposite Mary Claire, fresh tears budding in her eyes. ''What am I going to do?'' she moaned.

''What do you want to do?''

Leighanna wearily wagged her head. ''I don't know,'' she said, sniffling. ''He wanted me to stay with him, but I couldn't, not after what he did.''

''And what exactly did he do?''

Leighanna lifted her head, looking at Mary Claire in amazement. ''Well, he kissed her, that's what!''

"Did he kiss her, or did she kiss him?"

Leighanna frowned, not liking the direction of Mary Claire's gentle probing. "Well, he certainly didn't put up much of a fight," she muttered defensively.

"And neither did you," Mary Claire replied, looking at Leighanna from beneath an arched brow. Her expression softened at the stricken look on Leighanna's face. Taking her friend's hand in hers, Mary Claire sought to soothe. "It would be foolish to think that Hank didn't have a life before he met you. And even more foolish to let his past stand between you and what you so obviously want."

The silence was painful, pricking at the back of Leighanna's neck and making her nerves burn in frustration. She'd tried to fill it over the past few days by smiling and chatting with the customers that drifted in and out of The End of the Road, but the silence was still there, stretching between herself and Hank like a wire strung too tightly.

Even when away from Hank and working at Mayor Acres's office she felt the oppressive silence. She'd transferred all her things from Hank's apartment back to the mayor's office, but every time she looked at them, she was reminded of him and his apartment and the hours they'd spent together while she'd simultaneously nursed him and planned the festival. Though it had been a strain on her physically, she'd enjoyed caring for him, laughing with him, loving him, and would give anything to be able to return to those days when everything was so easy between them, so relaxed.

Wearily she rubbed a hand across the back of her neck. She hadn't slept a total of four hours since the night Betty Jo had appeared at the bar. And with the exhausting schedule she was maintaining, working for both Hank and the mayor, the lack of sleep was taking its toll.

Sighing, she stripped off her apron and retrieved her purse from beneath the bar. She stole a glance at Hank where he stood before the cash register, calmly counting the night's proceeds. Emotion wedged in her throat at the mere sight of him, nearly choking her.

Had Mary Claire been right, she wondered, when she'd suggested that Leighanna should have put up a fight for Hank?

No, she told herself and gave herself a hard shake. She'd done the right thing in leaving. She refused to be just another notch on his bedpost.

"I'm leaving," she said, hoping that he'd at least look her way.

But Hank never so much as lifted his head. He merely grunted his acknowledgment and went on with his counting.

Though he remained behind the bar, his gaze fixed on the money spread before him, Hank followed the sound of Leighanna's departure: the squeak of her tennis shoes on the freshly mopped floor, the click of the door handle as she twisted it open and the soft shoosh of wind that swept inside before she stepped through and closed the door behind her again.

"Damn!" he muttered, tossing the money aside. "Damn, damn, double damn, hell!"

He raked his fingers through his hair, turning away

from the sight of her retreating figure. He couldn't stand much more of this silence. The woman was slowly driving him nuts! She sashayed around the bar, laughing and talking with his customers, but she treated him as if he wasn't even there. When she did bother to address him, it was with a coolness that bordered on disdain. He had retaliated with the same, refusing to knuckle under to what he considered her female coercive tactics.

And what in the hell had he done to deserve her silent snubbing, anyway? Nothing! he told himself. Absolutely nothing! Was it his fault that Betty Jo had decided to pay him a visit? Hell, no! And was it his fault that Betty Jo had plastered herself all over him? Absolutely not! He'd been an innocent victim, trapped between a woman with whom he'd enjoyed a short, if memorable, fling and the woman who currently had his heart caught in a wringer.

He paused, listening, waiting for the sound of that clunker of Leighanna's to spark to life, but heard nothing but silence. Silence again, he thought with a growl of irritation. And he was damn sick and tired of the silence. Striding to the door, he peered through the glass. In the corner of the parking lot, Leighanna stood at the front of her car, spotlighted by the security light, struggling to lift its hood.

"What in the—" He jerked open the door and marched across the parking lot, grinding gravel beneath his boots with each angry step.

"What in the hell do you think you're doing?"

Leighanna lifted her head, wearily pushing her blond hair from her face as she turned to look at him.

He'd finally spoken to her, but, naturally, it was only to curse her. "It won't start," she said miserably, then bent her head over the open hood again.

Hank huffed an impatient breath, then moved closer to look over her shoulder. He shook his head at the grimy condition of the engine and the tangle of baling wire that seemed to hold everything in place. "No wonder," he muttered in disgust. "When was the last time you had this hunk of junk worked on?"

When Roger fleeced me of my money when he took it to have the transmission repaired, Leighanna remembered morosely. But she wouldn't tell Hank that. She was sure he already considered her a fool, after the way she'd reacted to Betty Jo, and she wasn't about to prove him right. "About a month before I moved here," she said instead.

Hank grunted, shouldering her out of his way. "Give it another try," he ordered gruffly as he bent his head over the engine.

Reluctantly Leighanna slipped behind the wheel and turned the key. *Waaaa...waaa...waaa.* "Come on," she urged, pumping the accelerator, "please start."

But in spite of all her prodding and Hank's tinkering under the hood, the engine refused to turn over. Biting back tears of frustration, she climbed from the car.

Hank watched her out of the corner of his eye, seeing the weary slump of her shoulders, the dark circles beneath her eyes, the glimmer of unshed tears...and his anger melted away. "Why don't you go to my apartment and put your feet up? As soon as I get it started, I'll give you a holler."

Too exhausted to argue, Leighanna turned and headed back to the bar.

Hank watched her and swore under his breath. "She's going to kill herself if she keeps up this pace," he muttered as he ducked under the hood again. "If I don't wring her pretty neck first."

Hank had known it would be a waste of his time, but he tried his damnedest to get Leighanna's car running for her again. After fooling with the cantankerous engine for over an hour, he finally admitted defeat, slammed down the hood and headed for the bar.

After locking the door behind him, he stopped in the kitchen long enough to wash the grease from his hands, then walked on to the apartment, ready to offer Leighanna a ride back to Mary Claire's.

But when he opened the door and found her curled on his bed asleep, he didn't have the heart to wake her. Knowing full well that she'd probably be madder than a wet hen when she awakened and found herself in his bed, he left her there and went into the bathroom, closing the door softly behind him. He stripped off his clothes, then stepped inside the shower and twisted on the faucet, letting the cold beads of water sting his face. With a shiver he adjusted the temperature to a warmer setting, then moved it right back, deciding a cold shower might be what he needed after all.

When he finally climbed into bed beside her, Leighanna rolled, curling against his chest in her sleep. With a sigh Hank hooked an arm at her waist and pulled her close.

* * *

"Leighanna? Sweetheart, wake up. It's time to go to work."

Leighanna fought the intrusion to her sleep and dragged her pillow over her head. "Go away," she mumbled.

Hank chuckled and lifted the edge of the pillow just high enough to see her face. "Can't. Not until you're on your feet and alert."

Leighanna swatted at his hand, but refused to open her eyes. "Leave me alone," she grumbled.

Hunkering down beside the bed, Hank raised the pillow higher and waved a steaming cup of coffee beneath her nose. She lifted her head, though her eyes remained closed, and sniffed.

"Is that coffee I smell?"

Chuckling, Hank kept the cup just out of reach. "Open your eyes and see for yourself."

Though it was an effort, Leighanna forced her lids open, squinting against the sunshine streaming into the room. Moaning, she reached for the cup and grasped it between her palms. "Thank you," she murmured before taking the first greedy sip. Hiking herself up to a sitting position, she eased back against the headboard, gradually taking in her surroundings. "I take it I fell asleep," she said with a self-conscious glance at her wrinkled clothes.

Hank dropped down on the foot of the bed. "Passed out would be more like it."

She lifted her gaze to his, remembering her reason for being in his apartment. "My car?"

He snorted. "What car?" Then waved away her

look of concern. "Don't worry, I've already called Mitch. He's on his way over to tow it to his garage."

Her eyes widened in alarm as she lurched to a sitting position. "But I've got to go to work at the mayor's office!"

Hank deftly snagged the coffee cup before she succeeded in spilling the hot liquid all over herself. "Don't worry. I'll take you."

Hank sat parked at the curb in front of the mayor's office with a picnic basket resting on the seat beside him. Nervously he drummed his fingers against the steering wheel while he waited for Leighanna to appear.

He'd never taken a woman on a picnic before, which in itself was a little daunting. The fact that Leighanna knew nothing of his plans and might very well refuse to go with him only added to his nervous state.

But Hank was determined to make things right between them. When he'd driven her to work earlier that morning, the atmosphere had been a little strained. *A little strained,* he reflected, choking back a laugh. That was an understatement. She hadn't said more than two words to him during the drive to Mary Claire's, where she'd quickly showered and changed clothes and mumbled only a quick "thank you" before she'd leapt from his truck and hauled ass into Acres's office like the devil himself was chasing her. And that bugged Hank enough to want to do something about it.

The whole picnic setup screamed of courting, and truth be known, Hank had never courted a woman in his life, had never felt the need to do so. In the past women had flocked to him, and he'd never had to put forth much effort to pursue one. Not that he was pursuing this one now, he told himself. He just wanted to set things right between them again.

At least he would if she ever showed her face beyond Acres's door. He glanced at the clock on the dash. The woman had to eat sometime, he told himself in growing frustration. He'd give her another five minutes and if she didn't appear, he'd—

At that moment the door to the mayor's office opened and Leighanna stepped through, shoving a pair of sunglasses across the bridge of her nose. She stopped cold when she saw Hank's truck parked at the curb.

He stretched across the seat and rolled down the window. "Need a ride?" he asked.

"W-w-well, no," Leighanna stammered, wondering why he was there. "I was just going to walk over to the mercantile and grab something for lunch."

Hank pushed open the door. "No need. I've got enough here for two." He pulled the basket to his side, giving Leighanna room. When she hesitated, he dipped his head down to peer at her. "You like fried chicken, don't you?"

"Well, of course I do," she sputtered. "Everybody likes fried chicken."

"Then what are you waiting for." He patted the seat beside him. "Climb in."

Not at all sure what was going on, Leighanna climbed onto the seat and closed the door, eyeing the picnic basket suspiciously. "You cooked fried chicken?"

Hank shifted into drive and eased away from the curb. "No. Mary Claire did."

Leighanna rolled her eyes heavenward. She should have known that her friend was behind this. "So this was Mary Claire's idea," she said wryly.

Hank glanced at her, pressing a hand over his heart as if wounded. "No, it was mine. I was over at Mary Claire's with Harley, helping him fix that leaky pipe in the upstairs bath, and Mary Claire was in the kitchen frying chicken. You know how she is," he added, turning his attention back to the road. "She cooks for a damn army. She invited me to stay for lunch, but I told her, no, that I was coming over here to see if you needed a ride to lunch, and she insisted on making up this picnic basket."

Leighanna simply stared at him, unable to believe he would do something so thoughtful. "How sweet," she murmured.

Hank gave his head a quick nod. "Yep, that Mary Claire's sweet, alright."

Leighanna rolled her eyes again, shaking her head. "No, silly. I meant you."

He twisted his head around to look at her and grinned when he saw her amused smile. "No, just selfish. I'm trying real hard to get back on your good side."

The door of resistance that Leighanna had slammed between them squeaked open a bit. Wanting to take advantage of the opening he'd offered, but unable to meet his gaze, Leighanna dipped her chin. "Hank, I'm sorry. I know I overreacted when I saw...well, when I saw Betty Jo—"

Before she could finish, he stretched across the seat and caught her hand, squeezing it within his own. "You don't have anything to be sorry about. You reacted just fine." He chuckled, taking the wheel with two hands again as he turned his attention back to the road. "In fact, if the situation had been reversed, and I'd been forced to watch some strange man kissing you, I might have been tempted to rearrange the guy's face."

Leighanna bit back a smile. "The thought did cross my mind."

Hank tossed back his head and laughed. "Lucky for Betty Jo that you didn't." He cocked his head to look at her and shot her a wink. "As I recall, you've got a mean right hook."

Leighanna saw the gleam of humor in his eyes and let that door of resistance swing all the way open. "Yeah, I do, don't I?" she said smugly.

Leighanna neatly packed away the remains of their picnic, then turned and glanced at Hank, who was stretched out on the blanket beside her, his hands folded beneath his head. The desire to lie down beside him was strong, but even though he'd made the first step in repairing the rift between them, Leighanna was hesitant to seek such an intimacy.

As if sensing her uncertainty, Hank withdrew a hand from beneath his head and held it out to her, palm up in invitation. With a sigh, Leighanna placed her hand in his and let him draw her to his side. Nestling her head in the crook of his shoulder, she snuggled against him, placing a hand on his chest. Beneath her fingers, his heart beat in a steady, comforting rhythm.

She'd missed this, she thought as the heat from his body permeated hers. Missed lying beside him, missed his constant teasing, missed the comforting warmth of just being near him.

"Leighanna?"

"Hmmm," she murmured, her voice lazy with contentment.

"I've been thinking.... You know, with your car out of commission and with you working two jobs and with that long drive out to Mary Claire's and all... Well, I was thinking that it might be easier if you stayed with me for a while."

Leighanna's fingers stiffened on his chest. Slowly she lifted her head high enough to look at him. "Stay with you?" she repeated, her heart thudding against her ribs, wondering what he was offering.

Hank raised his head, meeting her gaze. "Yeah. That way I could drive you to work and save you the hassle of having to find a ride back and forth every day."

Leighanna hadn't thought anything could hurt as much as seeing Hank kiss another woman. But she was wrong. She scrambled to her feet, whirling away from him, then just as quickly back. "Just like that?" she cried, snapping her fingers. "You expect me to move in with you?"

Frowning, Hank pushed himself to an elbow, wondering what he'd said that had set her off. "Well, yeah," he mumbled uneasily. "Makes sense to me."

Leighanna fisted her hands at her sides, the implication behind his offer crystal clear in at least *her* mind. "You scratch my back, I'll scratch yours. Is that what you're thinking?"

Hank's frown deepened. "What in the hell are you talking about? I just asked you to move in with me. I don't recall saying anything about scratching anybody's back."

"Well, that's what you intend, isn't it? You taxi me around, and in exchange I'll serve your more basic needs?"

The hurt in her voice slowly registered. Without meaning to, once again Hank had screwed up royally. He pushed himself to a sitting position and dragged his hands down his face. With a sigh, he looked up at her. "No, Leighanna, that's not what I had in mind at all." Determined not to let this misunderstanding stretch into another war of strained silence, he reached out and snagged her ankle, hauling her down across his lap. Before she had a chance to react, he locked his arms tight around her, holding her in place, though she stubbornly refused to look at him.

He pressed a finger beneath her chin, forcing her gaze to his. "I've never asked a woman to move in with me before. And you're sure as hell not making this first time very easy." He heaved a frustrated sigh when she continued to glare at him. "The deal about your car was just an excuse. I want you to move into my apartment, for no other reason than I want you with me. It's as simple as that."

Though she tried to hang on to her anger, Leighanna felt it slipping away, giving way to another emotion, one that responded to the sincerity in the brown eyes that gazed down into hers. "But, Hank. It isn't simple. It's—"

"What I want," he finished for her. "And what I think you want, too." He shifted, settling her more snugly in his lap. "I've never asked a woman to live with me before, never felt the need to until now." He laid a hand at her cheek and drew his fingers downward in a slow caress. "But I'm asking you, Leighanna. Only you. Tell me that's what you want, too."

Eight

Digging his fingers through his hair, Hank paced his small apartment, silently cursing himself under his breath. He should have gone with her, he told himself. He should've never allowed her to go to Mary Claire's without him to pack her things. What if during the drive she had second thoughts and decided she didn't want to move in with him after all? What if Mary Claire convinced her that moving in with him was a mistake?

A sound outside had him spinning toward the window. Leaning to peer through the glass, he saw Leigh-anna climb down from his truck. Heaving a sigh of relief, he charged for the side door located in the bar's kitchen.

"Here, let me," he said, taking the suitcase from

Leighanna's hand. He felt the tremble in her fingers and was glad to know he wasn't the only one suffering a bad case of nerves. He glanced over her shoulder, then back at her. "Is that all?"

She smiled shyly, and the innocence in that smile touched a spot on Hank's soul he hadn't known existed. "Yes," she said softly. "Most everything I own is in storage in Houston."

He held the door, allowing her to pass in front of him. "I guess we won't be fighting over closet space, then, huh?" he teased, hoping to put them both at ease.

He set the suitcase on the floor, and Leighanna immediately reached for it. He stilled her with a touch of his hand. "That can wait," he said, his voice growing husky. He wove his fingers through hers. "First, I thought I'd give you a tour of your new home."

Leighanna glanced up at him in surprise, then laughed as she scanned the small room. "I don't think that's really necessary, do you?"

"Oh, very," he said in mock seriousness. Dragging her behind him, he crossed to the kitchen nook. "This is the kitchen," he said, then gestured to a closed door. "And that is the bathroom." He took three steps, tugging her along behind him. "And this," he said with an expansive wave of his hand, "is the bedroom."

Laughing fully now, Leighanna turned to him, grateful to him for recognizing the awkwardness she was experiencing and allaying it with his teasing. "Nice place you have here, Mr. Braden."

His lips curved in a slow grin as he wrapped his arms at her waist and pulled her to him. "I like to think so." He lowered his head to hers. Their lips touched, then touched again, and Leighanna sighed, stretching to loop her arms around his neck as that familiar warmth spread through her abdomen.

His hands dipped to cup her bottom, drawing her fully against his groin, and the swell of his manhood settled in the curve of her pelvis...and Leighanna truly felt as if she'd at last come home.

"You know, I'd really like to make love with you right now," Hank murmured, brushing the tip of her nose with his. "But I sure wouldn't want you to think that's the only reason I invited you to move in here."

Leighanna chuckled, sliding her hands from around his neck. "Since I want that, too, I could hardly accuse you of taking advantage of me."

With a provocative smile, she slid her hands from his neck, found the first button on his shirt and won a moan from him as she quickly worked it through its hole. Smiling against his lips, she slowly moved her hands down his chest, freeing each button until his chest was fully bared. Loving the feel of him beneath her inquisitive fingers, she pushed his shirt over his shoulders and smoothed her hands across the muscular expanse she'd bared, her fingers lightly grazing the tape that still wrapped his ribs. At his waist, she tugged open the snap of his jeans, then slowly unzipped them, thrilling at Hank's sharp intake of breath when her knuckles grazed the swell of his manhood.

"I want to make love with you," she whispered against his lips as she took him into her hand.

"I think that was my line," he replied, his breathing ragged.

Leighanna chuckled and increased the pressure of her fingers around him.

"Oh, Leighanna," he moaned as she stroked him. "You're killing me."

She gave his chest a shove, pushing him down on the bed. "Prepare to die, then, because I'm not planning on stopping anytime soon." Hiking her skirt up in her hands, she followed him down, straddling him while she sought his mouth again.

And Hank was sure that somehow, when he wasn't looking, another woman had snuck into his room and into his bed. This couldn't be Leighanna. Not his Leighanna. The Leighanna he knew was shy and totally unaware of her feminine power. Whereas, *this* woman was aggressive, a seductress bent on having her way with him.

And Hank couldn't have been any more willing to give her what she wanted.

Hooking his thumbs in the waist of her skirt, he dragged it over her hips and down her legs, taking her panties along with it, then just as quickly divested her of her blouse and tossed it all carelessly to the floor. On a moan of sheer pleasure, he felt her hips meet his, the mound of her femininity grinding against that part of him that throbbed for her. Impatient for the feel of her honeyed softness around him, Hank grasped her hips within the span of his hands and lifted her, guiding her to him. She gasped at the first urgent thrust and dropped her chin, her long blond hair falling to curtain her face, then tossed it back, passion building on her face and in the blue eyes that gazed down at him.

Flattening her hands against his chest, she rode him, taking her pleasure from him and giving a ton of it in return. Hank felt the pressure building and cursed his own lack of control. He wanted this to last forever, this feeling of oneness, this building of passion that blinded him to everything but the woman he held in his arms. But the sight of her before him, her cheeks flushed with the passion they shared, her skin beneath his roving hands slick with perspiration, her swollen breasts swinging only inches from his face, was more than he could withstand. Reaching out, he grasped her breasts in his hands and drew her to him, catching a nipple with his teeth and drawing her deep into his mouth. She arched, crying out, and he felt the pulsating heat of her climax tighten around him, drawing him with her to that razor-sharp edge.

With a shudder that wracked his body from temples to toes, he slipped over that edge, spilling into her. With a groan, he released her breast, but only to seek her mouth with his. Folding his arms around her, he drew her to his chest. Her breath warmed his neck on a sigh of utter contentment…and Hank wondered why he'd let his stubbornness allow so many days to pass without mending the rift between them. He'd missed her, and not just for the sex. He'd missed *her,* her gentleness, her softness, the strength of her spirit. Tightening his arms around her, he pressed his lips to her hair, not wanting to let her go.

"Hank!" Leighanna called. "Breakfast is ready!"

Fresh from a shower, Hank tugged on his jeans and opened the bathroom door. Leighanna stood before the stove, wearing one of his shirts, and from what he could tell, nothing beneath it. Crossing to stand behind her, he nuzzled the back of her neck with his nose. "Ummmm. Smells good."

Smiling, Leighanna levered a heaping stack of pancakes onto a plate and turned to hand it to him. "Me or the pancakes?" she teased.

Hank took the plate, grinning. "Both." He dipped his face over hers to steal a quick kiss, then turned and headed for the bed.

"And where do you think you're going with that?"

Hank stopped and turned to find Leighanna standing where he'd left her, her arms folded beneath her breasts, her mouth curved in a disapproving frown. "To bed to eat," he said innocently.

She lifted a hand and pointed. "That's what tables were made for."

Hank followed the direction of her finger and discovered that Leighanna had been busy while he'd been in the shower. She'd dragged a table in from the bar again, and shoved it underneath the window. A vase of sunflowers sat in the center of the table and two places were set on opposite sides.

With a guilty smile, he detoured by the bed and crossed to the table. "Sorry. Old habit."

She nodded her approval as he placed his plate on the table, then fixed her own and moved to sit opposite him, neatly sidestepping her still-unpacked suitcase. Picking up the bottle of syrup, she squirted a generous amount over her pancakes...then shivered when something cold brushed her bare toes. Snapping up her head, she looked at Hank and saw him grinning at her.

"What are you doing?" she asked as that 'something' smoothed a slow path up her leg, sending ripples of heat skimming all the way to her abdomen.

"Touching you." He popped a forkful of pancakes in his mouth, still grinning. "I'm not used to having a beautiful woman around in the morning. Just checking to make sure it wasn't a mirage."

Laughing, she reached beneath the table and gave his foot a playful shove. "Trust me, I'm no mirage."

His grinned softened, taking on a seductive look. "No," he said, and slipped his foot between her knees to tease her thighs apart. "I can definitely tell you're real. I can feel your pulse beating."

Already feeling herself weakening, Leighanna struggled to breathe. "Your breakfast," she reminded him, with a gesture toward his plate, then gasped when his toe gently prodded the juncture of her thighs.

His eyes turned a smoky brown and he laid his fork aside. "I'm not really very hungry, are you?"

Leighanna had only been in the apartment a week, but she was slowly making her presence known. Dresses, skirts and blouses added about a foot and a half of color to Hank's otherwise dreary closet. With Hank's permission, she'd claimed the top right dresser drawer as her own, relegating his underwear and socks to a lower drawer. Three pots of geraniums bloomed on the window sill above the table, and the refrigerator, once holding only the bare necessities—a gallon of milk and a six-pack of beer—was now filled with fresh vegetables, fruits and a covered dish containing a leftover meat loaf.

Hank shook his head as he turned his gaze to the bed. He couldn't remember the last time his bed had been made up. Probably never, he thought with a chuckle.

The only thing in the room that remained the same was the television propped up on the dresser for easy viewing from the bed. But he figured she'd change that, too, if she ever figured out how to fit a sofa into the small apartment.

But he didn't mind the changes, he told himself as he stripped off his shirt. In fact, he kind of liked the homey look his apartment had taken on since Leighanna had moved in. Eating regularly wasn't so bad, either, he reflected as he gave his flat stomach a sound pat. And, boy, could that Leighanna cook. He figured he'd put on a good five pounds in the week that she'd been there.

As he pulled a fresh shirt from the closet in preparation for the arrival of his poker buddies, he heard the shower shut off and smiled. The nights weren't too bad, either, he thought with a flicker of anticipation. Going to sleep with Leighanna curled at his side and waking up with her in the morning...well, a man could get used to that.

At that moment the bathroom door opened and Leighanna stepped out, her skin flushed from the heat of the shower...and Hank's mouth went slack. Dressed in a blue satin nightgown that matched her eyes and dipped into the provocative shape of a heart between her breasts, she crossed to him, the satin gown whispering against her bare skin. His mouth suddenly dry, he cupped his hands at her shoulders and drew her to him, burying his nose in the silky tresses of her hair.

"Wow," he murmured appreciatively. "What's the occasion?"

She lifted a hand, cradling his cheek and stepped back to look up at him, her eyes filled with a warmth that made Hank's blood heat. "We're celebrating. Tonight is the anniversary of our first week together."

Hank tensed, remembering his poker game. He hadn't thought to mention it to Leighanna, wasn't in the habit of sharing his plans with anybody but himself. He lifted his wrist behind her head and glanced at his watch. If he hurried, he might be able to call the boys and tell them the game was off for the night.

"Leighanna, sweetheart," he began. But before he could finish the statement, he heard the clump of boots outside his apartment door. A loud knocking followed.

"Hank? You in there?" Cody called.

"Hurry up!" Harley echoed. "I'm feeling lucky tonight!"

Leighanna's expression turned from dreamy to dismay in the time it took to bat an eyelash. "What are they doing here?" she whispered.

Hank lifted his shoulder in a self-conscious shrug. "It's our poker night." When he saw her face fall in disappointment, he hurried to reassure her. "But don't worry, I'll get rid of 'em."

He started to spin away to do just that, but Leighanna caught his arm. "No. Don't. We can celebrate another time."

"But, Leighanna..."

She tipped her face to his, forcing a smile to hide

her disappointment. "No, really. I don't mind." She gave him a gentle shove toward the door. "Now go on and strip those men of all their money."

Blue, red and white chips lay clumped in the center of the table, sharing the space with several empty long-neck beers. Four men sat around the table, their backs slumped, while a fan of cards blocked their faces.

Cody smiled beneath the cover of his cards, then plucked several chips from the pile in front of him. "I'll see your ten, and raise you five."

Harley glanced up from his cards to frown at Cody. "If you've got another damn straight, I'm gonna have to shoot you for the cheater you are."

Cody chuckled. "Don't have to cheat to beat you."

Frowning, Harley tossed the required chips down on the table. "I call."

Fanning his cards out on the table, Cody revealed three kings, the four of spades and the ace of hearts. He let out a whoop of victory and grabbed for the pile of chips.

Harley snagged his wrist. "Not so damn fast." He nodded to the other two men. "What've you got, Newt?"

The tall, rangy cowboy just wagged his head and tossed his cards on the table. "A lousy pair of threes."

Harley turned his attention to Hank. "How 'bout you, Hank? What've you got?"

When Hank didn't respond, but kept staring at the door to his apartment, Harley gave him a sound kick under the table. "You in this game or not?"

Hank shook his head to clear the vision of Leigh-anna dressed in nothing but shimmering blue satin, lying on his bed, waiting. "Yeah, I'm in," he said, forcing himself to focus on the cards in his hands. He reached for a chip. "I'll raise you five."

Harley shook his head sadly. "Man, you've got it bad. Can't even keep your mind on a poker game."

Hank frowned, noticing for the first time the cards spread face up on the table. "Just tired, is all." He stood, kicking back his chair. "In fact," he said, faking a yawn and stretching his hands above his head, "I think I'm going to call it a night. You guys stay as long as you want, just lock up before you leave."

He turned away and strode for the outside door, the three men staring at him in puzzlement.

"You suppose he's so lovesick that he's forgotten the way to his own apartment?" Cody asked.

At that moment, the door opened again and Hank strode back in with a fistful of sunflowers clutched in his hand. With three sets of eyes boring into his back, he ducked behind the bar, nabbed a bottle of wine from the rack there, then headed for his apartment.

Harley tossed down his cards. "Well, I'll be damned," he muttered. "Never thought I'd see the day that old Hank would let a woman get between him and a poker game."

Hank stepped into the apartment and closed the door softly behind him. The only light in the room came from the television screen where an old movie played, but in its glow he could see Leighanna nestled against his pillow, her back to him, her shoulder rising and falling in the even rhythm of sleep.

Flicking off the television, he set the bottle of wine and the bouquet of sunflowers on the nightstand and quickly stripped out of his clothes. Grabbing the bouquet and tucking it behind his back, he buried a knee in the mattress and leaned over her. "Leighanna?" he called softly.

"Hmmm?" she murmured sleepily.

"Wake up, sweetheart," he urged gently.

She rolled to face him, pushing herself up on an elbow and opening her eyes to a squint. "What is it?" she asked, trying to bring him into focus.

"I have something for you." He drew the bouquet from behind his back and held them out to her. "Happy anniversary, sweetheart."

Leighanna's throat tightened at the sight. "Oh, Hank," she murmured tearfully, reaching for them. "How sweet."

He leaned to brush his lips across hers. "No, just crazy about you."

"Oh, Hank…" She dropped the flowers and threw her hands around his neck.

He gathered her close, sliding down her length until he lay beside her. He leaned back and combed his fingers through her hair, looking at her upturned face in the moonlight. He'd only been away from her a couple of hours, and that was only as far as the other room, yet it felt like years since he'd seen her, touched her. "I missed you," he said, his voice husky.

She smiled softly, catching his hand in hers and drawing it to her cheek. "I missed you, too."

He let his hand slip from beneath hers, following its descent with his gaze until his fingertips rested against her satin-covered breast. He slipped his hand inside the point of the heart, cupping her. "You're so soft," he murmured as if to himself. "So fragile." He flicked a nail over her nipple and watched it swell. Unable to resist the puckered tip, he dipped his head, taking her nipple between his teeth. "And so sweet," he whispered as he drew her deeper into his mouth.

Leighanna settled against the pillow on a sigh, offering herself more fully to him. Catching a wisp of hair from his forehead, she combed it back, enjoying watching the muscles in his jaw move as he suckled. Tears brimmed in her eyes. She loved him. The admission didn't frighten her as it once might have. She trusted Hank. Even with something as precious as her heart.

His suckling strengthened and she thrilled at the sensations he drew. They seemed to spiral in a red-hot line from her breast to burn at her deepest feminine core. No one had ever loved her so thoroughly, she thought, as her breathing grew ragged. No one had ever taken her so far so fast.

His fingers skimmed the satin fabric covering her abdomen and trailed down her leg until he found the gown's end. He lifted his head from her breast and looked at her, and she nearly wept at the longing she saw in his eyes. "As pretty as this piece of nothing is," he said, a slow smile curving at one side of his mouth. "I prefer your skin." Catching the hem, he drew it up, waiting while she lifted her arms for him, then raised himself to a kneeling position so he could peel it over her head.

Moonlight spilled over her body, and Hank sank back on his heels on a sigh. Reaching out, he touched a finger to her lips, then her breast, then let it drift slowly over the gentle swell and down to the mound of femininity at the juncture of her thighs. "So beautiful, Leighanna. So, so beautiful," he murmured before pressing his lips just below her navel.

Delicious shivers chased down Leighanna's spine as he pressed his hot lips against her fevered skin. Moaning her pleasure, she dug her fingers into his hair, needing that contact, no matter how slight. He wet his fingertip in her growing moistness, then gently separated the velvet folds of her femininity. Finding the button of her desire, he pressed and she gasped, bucking beneath his hand.

"Hank!" she cried almost desperately, then groaned again, arching, her back bowed as she sought an even more intimate touch.

Pressing hot kisses across her abdomen, he returned to her, crushing his mouth against hers, stabbing his tongue between her parted lips, mimicking the rhythm of his hand on her.

Desire clawed its way through her and, nearly crazed with her need for him, for release from the demons he'd unleashed inside her, Leighanna dragged her nails down his back, urging him to her.

With a feral growl, he slipped between her legs, kneeling, his manhood throbbing with the desire to make her his. Taking her hips in his hand, he lifted, gently guiding her until she was impaled on his staff...but even that wasn't close enough. He reached for her, bringing her body to his chest, crushing her against him as he began to move inside her. Perspiration beaded on their skin, blending as their bodies chafed with each wild thrust.

"Hank!" she cried, clawing at his back as the tension built to an almost unbearable crescendo. "Oh, Hank..."

"It's okay, baby," he soothed, clinging to that last thread of control. "Let it go. I've got you."

Because she trusted him, she did let go. She gave herself up to the void that sucked at her, knowing that he was with her every step of the way. His lips found hers in the darkness and she clung to him, nearly weeping with joy as shudders wracked his body, as his seed spilled hotly into her and her own climax exploded around him.

Tucking an arm behind her waist, he guided her down, then quickly reversed their positions so that she lay on top of him. Tucking her head beneath his chin, he pressed his lips to her hair.

Her heart filled to near bursting with her love for him, Leighanna lifted her head to look at him. Moonlight kissed his features, adding beauty to an already handsome face. "I love you, Hank," she whispered. She felt his body tense against hers and his fingers still on her hair.

"I care for you, too, Leighanna," he murmured.

His inability to say the words she longed to hear in return didn't hurt as she might have expected, because it was there, in his eyes, suppressed beneath his guarded expression. His love for her. She knew that a man like Hank who had never experienced love would have difficulty voicing his feelings. But he'd said he cared for her, and she knew he did. For now, at least, that would be enough. In time he would learn to trust her love for him and would find the courage to share his feelings with her, as well.

Sighing, she laid her head against his chest, content to wait for that moment.

Hank stood with his shoulder pressed against the open bathroom door, his hands tucked beneath his armpits, sporting a pout as big as the state of Texas. "How long are you going to keep this up?" he mumbled dejectedly. "You're hardly ever here."

Leighanna's hand froze on the mascara wand and she shifted her gaze from her own reflection in the mirror to Hank's...and had to smile. "Just a few more days," she promised, and quickly popped the wand back into the tube and laid it aside. With a last fluff of her hair, she turned to him. "By Saturday night the festival will be over, and my life will get back to normal."

He flattened himself against the door as she brushed past, then trailed her into the tiny apartment. "What's normal? This is all I've ever seen. You flitting in and out, then collapsing into bed, too exhausted to do anything but sleep."

Shrugging into a linen jacket, Leighanna turned, unable to suppress the laughter that bubbled up at the miserable expression on his face. "Oh, you're deprived, all right," she said dryly.

Hank had the grace to blush, knowing full well that

they made love every night and sometimes managed to squeeze in a nooner or an afternooner before the bar opened. And that was without considering those early morning trysts. "Well, so I exaggerated a bit," he admitted grudgingly. "But that doesn't mean I wouldn't like to see a little more of you."

Laughing, Leighanna caught his cheeks between her hands. "I don't know how you could possibly see any more of me," she said, arching a knowing brow. Giving him a quick kiss, she whirled away. "Gotta run, or I'm going to be late."

And with that she was gone, leaving Hank with nothing but the lingering scent of her perfume to haunt him and time on his hands.

"Hank!" Leighanna exclaimed as she burst through the front door of the bar. "Hank! Where are you?"

Hank strode from the kitchen carrying three cases of beer. "Right here. Where's the fire?"

"Oh, Hank! You aren't going to believe this," she gushed, her eyes bright with excitement as she climbed up onto a stool.

Hank levered the cases of beer onto the bar opposite her, then pulled out his knife to split the top box open. "Believe what?"

"Mary Claire and Harley are going to remodel Harley's house and they're going to move there after they marry!"

Hank looked at her, frowning, wondering what was exciting about that bit of news. "So?"

"So-o-o," she repeated dramatically. "Mary Claire is going to lease out her house again!"

Hank knew a moment's uneasiness, fearing where this conversation was headed. Pulling a beer from the box, he buried it in the ice, wishing he could bury his head there, too, and avoid this discussion.

"We could lease it from her," she continued, totally unaware of Hank's growing state of discomfort. "Just think," she sighed as she collapsed against the back of her stool, her eyes going dreamy. "A home. A real home, with room for both of our things. I've always dreamed of living in a house with a little white picket fence wrapped around it, with a place to plant flowers and maybe a small garden. Oh, Hank," she cried, sitting up straight and clasping her hands over her heart. "Isn't this wonderful?"

Hank slowly reached for another beer, averting his gaze from her expectant one. It didn't sound so wonderful to him. *Picket fences. Flowers. A garden.* The next rattle out of the box would be marriage. The whole setup reeked of commitment, and Hank was a little weak in the commitment department. It had taken all his nerve just to ask her to move in with him.

"What's wrong with where we live now?" he asked, frowning.

"W-well, nothing," Leighanna stammered, surprised by his lack of enthusiasm for her plan. "It's just that your apartment is so...well, so small. If we were to move into Mary Claire's house, then I could get my things out of storage. I don't have near enough furniture to fill that big house, but we could—" She broke off when she saw the storm clouds building on his face. "Is something wrong?" she asked, her stomach tying itself into knots.

"I'm not moving."

"But, Hank—"

"If you want to move," he ground out as he yanked a beer from the box, "fine, then move. But I'm satisfied right where I am."

His words were like a knife tearing through her heart. "Do you want me to move?" she whispered.

Hank slammed the beer onto the counter. "Hell, no, I don't want you to move. I'm satisfied with things just as they are. *You're* the one who's talking about moving."

Though still confused by his anger, Leighanna felt the knots in her stomach slowly unwind. He didn't want her to move, he was just scared, just as he was afraid to tell her he loved her. Slowly she stood, bracing her feet on the stool's rung. "It was just an idea. That's all." She leaned across the bar and wrapped her arms around Hank's neck. "It doesn't matter where we live. Wherever you are," she said, hugging him to her, "that's where I want to be, too."

Nine

Sounds from the festival drifted through the open door of the temporary office where Leighanna worked, distracting her from the long column of numbers she was double-checking. Giving up for the moment, she dropped her pencil and lifted her hair from her neck, sighing as the night breeze wafting through the open door cooled her damp skin.

Rearing back in the chair, she hooked a sandaled foot on the edge of the desk and stared through the window in front of her. Though darkness shrouded the area surrounding it, the park that lay beyond the small trailer was lit up like the sky on the fourth of July. Neon lights in a multitude of colors blinked on and off, luring fun seekers to lose their money on one of the games of chance, or their stomachs on one of the carnival's heart-stopping rides. Though it was nearing eleven and closing time, an amazing number of people still strolled through the carnival, eating cotton candy or holding a stuffed animal they'd won at one of the game booths.

I did it, she thought proudly as she watched the scene from the privacy of her office. Mayor Acres's festival is a success. And hopefully, she thought as she dragged her foot from the desk and picked up her pencil again, her life would get back to normal and she could spend more time with Hank.

"Leighanna?"

She stiffened at the sound of the husky and familiar male voice that came from behind her. Sure that she was mistaken about the identity of the person, she slowly turned, looking over her shoulder. But there he stood, his hands braced against the doorjamb, his hip cocked in that stance she knew so well. She squeezed her eyes shut, willing the image away as she would a bad dream, but as she did, his scent drifted to her. Polo. That spicy, sexy cologne he always wore. She forced her eyes open to find him watching her. A shiver chased down her spine.

"What are you doing here, Roger?"

He smiled that slow seductive smile of his and lifted a shoulder as he stepped inside the trailer. "I came to see you."

Leighanna spun back around, yanking up her pencil as she bent her head back over her work. "Well, you've seen me. Now leave."

"Leighanna, baby," he murmured as he crossed to her. "You don't mean that."

"Yes, I do, Roger. Now leave, or I'll call the sheriff and have him toss you out."

His hands lighted on her shoulders, and Leighanna stiffened as his fingers started a slow massage. He lowered his face to nuzzle her neck. "Come on, baby," he purred, making goose bumps of revulsion pop up on her skin. "You know you don't want to do that."

Leighanna bolted from the chair, whirling to glare at him. She lifted a hand, pointing a threatening finger at him. "You stay away from me, Roger. I mean it."

He lifted his hands, palms up in surrender. "All right. Whatever you say."

But instead of leaving as she'd hoped, he dropped down in the chair she'd just vacated, calmly studying the contents on the top of her desk. Leighanna lunged for the stack of money she'd just counted and quickly stuffed it into a zippered bank bag.

He slowly spun the chair around and Leighanna backed up a step, hugging the bag to her chest. Roger simply watched her as he propped his elbows on the chair's arms and templed his fingers beneath his nose. "Looks like you've done all right for yourself," he said with a nod toward the bag. "You've hit on a two-bit town just ripe for a picking."

Leighanna tightened her grip on the bag, knowing full well what he was thinking. "It isn't mine. I just work here."

He nodded sagely. "Yes, but who would be the wiser if you slipped a few of those bills into your purse?"

Leighanna's chin came up at his implication. "*I* would know."

He chuckled, then, and dropped his hands to lace them across his chest as he reared back in the chair. "Same old Leighanna. Honest as the day is long."

"And I see you haven't changed, either," she replied, her tone scathing. "You're still looking for easy money."

"Now, Leighanna," he chastened gently as he stood. "You know you love me."

She took a step back, recognizing that familiar gleam in his eye. "You're wrong, Roger. I don't love you. I'm not sure that I ever did."

"Oh, baby," he crooned softly as he lifted a hand to her cheek. "We were good together. It could be that way again. All we need is a little nest egg to buy us that house you always wanted."

Once she might have melted at his touch, at his promises, but now she felt only disgust. As she looked at him, she wondered how she could ever have thought herself in love with this man, and worse, how she could ever have compared Hank to him. Hank was nothing like Roger, he was good and kind and giving, nothing at all like the schemer she was confronted with now.

Slapping his hand away, she ground out, "In your dreams, maybe."

Roger arched a brow, obviously surprised by this new strength in his ex-wife.

"Leighanna?"

Leighanna whirled at the sound of the voice behind her. "Hank!" she cried, guilt flooding her cheeks with heat.

He took a step inside the trailer, his gaze going from

Leighanna to the stranger who stood behind her, then back to Leighanna. "Is there a problem?"

She forced a bright smile and quickly shook her head. "No. No problem." She twisted her head around to frown at Roger. "In fact, he was just leaving."

Though Roger's expression never once wavered, Leighanna knew him well enough to read the anger behind it. He gave her a tight nod. "It was good seeing you again," he said as he strode for the door. "Maybe we'll have a chance to get together again before I leave town."

Hank stepped out of the way to let the man pass. He watched him until he disappeared into the darkness outside the office, then turned his gaze back to Leighanna's. "Would you mind telling me what that was all about?"

Leighanna quickly shook her head. "It was nothing." Hoping to divert his attention from Roger, she hurried to the safe and placed the money bag inside. "It's almost eleven, isn't it?"

"Yeah," Hank murmured, frowning at her back. "The carnies are shutting everything down."

She straightened, raking her hair from her face with trembling fingers as she turned to look at Hank. "I'll be a while, yet. I still have some work to do."

Hank didn't have a clue what was going on, but he could see Leighanna's nervousness and wondered at it. "You're sure you're okay?" he asked again.

"Positive." She looped her arm through his and walked him to the door. "Are you going home now?"

"Yeah. Soon as I help Cody make a sweep through the park to make sure everyone's gone home."

She stretched to her tiptoes and pressed a quick kiss to his frowning lips, then changed her mind and deepened it. Hank was taken aback for a second at the urgency, at the almost desperation he tasted in her, but willingly gave himself up to her needs.

When at last she withdrew, she did so with a sigh that bordered on regret. "Don't wait up," she said, brushing a finger across his lips. "I'll probably be late."

She watched Hank as he walked away from the trailer, his hands shoved deep into his jeans pockets, then turned her gaze on the darkness beyond. A shiver chased down her spine. She knew Roger was out there somewhere. Waiting. Watching. She shuddered, drawing her hands up to rub at the goose bumps on her arms.

Why is he here? she wondered, choking back tears. Was he broke again and looking for money? She knew he'd seen the cash before she'd stuffed it into the bag. For Roger, that would be temptation enough to hang around.

Gulping, she turned and quickly closed the door, locking it behind her.

Hank did wait up, or at least he tried to, wanting and needing answers to the questions Leighanna had avoided before, but he finally fell into an exhausted sleep. When he woke up, the television was still on. Cartoons were now playing instead of the John Wayne movie he'd been watching when he fell asleep, and bright sunshine streamed through the apartment window.

With a frantic glance at the empty bed beside him, he rocketed from the bed and ran for the window, looking for Leighanna's car. His heart thudded to a stop when he discovered that it wasn't parked in its usual spot next to his truck.

"What in the—" Fearing that that damn unreliable car of hers had quit on her again and that she was stranded somewhere, he bolted for the bed. He snatched his jeans from the bedpost and yanked them on, then grabbed his shirt and shrugged it on. But when he stopped at the kitchen table to grab his keys, he saw it. A note propped against the vase of fading sunflowers he'd brought to Leighanna on their anniversary.

His fingers shaking uncontrollably, he picked it up.

"Dear Hank," he read. "I made a mistake in coming to Temptation. I'm going back to Houston. Please know that I will always love you." His eyes quickly scanned the note again, his heart slowly sinking. At the bottom it was signed simply, "Leighanna."

She'd left him. Without a word of explanation other than this sorry note...but then he remembered the man he'd seen her with in the trailer the night before.

It was good seeing you again, he remembered him saying. *Maybe we'll have a chance to get together again before I leave town.*

Anger surged through him, searing the wound on his heart. Curling the paper in his palm, he wadded it into a tight ball, then threw it as hard as he could against the opposite wall. It ricocheted back, rolling to a stop at his bare feet.

"Damn you, Leighanna," he roared, kicking at the

wad of paper and sending it flying again. "Damn you for doing this to me!"

Sagging against the table, he squeezed his forehead between the width of one hand, fighting back the tears that burned in his throat, choked by the same emotions he'd suffered as a child each time his mother had left him behind.

They gathered at The End of the Road, just as they had so many times in the past to discuss this newest tragedy to befall Temptation. Mayor Acres stood at the bar, his face mottled with anger.

"The money's gone. All of it!" he raged, shaking his fist at the ceiling. "And we all know who took it."

Knowing full well who Acres referred to, Cody glanced at Hank, expecting him to come to Leigh-anna's defense. But Hank kept his gaze on the table, his back slumped against the chair, stubbornly refusing to meet Cody's gaze. With a scowl at his friend, Cody pushed to his feet. "Now, Acres," he said, trying to keep a tight rein on his anger. "We don't know for a fact that Leighanna took the money."

The mayor whirled on him. "Then who in the hell do you think did? She was the last one in the office, and it was her job to lock it up in the safe."

"Leighanna didn't steal your money."

Every head turned to stare at Hank. Heat burned his cheeks as he saw the looks of pity that some of the folks turned his way. He didn't want their pity, he'd been pitied enough in his lifetime, a result of his mother's whoring ways. He may have made a mistake in trusting his heart to Leighanna, and he might be humiliated that all his friends were witness to her abandonment of him, but he couldn't remain quiet while they crucified her. She might be a lot of things, but he knew she was no damn thief. "She left me a note," he said gruffly. "Said she'd made a mistake in coming here to Temptation and was going back to Houston. A woman on the run sure as hell wouldn't have told anyone where she was going, not if she had anything to hide."

Cody heaved a sigh of relief, thankful that Hank had at last stood up for Leighanna. He quickly shifted his attention back to the crowd. "There were plenty of strangers in town last night. Any one of them could have broken into that office and stolen the money."

"They must have had the combination, then," Mayor Acres replied dryly. "Because you know as well as I do that that safe had not been tampered with. She probably was working with somebody on the outside."

Cody flattened his hands on the table to keep himself from punching the man in the face. "Did it ever occur to you, or to anybody else in this room," he said with a wave of his hand that encompassed the occupants of the bar, "that Leighanna might very well be the victim here? Did you ever consider the possibility that someone might have *forced* her to give them the money, then kidnapped her, or worse?"

Mary Claire, who was sitting next to Harley, made a strangled sound, then buried her face against Harley's shoulder.

The blood slowly drained from Hank's face. He'd

never considered the possibility that Leighanna might be in danger, at least not since he'd found her note. He lifted his head to look at Cody. "There was a man in the trailer with her last night," he said hoarsely, his throat raw from the fear choking him. "A stranger. I'd never seen him before. She seemed a little nervous, and when I asked her if anything was wrong, she said, no, she was fine."

Instantly alert, Cody turned his full attention on Hank. "What did he look like? Can you describe him?"

Hank frowned, trying to remember. "I don't know. Maybe. I'd guess him to be about five foot nine, or so, medium build, dark complexion." His frown deepened as the image grew. "Brown hair, kind of curly and combed straight back," he said, raking his fingers through his own hair to demonstrate. "He—"

Mary Claire lifted her head from Harley's shoulder to stare at Hank, her tear-filled eyes going round. "Roger," she murmured weakly.

Cody whirled. "Who?"

Mary Claire swallowed hard, shifting her gaze from Hank's face to Cody's. "Roger. Leighanna's ex-husband."

Hank felt his heart fall to land in his stomach like a lead ball. Her ex-husband. He remembered the man saying something about them getting together again before he left town. She'd probably gone back to him and hadn't had the nerve to tell Hank of her plans.

Cody's forehead plowed into a frown. "Would he…"

"I don't know," Mary Claire murmured, pressing

her fingers to her throbbing temples. "But I do know this," she added emphatically, making her hands into a white-knuckled fist on the table. "Leighanna would never willingly help him."

Cody turned to look at Hank. "Have you checked your safe, yet, to see if anything's missing?"

"I made my deposit yesterday," he said with a dismissive wave of his hand. "There's nothing there but the register drawer and a little start-up cash."

"Wouldn't hurt to check."

Though the thought of Leighanna stealing from him was a hard concept for Hank to swallow, he did as Cody instructed. He ducked beneath the bar to his safe and turned the dial, listening as the tumblers fell into place. Holding his breath, he wrenched the door open then sagged in relief when he saw the cash drawer lying on the shelf just as he'd left it. But as he started to rise, something else caught his eye. A bank bag lay on the bottom shelf...the same bank bag he'd seen Leighanna shove into the mayor's safe the night before.

His hand shaking, he drew it out, strengthening his grip on it as he took its full weight. Rising, he heaved it onto the bar, narrowing his eyes at the pompous mayor. "There's your money, Acres. I told you Leighanna was no damn thief."

With the mystery of the missing money resolved, there was no reason for anyone to stick around. Folks drifted out of The End of the Road, somewhat subdued, and headed for church or their respective homes. Only Mary Claire, Harley and Cody remained behind.

Silence hung over the foursome as they sat at a table, each consumed by the question that still remained unanswered. It was Mary Claire who finally found the courage to broach the subject of Leighanna's disappearance.

She reached over and covered Hank's hand with hers. "She loves you, Hank. I know she does. She would never purposefully hurt you."

Scowling, Hank pulled his hand from beneath hers, not wanting her pity. "She has a damn funny way of showing it."

Mary Claire shook her head. "I know this all must seem strange to you, but I think I understand why she did what she did."

Hank snorted. "Enlighten me. I'm still in the dark."

Mary Claire drew in a deep breath, wanting desperately for him to understand. "It all revolves around Roger. Knowing him as she does, Leighanna was probably worried that he might try something. By bringing the money here and putting it in your safe instead of leaving it at the office, I think she was trying to protect it."

When Hank continued to stare at her, his face an unreadable mask, she heaved a sigh before going on. "As to why she disappeared, I think that has to do with Roger, too. When she moved here from Houston, she hoped to escape him and the power he held over her. I'm certain that she felt responsible for his coming here and feared that if she stayed, he might, too, and she knew that it wouldn't be long before he'd figure out some new scam to run."

She lifted her hands in a helpless shrug. "In her

mind, if she wasn't here, then there would be no reason for him to hang around." She looked at Hank imploringly. "Her sole reason was to protect, not to harm." Once again she leaned to cover his hand with hers. "If you'd call her and talk to her, I'm sure that—"

Hank pushed to his feet, jerking his hand from beneath hers. "Nice try, Mary Claire," he muttered, then turned his back on them all and headed for his apartment. "But no cigar."

Unaware of the fact that her name was on the lips of every person within a fifty-mile radius of Temptation, Leighanna sat on Reggie's sofa, her knees pulled to her chin.

"I don't understand how he found me," she sobbed. "No one but you knew where I went when I left Houston."

Reggie laid a hand on Leighanna's back and rubbed in an effort to comfort. "Knowing Roger, he'd find a way. I wouldn't put anything past him." She continued to rub, her forehead pleating in a frown. "What I don't understand is why you left Temptation. Mary Claire told me you were head-over-heels for some bartender."

Leighanna hiccuped and dragged a hand beneath her nose as her thoughts drifted to Hank. Fresh tears flooded her eyes as she realized that by now he would have read the note she had left him. "I am," she said miserably. "But how could I stay after Roger said what he did, about how the town was ripe for picking?" She lifted her head, turning her watery gaze on

Reggie. "I would never be able to forgive myself if he took advantage of them in some way. They're good people, Reggie, and they're my friends. I couldn't just stand by and let Roger harm them when I could do something to prevent it."

Reggie heaved a frustrated breath. "You aren't responsible for Roger's actions, Leighanna."

"But I am," she cried. "If I hadn't been in Temptation, he would never have gone there."

"So what are you going to do, spend your whole life running? You have got to quit protecting him."

Horrified at the suggestion, Leighanna twisted around to stare at Reggie. "I'm not protecting him!"

"Sure you are."

"I am not!"

Reggie heaved a sigh. "Did you leave Temptation?"

"Yes."

"Did you leave to keep Roger from doing something stupid?"

Leighanna rubbed at her temples, trying to ease the ache there. "Well, yes, I suppose."

"Then you're protecting him. Let him do what he will and suffer the consequences alone." She cupped her hand beneath Leighanna's chin, tipping up her face. "Don't let him rob you of your happiness. Go back to Temptation and to Hank. Go back home."

Before Leighanna could argue the merits of Reggie's suggestion of returning to Temptation, the phone rang.

Reggie answered it, then held out the phone, cocking one brow at Leighanna. "It's Mary Claire," she said, her voice holding a gentle note of warning.

Leighanna's heart leapt to her throat. *Mary Claire?* If Mary Claire knew to call her at Reggie's, then she must have talked to Hank. He was the only one who knew of her departure for Houston.

"Hello?" she said, her voice quavering in uncertainty.

Reggie watched Leighanna's eyes widen in shock.

"Leighanna, what is it?" Reggie whispered in concern. Leighanna waved at the phone and Reggie quickly punched the speaker button so that she could hear the conversation, as well. They both listened, staring at each other in stunned silence while Mary Claire told them of the missing money and the mayor's assumption that Leighanna had stolen it.

"But I didn't take the money!" she cried, horrified that Mary Claire would think she'd do such a thing.

"I know you didn't," Mary Claire consoled her. "We all know," she said, then quickly added, "at least we do now. We were all gathered at The End of the Road this morning when Hank found the money in his safe."

Leighanna's eyes, if possible, widened even more. "All? You mean everyone in town thought I'd stolen the money?"

"Well," Mary Claire replied hesitantly, "you know how Mayor Acres is. He went off the deep end when he discovered it missing and called a town meeting. That's when he accused you of taking it."

Leighanna pressed a hand to her forehead. "Oh, my

God," she murmured, humiliated to think that everyone in town was privy to her disgrace.

"Don't worry, though," Mary Claire reassured her. "Cody came to your defense."

Leighanna wilted a little more. Not Hank, but Cody. That knowledge hurt more than anything she'd heard thus far.

"Cody refused to believe the mayor's theory," Mary Claire continued, "and was convinced that someone had forced you to give them the money, then kidnapped you, or worse. That's when Hank mentioned seeing a man in the trailer with you the night before. When he described him, I knew the man had to be Roger."

Leighanna's mind whirled with the possibilities that that news offered to her already damned character. "So then, naturally, everyone thought that Roger and I had planned this all along and that we had stolen the money, then escaped," she interjected miserably.

"Not for long. Cody had Hank check his own safe to see if anything was missing, and that's when Hank found the money bag from the festival."

Leighanna's eyes closed at the mention again of Hank's name. "Is he angry with me for leaving?"

She heard Mary Claire's sigh. "Angry or disappointed, I'm not sure. Why don't you call him, Leighanna, explain everything to him? I'm sure he'll understand."

Leighanna shook her head, at first unable to find the strength to utter a refusal. The fact that Hank had failed to defend her hurt more than she was ready to admit. "Maybe later. Not now." Before Mary Claire could argue, she quickly brought the conversation to an end. "Thanks for calling, Mary Claire. And I'm sorry for this whole mess." She quickly replaced the receiver, cutting the connection.

Mary Claire hung up the phone, her lips pursed in a frustrated frown. She glanced at Harley. "She's not going to call him."

Harley just shook his head. "There's nothing more you can do."

Mary Claire clasped her hands in a fist at her waist and paced away from the phone. "There has to be something. They need each other." She turned to face Harley. "You saw Hank. He was hurting, I just know he was. And Leighanna," she added, tossing up her hands. "She sounded as miserable as Hank looks."

"Now, Mary Claire," Harley soothed. "You've done all you can do."

Mary Claire turned her gaze to the window, her gaze narrowing in contemplation. "There has to be some way we can get them together again."

Working through a blind rage, Hank jerked Leighanna's clothes from the hangers in the closet, her lingerie from the top dresser drawer and stuffed it all into the single suitcase she'd brought with her when she'd moved in. Grabbing a sack from the kitchen, he raked all her toiletries from the bathroom counter, twisted the sack's neck as he'd like to twist her lying neck, then tossed it, too, into the suitcase before slamming it closed.

He marched angrily for the shed out back, ripped

open the door, tossed the suitcase inside, then slammed the door on the unwanted reminder. Returning to his apartment, he caught a glimpse of the geraniums blooming on the windowsill and with a growl, jerked open the window and gave the pots an angry shove. He listened to the sound of the clay pots shattering on the ground below and felt the same fissures splintering his heart. Bracing his hands on the windowsill, he dipped his head, his shoulders heaving, his anger slowly giving way to misery.

He loved her. Even though he'd never found the courage to tell her, he loved her. And now she was gone.

Heaving himself away from the window, he strode for the door and the outside. The geraniums lay amongst the shards of broken pottery and clumps of dirt. Carefully, he picked the plants up, dusting the soil from the blooms and carried them back inside.

"Have you talked to Leighanna?" Cody asked.

Hank stuck a mug beneath the spigot and filled it with beer. "No. Was I supposed to?" he asked sourly as he shoved the mug Cody's way.

Cody glanced at Harley who sat on the stool beside him then shrugged. "No. Just thought you might have called her."

Hank filled another mug and plopped it down in front of Harley. "And why would I do that?"

"I don't know. Just thought you might be curious to know why she up and left so unexpectedly. She seemed happy enough while she was here."

Hank bit back a frown. He'd wondered all right, but

his pride wouldn't allow him to admit that to his friends.

Harley lifted his mug and took a sip, eyeing Hank over its rim. "Mary Claire talked to her," he said quietly.

Hank snapped his head up to look at Harley, then quickly turned away, refusing to ask the questions that burned in his mind.

Cody didn't feel the same compunction. "Where is she?"

"In Houston," Harley replied. "She's staying with a friend."

"Is she planning on coming back to Temptation?" Cody asked.

Harley watched Hank's shoulders stiffen reflexively and said, "Didn't say, though I've wondered about that. Not more than a day or two before she left, she talked to Mary Claire about leasing her house after we get married. Seemed real excited at the prospect, too."

Hank had heard about all he could stand. He wheeled back around to glare at his two friends. "If you two came here to try to pressure me into calling Leighanna, you can haul your asses right back out, because I'm not going to. *She's* the one who left. *She's* the one who'll have to call me. Hank Braden crawls to no woman!"

"Damn nosey busybodies," Hank muttered as he carefully poured water over the geraniums he'd replanted. "Coming over here, thinking they can coerce me into calling Leighanna. Humph," he snorted, and tossed the plastic watering can into the sink. "They're wasting their time."

Opening the refrigerator, he pulled out a beer, then grabbed the plate with the sandwich he'd made. Heading for the bed, he stretched out, balancing the plate on his stomach. He refused to eat at the table where he'd shared his meals with Leighanna, reverting instead to his old habit of eating in bed. He knew it was a childish act of defiance, especially since Leighanna wasn't even there to witness his rebellion, but it made him feel a little better knowing he was doing something she wouldn't approve of.

Just thought you might be curious to know why she up and left so unexpectedly. She seemed happy enough while she was here. Cody's comment came out of nowhere and settled itself in Hank's mind.

Yeah, he'd wondered all right. Had spent hours, lying awake in his bed at night, weighing all the possibilities.

Not more than a day or two before she left, she talked to Mary Claire about leasing her house after we get married. Seemed real excited at the prospect, too.

Hank's grip on his sandwich slackened and it slipped from his fingers and fell back to the plate as Harley's words wormed their way into his conscience to replace Cody's. He remembered well the afternoon that she'd approached him about the two of them leasing Mary Claire's house...and remembered, too, her disappointment when he'd refused to consider her suggestion.

Was that why she'd left him? he wondered. Was it because she wanted more than he was willing to give?

Fearing that he was the one who was responsible for her leaving, he set aside the plate and sat up.

He wanted to hate her, rail at her for what she'd done to him...but for some reason he couldn't work up the strength required to do even that. Not any more. He missed her. Missed the warmth of her smile, the satisfaction of waking up with her beside him each morning, missed her working alongside him at the bar.

He loved her...but he'd never had the courage to share those feelings with her.

He dug his fingers through his hair, cursing himself for allowing his own fears of commitment to rob him of the only happiness he'd known in his whole sorry life.

Hank set his purchases on the counter and waited while Mrs. Martin rang them up.

"Have you seen or talked to Leighanna since she left?" Mrs. Martin asked as she weighed a sack of tomatoes.

Hank felt heat crawl up his neck as he heard almost the same question Cody had posed to him asked again. "No," he replied, hoping the inquisition would stop there.

Mrs. Martin pulled the sack of tomatoes from the scale and punched in the price on her cash register. "You're just gonna let her go, then?"

"She's the one who left," Hank reminded her.

"Humph," was Mrs. Martin's reply. She picked up a frozen TV dinner and frowned at it. "I'd imagine that it would be hard for her to make the first move, considering all that happened.''

Hank's forehead plowed into a frown, unable to follow her line of thought. ''And why's that?''

Mrs. Martin punched in a couple more items and dropped them in a sack before lifting her shoulder in a shrug. ''What with all Mayor Acres's ravings, accusing her of being a thief, I'm sure she'd just as soon forget she ever set foot in this town.'' She glanced at Hank over the top of her smudged glasses and gave him a knowing look. ''Can't say as I blame her, either, with everybody ready to hang her, and her being innocent and all.''

When he didn't reply, she merely lifted her shoulder in a shrug again and pushed his sack of purchases toward him. ''I suppose you'll be going to Harley and Mary Claire's engagement party Sunday night?''

He picked up his sack. ''Plan on it.''

''Wonder if Leighanna will show up?'' Mrs. Martin mused, eyeing him curiously. ''A person would think she might, since she's one of Mary Claire's best friends.''

Hank turned for the door without answering, his thoughts spinning crazily. He'd never considered the possibility of Leighanna returning for the party.

Would she come? he wondered. And what would he do if she did? What could he say to make up for ever doubting her? For not having had the courage to tell her he loved her? For not immediately following her and begging her to return?

A thought began to take shape in his mind, and he pushed through the door, dumped the sack of groceries in the back of his truck and headed for the hardware store across the street.

Reggie tossed the invitation onto Leighanna's lap and strode for the kitchen. "As much as I hate to miss it, I can't go."

Leighanna picked up the invitation she'd just handed to Reggie and stared in dismay at her retreating back. "But one of us has to go!" she cried. "Mary Claire's our friend."

Reggie's reply was muffled by the refrigerator door. "Then you go. I'm sorry, but I've got to work."

Leighanna dipped her head, staring blindly at the invitation. "I can't," she murmured miserably, knowing that if she went she was bound to see Hank. She didn't think she could bear it if he shunned her. "At least not yet."

Reggie appeared in the kitchen doorway, cradling a bottle of mineral water in one hand. "And waiting is going to make seeing him any easier?"

Ten

***

By Sunday morning Leighanna was a wreck, torn by her obligation to Mary Claire and her reluctance to confront Hank and all the other people of Temptation again.

I'm a coward, she told herself as she paced furiously around Reggie's guest room. Nothing but a sniveling little coward. Mary Claire is my best friend. How can I possibly let her down on such a special occasion such as this?

I won't! she told herself defiantly. She stripped her borrowed nightgown over her head and tossed it to the floor. She hadn't done anything wrong. She had nothing to be ashamed of. She'd wanted only to protect the people of Temptation, including Hank, and if they wanted to condemn her for that, well let them!

Besides, she told herself, as she jerked on some clothes. She missed Hank. She loved him, for heaven's sake! And if she had to fight for him as Mary Claire had once suggested, then she was prepared to duke it out with whomever necessary, even Hank if that's what it took to knock some sense in his head. He loved her, she knew he did, and she wouldn't let him get by without admitting it. Not this time.

She stopped in front of the dresser mirror, narrowing her eyes at her reflection as she drew her right hand into a fist and pounded it into her left. After all, she told herself, I have a pretty mean right hook. Hank had said so himself.

Hank knelt in front of the freshly planted shrubs in front of The End of the Road, frantically nailing pickets into place. He paused long enough in his work to wipe the sweat from his brow and glance at his wristwatch. Just past five and the party started at six. He twisted his head around to look at the road behind him where the sun created a hazy mirage on the hot asphalt. He knew that if she was coming, she had to pass by this way, as this was the only road that led to Harley's from Temptation.

He frowned, shoving back the doubts that suddenly crowded his mind. She'd be there, he told himself and picked up his hammer again. Leighanna was too good a person to let Mary Claire down.

But would she come by to see him? Would she stop when she saw what he'd done? Would she even bother to glance this way? He tightened his fingers on the hammer. Didn't matter whether she noticed or not, he told himself as he slammed another nail into the picket he held, because he was going to that party and if she was there, he was going to talk to her and insist that she come home to The End of the Road where she—

Before he could even finish the thought, he heard a car on the highway in the distance and knew without even turning it was Leighanna. He'd recognize that clanking engine anywhere. He held his breath as the sound of the car drew nearer and thought sure his lungs were going to burst wide open when he heard the car slow. Twisting at the waist, he turned and saw that she'd stopped right smack-dab in the middle of the highway at the entrance to the bar's parking lot.

With his heart in his throat, willing her to come to him, needing that sign that she still cared, he stood and waited. It seemed an eternity passed before she made the turn, swinging her car onto the gravel lot...and Hank finally breathed his first full breath that day.

She braked to a gravel-spitting stop in front of him and climbed out, that dang door of hers screeching on its unoiled hinges, sending a shiver down his spine, before she slammed it shut. He watched her stomp toward him and slowly became aware of the stiffness in her shoulders, in the determined, angry slant of her mouth.

She stopped in front of him, her chin cocked high as she glared at him through narrowed eyes. "You know what, Braden?" she ground out. "You always took pleasure in calling me a coward. Me!" she repeated, her voice rising an octave. "When you're the one who's the coward!'' She lifted a hand to poke a stiff finger at his chest. ''*You're* the one who's afraid. Afraid to share your feelings for fear you'll get hurt. Afraid to commit yourself to something that has no guarantees. Well, I'm not afraid,'' she raged on. ''I love you. I told you that before and my feelings haven't changed. I'm—''

''I love you, too.''

''—not afraid to admit that. I—'' She suddenly stopped as what he'd said soaked through the red haze of her anger. Her mouth went round in a silent ''oh'' and she fell back a step. ''What did you say?''

Smiling, Hank took a step toward her, closing the distance she'd put between them. ''I said, I love you.'' He cupped his hand along the line of her jaw, tipping her face to his. ''And you know what? Saying it isn't nearly as scary as the thought of losing you.''

She sucked in a breath, not trusting her ears. ''But I thought…''

''That I didn't love you? That I'd let you go without putting up a fight?'' he asked softly.

Leighanna closed her eyes and turned away from his hand, her mind whirling in confusion. She was the one who was supposed to be fighting for him. Hadn't she made that decision that very morning while staring at her own reflection in Reggie's mirror? With the tables reversed on her, she didn't know what to say, what to do.

She opened her eyes…and saw for the first time the newly planted shrubs…and the fence. Her hand went instinctively to cover her heart. When she lifted her face to look at Hank, there were tears on her cheeks...and Hank was sure that his heart was going to split right in two.

He took a step toward her, then stopped, unsure of what to say.

She looked at him, her eyes filled with questions. "You planted the shrubs," she murmured.

He lifted a shoulder in a shrug. "You said it was what the bar needed."

She swallowed hard, turning her gaze to the newly erected fence, wondering what all this meant and afraid to put more meaning behind its appearance than Hank had intended.

Hank saw the direction of her gaze and took another step closer. "I know the fence isn't exactly what you had in mind, but it was the best I could do at the moment."

Her mouth opened as if she was about to say something, then closed again. She pressed trembling fingers to her lips, and new tears came to chase those that already dampened her cheeks. This time Hank couldn't keep himself for reaching out to her. She fell into his arms on a strangled sob.

"Oh, Leighanna, baby," he murmured, holding her close. "Please don't cry." He rocked her in his arms, burying his nose in her hair, glorying in the feel of her again in his arms after so many days without her. "I'm sorry I didn't come after you. I know that I should have, that I shouldn't have let pride stand in my way." He pushed her to arm's length, needing to see her face, his heart nearly breaking all over again at the pain he saw there when he knew he was the cause. "Tell me you'll forgive me?"

Leighanna looked up at him through watery eyes and shook her head. "N-no," she stammered, scraping the tears from beneath her eyes. "You don't have anything to be sorry about. I should never have left." Fresh tears swelled as she closed her hands over the arms that held her. "I didn't want to leave you. I swear I didn't. I just wanted to protect everyone from Roger."

"I know, I know," he soothed. "Mary Claire told me the same damn thing, only I couldn't see beyond the hurt to believe it. Oh, God, Leighanna," he said, crushing her to him. "I've missed you so much."

Laughing through her tears, she threw her arms around his neck and clung. "And I missed you, Hank. More than you'll ever know."

They stood, the sun shining warm on their backs, their hearts thundering against each other. It was Hank who finally pulled away. He took a step back and dipped his head down, suffering a sudden attack of nerves and unable to meet her gaze. "Leighanna," he said, nervously digging the toe of his boot into the gravel. "I have a confession to make."

Her eyes grew round, and her heart stuttered to a stop. "A confession? What kind of confession?"

"I've been eating in bed again."

Expecting something much worse, like maybe Betty Jo had been back in town, Leighanna nearly collapsed in relief. "Shame on you," she chided, unable to keep from laughing.

He looked up at the sound of her laughter and grinned. He reached out and caught her hand in his, lacing his fingers through hers, and the grin slowly melted. "I just couldn't bring myself to sit at that table without you there with me."

Emotion rose to Leighanna's throat. "Oh, Hank..."

"I did water your geraniums, though I think they've lost a few blooms." His fingers tightened on hers. "We need you, Leighanna. Me and those dumb geraniums. We're liable to just wilt and die without you here to care for us."

"Oh, Hank..." she said again, fighting back tears.

"I love you, Leighanna. I want you to move back in, I—"

"Yes," she cried before he could finish. "I—"

He squeezed her hand, silencing her. "Let me finish. I want you to move back in, all right, but I want you to move back in as my wife."

Leighanna's eyes grew round, her mouth dropping open. "Your wife?" she gasped out on a hoarse whisper.

Hank frowned. "I know I'm not much of a catch, and I'm barely housebroke by most women's standards, but I promise that I'll give you all your dreams. We'll start with that house you've always wanted, the one with the white picket—"

Before he could say more, Leighanna was in his arms, her hands cinched tight around his neck. "Oh, Hank," she sobbed. "I don't need a house, or a picket fence. All I need is you."

And all of him was exactly what Hank was prepared to give.

* * * * *

Receive **75¢ off** your next

 *Silhouette*®

Desire®

book purchase.

75¢ OFF!

**Your next Silhouette Desire®
book purchase.**

**Coupon expires December 31, 2002.
Redeemable at participating retail outlets in the U.S. only.
Limit one coupon per purchase.**

109738

5 65373 00075 5   (8100) 0 10973

Silhouette®
Where love comes alive™

Receive **75¢ off** your next

book purchase.

75¢ OFF!
Your next Silhouette Desire®
book purchase.

52603974

Visit Silhouette at www.eHarlequin.com
PSNCP02SD-CANCOUPON
© 2002 Harlequin Enterprises Ltd.

Where love comes alive™

July 2002
IN BLACKHAWK'S BED
#1447 by Barbara McCauley
SECRETS!

Don't miss the latest title in
Barbara McCauley's sizzling and
scandal-filled miniseries.

August 2002
BECKETT'S CINDERELLA
#1453 by Dixie Browning
BECKETT'S FORTUNE

Be sure to check out the first book in
Dixie Browning's exciting crossline
miniseries about two families, four
generations and the one debt that
binds them together!

September 2002
RIDE THE THUNDER
#1459 by Lindsay McKenna

Watch as bestselling author
Lindsay McKenna's sexy mercenaries
battle danger and fight for the hearts
of the women they love, in book two
of her compelling crossline miniseries.

MAN OF THE MONTH

Some men are made for lovin'—and you're sure to love
these three upcoming men of the month!

Available at your favorite retail outlet.

Where love comes alive™

Silhouette® Desire®

Continues the captivating series from
bestselling author

BARBARA McCAULEY

SECRETS!

Hidden legacies, hidden loves—revel in the
unfolding of the Blackhawk siblings' deepest, most
desirable SECRETS!

Don't miss the next irresistible books in the series...

TAMING BLACKHAWK
On Sale May 2002
(SD #1437)

IN BLACKHAWK'S BED
On Sale July 2002
(SD #1447)

And look for another title on sale in 2003!

Available at your favorite retail outlet.

Silhouette®
Where love comes alive™

SDSEC02

FREE
Gourmet Garden Kit!

With two proofs of purchase from any four Silhouette® special collector's editions.

Special Limited Time Offer

YES! Please send me my FREE Gourmet Garden Kit without cost or obligation, except for shipping and handling. Enclosed are two proofs of purchase from specially marked Silhouette® special collector's editions and $3.50 shipping and handling fee.

Name (PLEASE PRINT)

Address   Apt. #

City   State/Prov.   Zip/Postal Code

IN U.S., mail to:
Silhouette Gourmet Garden Kit Offer
3010 Walden Ave.
P.O. Box 9023
Buffalo, NY 14269-9023

IN CANADA, mail to:
Silhouette Gourmet Garden Kit Offer
P.O. Box 608
Fort Erie, Ontario
L2A 5X3

FREE GOURMET GARDEN KIT OFFER TERMS
To receive your free Gourmet Garden Kit, complete the above order form. Mail it to us with two proofs of purchase, one of which can be found in the upper right-hand corner of this page. Requests must be received no later than December 31, 2002. Your Gourmet Garden Kit costs you only $3.50 for shipping and handling. The free Gourmet Garden Kit has a retail value of $17.00 U.S. All orders subject to approval. Products in kit illustrated on the back inside cover of this book are for illustrative purposes only, and items may vary (retail value of items always as previously indicated). **Please allow 6-8 weeks for delivery. Offer good in Canada and the U.S. only.** Offer good only while quantities last. Offer limited to one per household.

© 2002 Harlequin Enterprises Limited
598 KGJ DNCX

PSNCP02-OFFER